"HELLO, MO."

The skillet slipped from Morgana's hand, landing with a dull thud on the countertop. Franklin stood under the arched entrance to the kitchen.

"What the hell are you doing here?" Her voice, low and raspy, trembled with repressed rage.

Franklin smiled, extending his right hand, offering her a small blue shopping bag. There was no doubt it contained a piece of jewelry from Tiffany's. "Happy anniversary, darling."

"Whatever it is, you can give it to your whore!"

Lowering his arm, his face suddenly went grim. "I'm sorry, Morgana!" he shouted. "Is *that* what you want to hear? I'm sorry I slept with *that woman*."

Morgana was beyond being reasonable. "If you don't leave I'm going to call the police and have you arrested for trespassing."

"No, you're not," Franklin stated confidently. "You're going to stand right there and listen to what I have to say."

Secrets Never Told

ROCHELLE ALERS

POCKET BOOKS
New York London Toronto Sydney Singapore

An *Original* Publication of POCKET BOOKS

POCKET BOOKS, a division of Simon & Schuster, Inc.
1230 Avenue of the Americas, New York, NY 10020

ISBN: 0-7394-3588-4

Printed in the U.S.A.

Acknowledgments

I would like to acknowledge Veronica Mixon—thank you for giving me the opportunity to become a published author.

Marsha Ann Tanksley who has walked the long walk with me.

Brenda J. Woodbury. You are a publicist extraordinaire. Many thanks for all that you do.

Gwendolyn "Diva" Osborne—Eve has run amuck!

Dianna M. Collier—agent and friend. We're on a roll!

And last, but certainly not least, my editor Selena James—my sincerest gratitude because you believed in my dream.

Your joy is your own; your bitterness is your own. No one can share them with you.

—Proverbs 14:10

Good News Bible—Today's English Version

Secrets Never Told

PROLOGUE

Salvation, Georgia
September 1945

The lengthening ember on the tip of a fragrant hand-rolled Cuban cigar went unnoticed as Edward Joseph Graham squinted through the blue-white haze swirling around his face at the five cards cradled lovingly in his smooth, manicured hand.

Tonight's the night!

The three words echoed in his head, much like the sensual whisper from a seductive woman. But the numbers and faces on the cards were a woman—a lying, cheating, duplicitous, and sometimes pleasurable woman—from which he could not free himself. He'd tried over the years to walk away, but the game of chance was a jealous mistress, refusing to free him from her spell.

Every Friday night, with the exception of New Year's Day, Good Friday, or Christmas Day, Edward and eight of the most influential colored men in Salvation meet for their weekly poker game. They'd been meeting for the past two years, ignoring and alienating others who felt they were entitled, by virtue of their social standing in the community, to become a part of the privileged group.

Edward loved his wife, their beautiful daughter, Katherine, playing poker, smoking and drinking premium bourbon, but not necessarily in that order.

It was the cards, the smooth taste of bourbon on his palate, and the aromatic smoke wafting in his nose this night that had become as vital to him as breathing was to sustaining life.

Stealing a glance at his cards, Edward smiled, the corners of his mouth inching upward to reveal teeth clamped tightly around the tightly rolled tobacco leaves. Seven of the nine in the group had bowed out and said their good-byes. Tonight, as with most Fridays, only Edward and Randolph Johnson remained. He was heavily into debt to Randolph, but that would soon change.

Randolph, ten years Edward's junior, was thought of as a handsome man. He claimed a dark brown complexion, reminiscent of supple, highly polished calfskin. A thin, neatly barbered mustache made the contrast between a thin upper and fuller lower lip even more obvious. His close-cropped black hair was brushed back off a high forehead. And even though he wore a short-sleeved shirt open at the throat and sharply creased tan slacks, the businessman was the epitome of sophisticated elegance. This card game, like all the others, was held in Randolph's wood-paneled library, and the room's furnishings were as elegant as its owner.

"What do you have, Graham?" Randolph's deep voice was deceptive, soft as sterile cotton. He'd learned over the years to control the timbre to suit his mercurial moods. Nothing in his expression revealed the shiver of excitement racing along his nerve endings. He couldn't have been dealt a better hand if he'd cheated.

Closing his eyes, Edward mumbled a silent prayer. This was it—the moment he'd been waiting for. It was time for his luck to change, to regain his self-respect.

He placed his cards on the felt-covered table. "Four of a kind."

Randolph glanced down at the cards spread out on the table, his gaze narrowing. A muscle in his jaw twitched as he noticed Edward's right hand inch toward the pile of bills on the table's surface.

"Don't you want to see what I have?"

Edward jerked his hand back as if he'd touched a piece of hot coal. "Yes . . . of course."

Slowly, methodically, Randolph laid his cards down, fanning them. He almost felt sorry for the man staring numbly at the cards. "Royal flush." His voice held a mocking tone.

Closing his eyes, Edward slumped back against the tufted chair, trying unsuccessfully to stem the hot tears welling up behind his eyelids. He had been so certain, so damn sure that he would beat Randolph this time. He owed the man nearly three thousand dollars. Where was he going to get that much money to pay off his gambling debts? He had barely earned a little more than twice that amount last year.

Every week he told himself this was going to be the last time; that he would never gamble again. But every Friday night at seven-thirty he found himself in Randolph's library, sipping bourbon, puffing cigars, shuffling cards, and praying his string of losses would end.

The tears overflowed, running down his cheeks, and dotting the front of his starched white shirt. Edward cried silently, his chin quivering as he tried to regain his composure. Unsuccessful, a sob escaped his parted lips and the cigar fell onto the table. Randolph reached over, picked it up, and put out the burning embers in a large glass ashtray.

"I told you last week that I wasn't going to allow you to add to your tab. It ends tonight. You now owe me twenty-nine hundred dollars, and I want my money." The words were issued in a low, threatening tone.

Sniffling, Edward reached into the back pocket of his slacks and withdrew a handkerchief. Nodding, he blotted the moisture from his cheeks and chin. He picked up his glass half-filled with the golden liquid, put it to his lips, draining it with one swallow. The bourbon slid down the back of his throat, numbing the pain and his shame.

Squaring his shoulders, he stared directly at Randolph. "I don't have it."

"Yes, you do."

Edward blew his nose, red-rimmed eyes widening in puzzlement. "What do you mean?" he asked through the square of cotton.

"You have something I want."

He panicked. "Not my house."

Leaning forward, Randolph laced his fingers together. "What the hell do I need with your *house* when I have my own?" *A much larger house,* he added silently.

A wave of heat darkened Edward's burnished gold face. "But . . . but you're holding the deed to it." A month before he'd handed Randolph the deed as collateral against the money he owed him.

Randolph waved a hand. "That's before I realized that I actually like my own home. It has everything I want except for . . ." His words trailed off.

"Except what?" Edward held his breath, ignoring the increasing constriction in his chest.

"A wife. I need a wife." His dark eyes burned with a strange light. "I'm prepared to forgive your gambling debts, return the deed, but you have to give me something in return."

Edward's forehead wrinkled in a frown as he stared at Randolph with bloodshot hazel eyes. He knew he was slightly intoxicated, but he wasn't completely drunk. "What do you want?"

Randolph plucked a cigar from a humidor, cut off the tip, moistened the cylinder of tobacco with his tongue, taking his time lighting it. There was no need for him to hurry. After all, he was the victor. He inhaled deeply, drawing smoke into his mouth, savoring the heat and the sweet musky taste on his tongue before he blew out a perfect smoke ring. Squinting through the rising haze, he stared at the defeated man sitting across from him.

He hated Edward Graham: his polished manners, impeccable lineage, family name, and his education. He even hated his fair skin coloring. Edward had attended college and law school, while Randolph had to shine shoes, repair cars, muck out barns, and on occasion chop cotton to earn enough money to set up his own business.

One business became two, and now at thirty he and his brothers were partners in a funeral home and a real estate company. He had literally worked like a slave while Edward never had to worry about tuition, books, or room and board because of his family's money. But all of that was about to change because of five cards. He would exact his revenge on everyone who represented the class of Negroes into which the Grahams were born.

"Not what, but who. I want to marry your daughter."

Weaving slightly on his chair, Edward smiled, his eyebrows

shifting upward. "I believe you have me confused with someone else. My daughter is only fifteen."

"I know how old she is, Graham." He'd spat out the last name. "I'm willing to wait for her."

Pushing away from the table, Edward attempted to stand up. "Go to hell! You're fifteen years older than my Katherine."

Moving quickly, Randolph reached across the table. Holding tightly to the front of Edward's shirt, he slapped him savagely with his free hand. A trickle of blood dotted Edward's chin from a split lip. Randolph almost laughed aloud at the stunned expression on his captive's face.

"Watch your mouth with me. Either you bring me my money by twelve o'clock tomorrow, or I'm going to evict you, your wife, and your lovely young daughter. And don't think I won't do it."

At that moment Edward wished he'd been carrying a gun. He would've shot Randolph Johnson through the heart before he turned himself into the sheriff.

"You have until tomorrow to let me know if we have a deal." Randolph released Edward and the man slumped back down to his chair. "No one has to know," he continued, deciding to press his attack. "I'll wait until she's eighteen before I begin to court her."

Shaking his head, Edward tried to make sense of Randolph's preposterous proposal. He glared at the man who within an instant had changed from friend to enemy.

"You're asking me to sell my daughter."

"It's not the first time it's been done, and it won't be the last."

The soft ticking from a clock on the fireplace mantel measured the seconds. Edward closed his eyes in resignation, the gesture seemingly aging him by twenty years.

"I can't. As God is my witness I can't."

Randolph sat down again. "Sleep on it. You'll see things more clearly in the morning."

He opened his eyes. "Why are you doing this?"

"Isn't it obvious to you?"

"No."

"Marrying a Graham will give me respectability."

"But you and your brothers have a stake in every important business in Salvation," Edward argued.

Randolph silently acknowledged that fact. Like him, two of his brothers were astute and savvy businessmen, while the youngest had expressed a desire to become a doctor.

"We have money, but people still see us as the sons of a sharecropper daddy and a laundress mama. Your daughter comes from a line of teachers, lawyers, and doctors. Right now, you sit here broke as a convict, yet you still get respect because you're a lawyer, as was your daddy. I want my children to have money *and* respectability."

What he didn't say was that Katherine Graham was also the right complexion. If she bore his children, then her pale coloring, wavy dark auburn hair, and sparkling light gray eyes would offset his dark skin and kinky hair. He'd managed to tame his tightly curled hair with water, hair pomade and a nylon stocking cap, but there was little he could do about his own sable-brown coloring. He knew several dark-skinned Negroes who had taken to bleaching creams to lighten their skin, but he wasn't one of those. If he had children with a high-yellow woman, then he was certain to have one or two who would inherit her light complexion.

"What if she doesn't like you?"

"I am not without charm." There was no boastfulness in the statement. He did not want to tell his future father-in-law about the number of women who were more than willing to share their beds with him. "I'll even wait for her to graduate from college. A month after she graduates I expect her to become my wife."

Edward knew he had to agree or be disgraced. Katherine was only fifteen, and if she attended college then she would graduate at twenty-two. A lot of things could happen in seven years. Maybe he would get enough money to repay Randolph. Or . . . maybe some unfortunate accident might befall the arrogant piece of shit whose only focus was respectability when most Negroes were concerned about their survival in a region of the country where Jim Crow and the Ku Klux Klan were evil threads tightly woven into the fabric of the Southern landscape.

Seven years. The two words were branded on his brain. He had time. He was given a reprieve.

"Okay." The single word was pregnant with resignation.

Randolph refilled Edward's glass with the bourbon he kept especially for his card games, then poured a splash into his own snifter. "I'll be good to her, Edward. She'll become my queen."

Edward stole a lingering glance at his cards, then rose slowly to his feet and walked unsteadily out of the library. He left the house, mumbling an incoherent farewell to Randoph's housekeeper who'd opened the door for him, stumbled to his car, and managed to make it home without wrecking the vehicle or injuring himself.

His footfalls were heavy as he climbed the winding staircase to the second floor. He stood outside the door to his wife's bedroom, wanting to go to her and confess all of his sins, but couldn't. He made his way down the hallway to another bedroom where he slept whenever he came home smelling of stale cigar smoke and bourbon. Lauretta forbade him to come to her bed whenever he drank.

She was lucky gambling and drinking were his only vices, because she had given him every right to take up with other women. It had been more than four years since Lauretta had permitted him to make love to her. He was only forty—much too young to stop taking his pleasure with his wife.

The light from a lamp on a table outside the bedroom provided enough illumination to make out the bed. Falling facedown on the firm mattress, fully clothed, Edward Joseph Graham berated himself for his weaknesses. He'd lost thousands of dollars on a card game and now he was using his daughter—his beautiful, delicate, and trusting Katherine, to pay off his gambling debts.

Edward wondered, before he succumbed to a tortured sleep, whether he would ever be forgiven for his many sins.

It was the end of something and we both knew it. We would come back again but it would never be the same.

—Cornelia Otis Skinner
and Emily Kimbrough

ONE

CHEVY CHASE, MARYLAND
PRESENT DAY

Morgana Wells stepped into the strapless dress, pulling it up her legs, thighs, hips and up over her breasts.

"Please zip and hook me up, darling." Shifting, she presented her husband with her bared back.

Taking several steps, Franklin curved an arm around his wife's waist, pulling her hips against his belly, as he lowered his head and brushed a kiss over her velvety shoulders. "You look and smell wonderful."

She smiled at him over a shoulder. "Thanks."

Franklin eased back and zipped and hooked the delicate fabric while admiring the way it clung to Morgana's toned, trim body. He still marveled that he'd been married for nearly three decades, because with each anniversary he deemed himself blessed that he was able to balance a career, marriage and fatherhood without sacrificing one for the other.

He and Morgana were living the American dream—she a co-owner of an elegant gift shop in Chevy Chase, Maryland, while he'd become Washington, D.C.'s most celebrated African-American criminal attorney. Their son Justin had graduated Annapolis and was currently attending flight school, and Sandra had just completed her second year at Georgetown Law. His wife and children were perfect, his home perfect, but on the other hand he hadn't always been the perfect husband. In twenty-eight years of marriage he'd had one long-term affair; he'd found it virtually impossible to avoid the temptations to which he was continually exposed. His high-profile status had become a beacon for women—especially the young and ambitious ones—seeking to advance themselves. They needed connections, and he had them.

Despite the fact he'd slept with other women, Franklin loved his wife unconditionally and would never forsake her for another woman. His father, Albert Wells, had walked out on his mother, leaving her with the responsibility for rearing four young children. Franklin hated his father for deserting his family because he'd left Erna Wells and their three daughters without male protection. His hate and resentment had run deep. When Albert had summoned his children to his deathbed, Franklin's sisters were reunited with their father for the first time in more than twenty years, but Franklin had refused to join them. In the end he forwarded his sisters a check to cover the cost of the funeral.

Morgana turned and stared up at her suddenly pensive husband, meeting his gold-brown eyes before she lowered her gaze to sweep over the stark-white dinner jacket stretched over a pair of broad shoulders.

She had fallen in love with Franklin on sight when they were sophomores at Howard University, and thirty years later she still loved him with an intensity that at times frightened her. Six-two and an even two hundred pounds, Franklin was as good-looking as he was brilliant. His professionally barbered coarse hair was now salt-and-pepper. There were distinctive lines bracketing his full sensual mouth, and because he'd recently excluded all meat from his diet his face was leaner, which made his high cheekbones more pronounced.

She picked a tiny piece of dark thread off his lapel. "I thought you were going to wear a tux."

He shook his head, pulling down the cuffs to his dress shirt. A pair of onyx and mother-of-pearl checkered cuff links showed beneath the jacket's sleeve. "The tux is too sedate for this time of year." It was a week before the Memorial Day weekend, and summer had come early to the Capitol district area. Most daytime temperatures peaked in the low-nineties.

Morgana smiled again, her large gray-green eyes crinkling. "I just have to get my wrap."

Franklin watched her cross the pale plush carpeting to a burgundy-hued, brocade-covered armchair. Morgana had personally selected every piece of furniture in the house, turning their home into a showplace worthy of a layout in *Architectural Digest*.

And it had been months since they'd entertained. The last time had been a New Year's Eve celebration. Barely a month would go by that he and Morgana did not host a cocktail or dinner party. During the warmer weather they usually held outdoor barbecues that were so well attended that their expansive backyard overflowed with friends and business associates.

Franklin's eyes narrowed slightly. He and Morgana were seeing less and less of each other. Lately, he was spending more time at the hotel in D.C., where the firm rented a suite of rooms for its partners. And if he did not work weekends, then it was Morgana who alternated working weekends at The Registry—a small gift shop catering to brides-to-be. She picked up a black silk shawl and small beaded evening purse as the telephone rang.

He reached for the cordless phone resting on a bedside table before it rang a second time. "Hello." A frown furrowed his forehead. "What do you mean she's taking him away? We're scheduled to go to trial on Tuesday."

Morgana went completely still as she watched her husband's face. She'd clutched her purse so tightly the bugle beads and sequins left an imprint on her palm. She'd waited months for this night. It would be the first time in almost six months she and Franklin would attend a social event together. A chill raced up her spine as she watched him change before her eyes like a snake shedding its skin. An expression of hardness transformed him into a stranger. His voice lowered, his words cold and exacting.

"Get over to their place as soon as you hang up. Wait for them to pack enough clothes to last them at least a week. If the grandmother starts to bitch tell her we're going to hide her where no one can find her or her grandson until we go to court. Call Luther Vaughn and inform him we'll need one of his apartments for the duration of the trial, then contact Du-Lock and have him stay at the apartment with Mrs. Jackson and her grandson."

Franklin did not know Du-Lock's real name and chose not to know. Du-Lock was the nephew of a paralegal, and his background had been checked out by one of the firm's investigation associates. The man had no prior criminal history. What he did have was a short and less than illustrious career as a professional wrestler. A poorly executed leap off the top rope of the ring had resulted in torn tendons in both knees. The firm listed his job description as a chauffeur/messenger; however, he actually performed tasks best suited for his impressive strength. One glance at his six-six, two hundred seventy-five-pound frame was enough to send most men running in the opposite direction.

Franklin took a quick glance at the gold timepiece on his left wrist. "Traffic permitting, I should get to you within twenty minutes."

Waiting until he hung up, Morgana shook her head. "No, Franklin. Not tonight."

He stared at the look of distress on her face. "I'm sorry, Mo."

She held up a hand. "Say anything, but don't apologize, Franklin," she warned quietly. Turning on her heel, she walked out of the bedroom, leaving him to stare at her retreating back.

He caught up with her as she descended the staircase. His fingers curved around her upper arm. "Wait, baby."

She turned on him as they stepped off the last stair. "I'm not waiting for you anymore, Franklin." Her luminous eyes, darkening to a stormy gray, glittered with a lethal calmness. "You know how much *this* fund-raiser means to me."

He tightened his grip on her arm. "And you know the importance of *this* case."

Morgana thrust her face close to Franklin's, her breath sweeping over his exposed throat above the collar of his dress shirt. "When hasn't a case been important? *Every* case is important to you. Take your hand off me. I don't want to be late."

Franklin's hand dropped to his side. "Look, baby, if I finish up early I'll stop by."

Forcing a smile, she drawled, "Don't bother. Remember, I'm a big girl and I *can* find my way home."

For the second time within a span of minutes, Franklin Wells watched his wife turn her back on him. It wasn't until he heard the solid slam of the door leading to the garage that he followed her. Picking up a set of keys off a hook in the kitchen, he noticed Morgana had taken the keys to his Mercedes, leaving him to drive hers. Even though the cars were identical models, his was a gleaming black on black, Morgana's a dark green with saddle-tan interior. Clenching his teeth, he cursed to himself. Had she deliberately taken his car because she knew he hated the color of hers?

His aversion to green had stemmed from his childhood. He'd grown up poor, and every night of every week he'd eaten collard greens, string beans, or cabbage seasoned with bacon ends. The homegrown green vegetables were supplemented with cornbread and whatever meat his mother purchased with her meager earnings. Most selections had been pork: chops, ham, neck bones or ham hocks. The fare was always hearty, he and his three sisters never complained about not having enough to eat, but he'd promised himself he would never eat or own anything green once he became an adult.

He'd kept the promise but had been forced to make one concession: money.

Morgana hadn't realized she had taken Franklin's car until she slowed for a stop sign. The scent of his cologne mingled with the smell of new leather. She took a quick glance in the rearview mirror, watching headlights behind her come closer and closer until the front bumper of the dark green Mercedes touched the rear bumper of the one she was driving. Franklin had come after her. Shifting into park, she reached for her purse and shawl, pushed the door open and stepped out into the warmth of the late spring evening as Franklin's black patent leather dress slip-ons touched the roadway. Without saying a word, she walked past him, slipped into her car, and closed the door. Seconds later she backed up and maneuvered around Franklin's black sedan, heading for Washington, D.C. without a backward glance.

She'd wanted to scream at Franklin that their marriage was more important than any case Wells, Murphy and Curtis had or will ever handle, yet she'd held her tongue. She'd defied her parents to marry Franklin. Before exchanging vows she and Franklin had sworn a solemn pledge to each other: they would never quarrel about the path their careers would take.

Morgana did not know when it had happened, but something had changed—she and Franklin had changed. They were spending more and more time apart, and she could not remember the last time they'd made love. Her sex drive wasn't as strong as it had been in her twenties, thirties, and early forties; but on the other hand she wasn't ready to embrace celibacy.

When Morgana stopped in front of a small boutique hotel, she smiled at the young valet who opened her door, missing his admiring glance linger on the length of her long legs as she stepped out of the car. He handed her a stub, watching her as she made her way to the entrance.

A doorman in bottle-green livery touched the shiny brim of his cap and opened the door for her. "Good evening, Mrs. Wells."

Morgana flashed a warm smile. "Good evening," she said softly, returning his polite greeting. Walking into the lobby, her gaze swept over the Victorian Revival furnishings. As chairperson of the fund-raising committee for an organization of educators, she had been responsible for selecting the site for this year's dinner-dance. Two years ago she'd joined TWC—

Teachers Who Care—an organization whose sole focus was to keep young adults in school and off drugs. Even though she hadn't taught in years, she had been invited to join because she was Mrs. Franklin Wells. She'd accepted the fact that many in the group sought to capitalize on Franklin's name, but if it was for a worthwhile cause, then she was more than amenable to help TWC because of the success of their mentoring program.

Waiters were setting tables and filling water goblets, while the maître d' conferred with the board president, a heavyset woman with shimmering blue hair who wore a matching blue satin dress. Other board members were gathered on the dais, talking quietly to one another. Quickening her pace, Morgana joined them.

"Where's your gorgeous husband, Morgana?"

Forcing a smile, she tried not to glare at Belle Collins. Pretty and petite, the twice-married, twice-divorced D.C. high school principal had made it known she was looking for husband number three, and when Morgana had opened her home to host a board meeting last year, Belle had practically wet her panties when introduced to Franklin, who had come home unexpectedly because he hadn't been feeling well. Two days later another board member called Morgana to warn her that Belle couldn't stop talking about Franklin during their return drive. She had politely thanked the woman, filing away this information. Belle wasn't the first woman to find herself blinded by Franklin's celebrity status, and she certainly would not be the last.

"He's not certain whether he will be able to come tonight." Morgana took special delight in seeing disappointment pull Belle's pert vermilion mouth downward, but her words echoed her own disappointment. Opening her evening purse, she withdrew a check. "But he gave me this for the scholarship fund."

Belle, the organization's treasurer, took the check, her large dark eyes widening in shock. "Mercy," she whispered, fanning herself with the check before waving it above her head. "Ladies, gentlemen, the firm of Wells, Murphy and Curtis has just put us over our goal with their generous donation of fifteen thousand dollars."

A rousing round of applause followed Belle's announcement. Morgana had asked her husband to get his partners to match his five thousand dollar pledge to the scholarship fund, and they had come through. Franklin had also agreed to accept three high school seniors who'd expressed an interest in law. One had dropped out after a month, but the remaining two were near to completing their ten-month commitment. TWC had been instrumental in placing more than sixty-five high school students with businesses throughout the city as work-study interns. All were offered stipends above the minimum wage for up to twenty hours of work each week.

A quartet of musicians arrived and they were directed to the ballroom where they would set up their equipment. The evening's program included a cocktail hour, a sit-down dinner, a minimum number of speeches and several hours of dancing.

Morgana waited until the dancing began, then slipped out surreptitiously, giving the valet the stub so he could retrieve her car. It was after eleven o'clock, and she knew Franklin wasn't coming.

She and Franklin could not continue to live together, yet exist in separate worlds, passing each other like strangers in Union Station who took the same train to work each day.

She had to talk to him.

Tonight.

She left the main thoroughfare and turned onto a private road. Streetlights reminiscent of gas lamps from the late nineteenth century cast a warm glow on the street that led to her home—a home that was empty despite the fact that she slept there every night.

As Morgana parked her car in the garage, she saw the bay where Franklin parked his car was empty, confirming he hadn't and probably wouldn't come home tonight. She left the garage and walked up the stairs leading into a small space outside a large modern kitchen. Placing her keys on a hook under a cabinet, she took a quick glance at the wall telephone. A flashing red number one indicated an incoming message. She walked over to the answering machine and pressed the play button.

"Morgan, I am sorry for the lateness of the hour. But I *need* you to call me as soon as you get this message. It's very important."

Picking up the receiver, she pressed two digits, listening to the automatic dialing of the programmed number.

The call was answered after the first ring. "Hello." Julian's soft voice was layered with the seductive drawl of southern Georgia.

Morgana smiled. "Hi, Uncle Julian." There came a silence, punctuated with the whisper of breathing. Her smile faded. "Uncle Julian? Are you there?"

"I'm here, Morgan." His voice was low, tired. "She's gone."

The purse she held in her hand fell to the black-and-white tiles on the kitchen floor, opening and spilling its contents. "What are you talking about?"

"It's your mother. I tried to wake her, but . . ." His words trailed off.

Morgana's knees gave way and she sank to the floor. The tears flooding her eyes overflowed.

"Are you certain, Uncle Julian?" She knew the answer before she'd asked the question. Of course he would know. Her uncle was a doctor. "Mama, Mama, Mama," she whispered over and over, the name falling from her trembling lips as she struggled to digest the shocking news. Her mother couldn't die. Not now. She was only seventy-four. And she hadn't been sick. "No . . . no!"

"Morgan. Morgan!" Julian's voice had taken on a sharp edge.

Her hands were shaking so badly she almost dropped the phone. "Yes-s-s-s."

"Where's Franklin?"

"I . . . I don't know."

"What the hell do you mean, you don't know where your husband is?"

Hearing her uncle snap at her temporarily pulled Morgana from her shocked stupor. She'd never heard him raise his voice or utter a profanity.

"What I mean is that he's not here with me. If he's not at his office, then he's probably at the hotel." She wiped her nose with the back of her hand.

"Pull yourself together and call him, Morgan. Nothing can be done here until you arrive."

Pressing the back of her head to the wall, she stared across the room with unseeing eyes. "I'll be there as soon as I can arrange for a flight."

"Call me when you get to Savannah. I'll come and pick you up."

"Uncle Julian?"

"What is it, Morgan?" His voice was softer and soothing.

"Thank you."

"I love you, Morgan." That said, he hung up the phone.

Listening to the dial tone, she tried valiantly to stave off another wave of sobbing. It took several attempts before her fingers were steady enough to hit the programmed speed dial to the offices of Wells, Murphy and Curtis. It rang three times before sending her call to voice mail.

Regaining a modicum of self-control, she called Franklin's hotel suite. For the first time she cursed him for his reluctance to wear a pager or carry a cell phone.

The telephone at the Marriott suite rang three times before she heard a break in the connection. A ragged sigh escaped her parted lips. He was at the hotel.

"Hello." The sultry voice of a woman came through the earpiece.

Morgana went completely still, then pressed a button and disconnected the call. She'd dialed the wrong number. Normally she would've apologized, but because of shock she'd forgotten her manners.

Taking her time, she punched in the programmed code a second time, certain she'd gotten it right. It was answered on the first ring.

"Hello." It was the same woman's voice.

"I'd like to speak to Franklin Wells." Her voice was low, calm.

"Frank's in the shower. Would you like to leave a message?"

A new anguish gripped her heart; a suffocating sensation wouldn't permit her to breathe. Franklin had showered before dressing for the fund-raiser, and *if* he'd showered again it was because he'd had sex with the woman who had answered the phone. Morgana hadn't slept and lived with the man for thirty years without knowing most of his idiosyncrasies.

The knowledge that her husband had been sleeping with another woman twisted inside her. "Tell *Frank* to call his *wife* at her mother's house." She ended the call and threw the phone across the kitchen. It bounced off a wall, gouging out a piece of wallpaper. Staring at the damaged wall, she laughed—the sound high-pitched and maniacal.

Still sitting on the floor, Morgana covered her face with trembling hands and drowned in the agony of her loss. And at that moment she wasn't able assess which loss was more profound—that of her mother or her marriage.

TWO

Franklin walked out of the bathroom, his toes sinking into the deep pile of the suite's carpeting as he entered the bedroom. Valerie had turned off all the lights except for the subdued ceiling fixture in the entryway. He made his way to the king-size bed, pulled back the sheet and slipped in beside the young woman who never failed to surprise him with her ardor. It was only the third time the law clerk had shared his bed. Just looking at her he never would've imagined she would be so talented between the sheets. Since their first encounter, he found everything about Valerie Garrett voluptuous: mouth, hips, breasts, and legs. Her skin was dark, dewy and satiny as polished mahogany. She was young, beautiful, smart, and very sexy.

Curving an arm around her middle, he pulled her buttocks to his groin. She sighed, and then moved her hips sensuously against his flaccid sex. "You had a telephone call." Valerie's husky voice still held a lingering trace of sleep.

Franklin pressed a kiss to the nape of her neck. "When?"

Valerie yawned. "About twenty minutes ago."

Sitting up, he reached over, turned on the bedside lamp and stared at the telephone. There was no blinking light. He picked up the receiver to call the hotel's message center when Valerie's hand stopped him. Wresting the receiver from his grip, she hung it up, running her tongue down his spine.

"I answered the call."

He shifted on the bed, staring at her as if she'd lost her mind. "You did what?"

She schooled her expression to remain impassive. "It was your wife. She said you can call her at her mother's house."

Franklin's fingers curled into tight fists as a rush of blood darkened his cheeks. "You stupid bitch! I—"

At Franklin's words, Valerie's features contorted in rage and she shrieked, "Just because I let you fuck me, that doesn't give you license to call me a bitch. I was half-asleep when the telephone rang the first time, and I hadn't meant to pick it up. But now I'm glad I did, because now your wife knows exactly what you are," she ranted, a sneer curling her upper lip. "You're a phony piece of puffed-up shit, Franklin Wells. I don't mind using my body to get what I want from a man, but what I won't put up with is being called a bitch." Moving off the bed, she picked up the telephone on her side of the bed and requested a taxi. "I'll be in the lobby in five minutes." Without a backward glance, she reached for the underwear and dress she'd folded neatly on a chair. Five minutes later she left, slamming the door to the suite behind her.

Franklin called his house, hoping Morgana would answer the phone. He got the pre-recorded generic message instead. "Mo, this is Franklin. Please pick up the phone. I know you're there, Morgana. Please talk to me, baby. I can explain everything." He pleaded until a beep indicated he had exceeded the two-minute time limit for his message.

The next few minutes came and went for Franklin Wells and he couldn't remember any of it. His drive from downtown Washington, D.C. to Chevy Chase was accomplished in record time, and once he parked his car next to Morgana's, some of his anxiety eased. She was home! He was prepared to plead, beg, do anything, but he had to get her to forgive him. He could not afford to lose his wife—not now, not ever.

Walking into the kitchen he saw the phone on the floor. He left it where it lay, bounding up the staircase, taking two steps at a time. He raced in and out of every room in the five-bedroom house, calling out Morgana's name, and it wasn't until he saw her wedding band on the slate-gray marble countertop in the bathroom adjoining their bedroom that he came to the realization that his wife was gone—she had left him.

Sinking down to the floor, he buried his face in his hands, hyperventilating. The tightness in his chest wouldn't permit him to breathe without pain squeezing his heart. He panicked. Was he having a heart attack? Slumping over, he lay on his back staring up at the ceiling, unable to believe that he was going to die. He never thought his life would end like this.

As quickly as the pain had begun it eased, but Franklin did not move. He recalled events from his childhood. He remembered with vivid clarity the sound of his mother's voice when she'd pleaded with her husband to stop running around with other women. His father's excuse was that his wife could not satisfy him, and that was why he saw other women.

You're just like your father. He looked around, thinking someone else was in the bathroom, but realized he was still alone. Now he was hearing voices.

Franklin had to admit the voice was right. His father had been an unfaithful husband and he'd followed in his footsteps. The only differences were the excuses for their infidelity. Albert Wells's wife may not have satisfied his sexual needs because she'd been too tired after working long hours at a meat-processing plant. Her priorities had been keeping her home clean and her four children fed.

Franklin's wife was not to blame for his adultery. From the first time they'd shared a bed he and Morgana had found themselves sexually compatible. She'd come to him a novice, but was a quick study.

His wife had never given him cause to seek out another woman's bed, yet just knowing women wanted to sleep with him because he was Franklin Wells, a celebrated criminal attorney, had turned into a dangerous game of conquest.

Waiting until his breathing returned to a normal rate, he pushed to his feet and retreated to the bedroom and fell across the bed. He would wait until the sun came up before he decided what he would have to do to save his marriage. He willed his mind blank, and an hour before streaks of light pierced the nighttime sky, he fell asleep.

Morgana called her uncle at his home after the red-eye flight from Baltimore-Washington International Airport touched down at the Savannah International Airport. It was four twenty-five in the morning, yet he sounded alert. "I'll be there within the hour."

Slipping the cellular phone into her purse, she stood up and made her way down the airplane's narrow aisle. Her steps were slow, halting, as if she were ninety-nine instead of forty-nine. She hadn't stopped to pack a bag after she'd called a carrier. She had just enough time to call a taxi, change her clothes and arrive at the airport to purchase her ticket and go through the security checkpoints.

Shock hadn't permitted her to sleep during the flight, and she spent the time staring through her sunglasses at the back of the seat in front of hers. Her uncle's statement, *"she's gone,"* and her husband's lover informing her that *"Frank's in the shower"* taunted her until she wanted to scream. But she hadn't screamed. What she'd done was cry—inside, silently. The urge to contact her children was very strong because she needed them.

Trancelike, she walked into a coffee shop, ordered a large cup of black coffee, and sat sipping it while she waited for Julian.

Morgana spotted her uncle as soon as he walked into the terminal. He'd lost weight since she'd last saw him at Easter in late March. However, his carriage was still elegant and erect for a man who would celebrate his eightieth birthday in July. His snow-white hair was close cropped, a style he'd affected all of his life. Small, oval, rimless glasses were perched on the narrow bridge of a nose that appeared much too delicate for a man over six feet tall. It was his eyes—dark and deep-set in an angular face the color of sable—that hadn't changed. They were still bright, alert, taking in everything around him. Rising to her feet, she forced a crooked smile.

Julian stopped less than a foot from his niece, extending his arms. He was not disappointed when she moved into his embrace. Tightening his hold, he pressed a kiss to her short curly hair.

"How are you holding up, Morgan?"

Resting her forehead on his shoulder, she shook her head. "I don't know." And she didn't know. The loss of her mother was compounded by the knowledge that her husband was sleeping with another woman. She was forced to grieve not once, but twice.

His hands moved up and down her back in a comforting gesture. "It's going to be all right."

"Where is she?"

Pulling back, Julian reached up and removed her sunglasses. Though red and swollen, Morgana's eyes reminded him of Katherine's. He hadn't cried for the loss of his sister-in-law because he knew he had to be strong for Morgana and his grandniece and nephew.

"At the hospital. They won't release her body until they get your signature."

Morgana held out her hand for her glasses. She gave Julian a tired smile. "Let's go and get this done."

He gave her the glasses, then placed a hand on her shoulder. "Aren't you going to wait for Franklin?"

Shielding her eyes with the dark lenses, she said, "Franklin will probably get here later."

Julian lifted an eyebrow. "Later?" He frowned when she did not respond. "Are you sure you're all right, Morgan?"

She gave Julian a level look behind her glasses. She knew he would never question her about her relationship with Franklin, because thirty years ago he'd assumed the role of peacemaker between her and her parents when she'd informed them she'd planned to marry Franklin. Their reaction was volatile, and Julian, the gentle family doctor, had become the recipient of their wrath.

Randolph and Katherine had vehemently voiced their disapproval, claiming Franklin was not socially acceptable to them. It hadn't mattered that Franklin Wells was intelligent and polite. What *had* mattered to them was his family's background: his father had deserted his family for another woman, his mother had worked in a factory, two of his sisters had borne children out of wedlock and the third had been in and out of jail and had a history of drug abuse.

It hadn't mattered that as the youngest child Franklin had decided he wanted a better life for himself and had attended Howard University on full scholarship. That he'd worked nights while he attended classes during the day, giving up any semblance of a social life. All that mattered to them was his less than illustrious pedigree.

Morgana hadn't needed her parents' permission to marry but had wanted their blessings. The stalemate ended when she told them she planned to marry Franklin despite their protests. A week following their graduation from Howard, she and Franklin exchanged vows in Salvation, Georgia.

Most of the invited guests were her family members. Franklin's mother and one of his sisters made the trip from Birmingham, Alabama. His youngest sister was in jail again for burglarizing a neighbor's house to fund her heroin addiction, and the oldest sister had just given birth to her third child without benefit of a husband.

"I'm fine, Uncle Julian. I am," she insisted when he continued to stare at her. Reaching for his hand, she steered him out of the terminal to the parking area. "I haven't told Sandra or Justin."

Julian squeezed her fingers. "It's still rather early. You can call them later." He gave her a sidelong glance. "Have you eaten?"

She smiled again. He was worrying about her when it was he who looked as if he hadn't had a substantial meal in weeks. "Not since last night."

"After we leave the hospital we'll stop and eat breakfast. Then I'll take you back to your mother's house."

Morgana stopped suddenly. "How did she die?"

He stared over her head. "It was heart failure. We were sharing dinner when she complained of feeling fatigued. I told her I'd clean up the kitchen, but she insisted on doing it. I stayed with her until she finished and then she went upstairs to lie down. I sat on the sunporch watching the baseball game. After the game ended I went up to check on her." He hesitated, drawing in a deep breath. "Her heart had stopped. I performed CPR, checked her vitals over and over, hoping and praying she was still alive. But she was gone. I called 911, then sat down beside Katherine to wait for the EMTs. And no, Morgan, she did not suffer. You only have to see her face to know that."

Leaving the airport, Julian followed the signs pointing west. Salvation, Georgia, a historically all-black town, was ninety minutes from Hilton Head Island and forty minutes from Savannah. It was where he'd been born and raised, and where he'd returned to set up a family practice more than fifty years ago.

He took a quick glance at Morgana. The corners of his mouth lifted in a smile. She had fallen asleep. Slowing, he left the highway for a local road. He would take the longer route, giving her time to get some rest before she initiated preparations to bury her mother.

It was daybreak before Morgana unlocked the door to the house where she'd grown up, feeling like a stranger for the first time because there was no one there to greet her. She had signed the necessary documents for the hospital's morgue to release Katherine Johnson's body to the local funeral home, and then she and her uncle had shared breakfast at a twenty-four-hour diner a mile outside of Salvation. The sight of food had made her nauseous, but she'd forced herself to eat a slice of toast and drink a cup of herbal tea.

The air inside the house was thick and stifling. The flowers cradled in a lead crystal vase on a table in the entryway had bowed their heads as if mourning their owner's passing.

Her uncle stood behind her. "I closed all the windows because I didn't know when it was going to rain."

Morgana smiled. "I'm going to turn on the air to get rid of the stuffiness before I open windows."

Pushing his hands into the pockets of his slacks, Julian angled his head. "Do you want me to stay with you?" She half-turned to face him, shaking her head, and Julian wanted to tell her that her husband should've come down with her, but held his tongue. Leaning down, he kissed her forehead. "Get some sleep, Morgan."

"I will."

A hint of a smile crinkled his dark eyes. Turning, he walked out, closing the door quietly behind him.

Morgana pressed several buttons on a panel near the door, activating the central air-conditioning. She had paid to have the house centrally cooled, despite her mother's protests, after a summer of dangerous heat resulted in the deaths of thirteen elderly Salvation citizens. Julian, who had found Katherine delirious and dehydrated, had called Morgana after he'd stabilized his sister-in-law. The decision to centrally heat and cool the house had caused a rift between her and her mother, but it had ended when Katherine called to confirm their annual Christmas family gathering.

The cooling air flowed through vents, sweeping over her body as she made her way to the sunporch, her favorite room in the house. Her father had had the house built before she was born, and at that time it was one of the finest homes in Salvation. The grandest had belonged to Morgana's grandparents Edward and Lauretta Graham. After they passed away Katherine sold it to a developer who razed it and erected six structures on the land where the historical house had stood for more than a century.

Sinking down to an overstuffed club chair covered with a polished cotton fabric in a sunny yellow, she kicked off her running shoes and rested her sock-covered feet on a matching footstool. An antique clock on the fireplace mantel chimed the hour. It was seven A.M.

Retrieving the tiny cell phone from her purse, Morgana called her daughter.

Sandra answered, her voice heavy with sleep. "This had better be good," she slurred.

"This is your mother."

"Mom! I'm sorry."

Morgana bit down on her lower lip before saying, "I'm calling to tell you that Grandma Katherine died in her sleep yesterday, and I want you to make arrangements to come to Salvation."

A gasp came through the wire, then the sound of soft

sobbing. Morgana heard her future son-in-law's voice in the background.

"Morgana?" Kenneth had picked up the telephone.

She told him what had happened, and that arrangements couldn't be finalized until the immediate family was in attendance. Kenneth assured her that he would take care of Sandra, and secure travel arrangements for both of them.As she ended the call the telephone next to the chair rang. She stared at it for several seconds before picking it up.

"Hello."

"Mo?"

She wanted to hang up, but knew she had to tell Franklin about Katherine. After all, she'd been his mother-in-law for twenty-eight years. "Yes, Franklin?"

"When are you coming home?"

Her delicate jaw tightened. "I'm not. I have to bury my mother."

"Oh no, Mo," Franklin moaned.

Morgana felt more in control than she had since she'd returned her uncle's call. "I just hung up with Sandra. Kenneth's taking care of their travel arrangements."

"Have you called Justin?" Franklin asked.

"No."

"I'll do that. As soon as I hang up with you I'll call the base, then I'll get in touch with Sandra and Kenneth. I'll see if we can all come down together." There was silence before he spoke again. "Are you all right?"

"I have my uncle." What she didn't say was that it shouldn't have been her uncle who'd had to comfort her, but her husband. "I'll talk to you later." She placed the phone on its cradle before Franklin could say anything else.

She sat on the chair until the room cooled, and then she got up and climbed the curving staircase to the second floor. She would take Julian's advice and try to sleep. But first she needed to shower before she called her best friend and business partner, Bernice Miller.

THREE

Morgana stepped out of the tub, reaching for a towel hanging on a nearby rack. She smiled a sad smile. Her uncle was right about Katherine not suffering. Even in death her mother had affected a mysterious smile.

Moving closer to the full-length mirror on the back of the door, she examined her face. The strain of the past day's events was obvious in the slight puffiness under her gray-green eyes. Her gaze moved lower as she examined her nude body. What she saw staring back at her was a tall, middle-aged woman with a firm body that belied her near fifty years. Although she'd given birth to two children her full breasts hadn't sagged, the skin over her belly was still taut and her hips were slim, toned. She claimed a few gray hairs, but the auburn strands she'd inherited from her mother made them appear more gold than gray.

It no longer mattered that she worked out at a health club three times a week, had a standing weekly appointment at a full-service salon for her hair, skin, hands and feet, or that she monitored everything she put into her mouth. She'd embarked on a beauty regimen that would rival a high-fashion model's—and for what? It hadn't stopped her husband from straying.

The fingers of her right hand curled into a tight fist before she hit the door frame, welcoming the pain radiating up her arm to her elbow. "Why, Franklin?" she said aloud, swallowing back a sob.

She'd wanted to be the perfect wife for D.C.'s celebrated African-American attorney. Both of them had worked hard to become a power couple.

Nagging questions attacked her relentlessly: Was the woman pretty, young? Was she the first woman Franklin had slept with, or was she merely one of many? Did he have a mistress? Had he fathered other children? The questions taunted until she was forced to ask herself how she had missed the signs: his sleeping at the hotel and their not making love for weeks. And why did she have to discover his infidelity the day she'd been given the most devastating news of her life?

A tight knot gripped her belly, followed by a rush of bile in her throat. Moving quickly, she bent over the commode, retching violently. Purging the contents of her stomach had helped her to feel better. It ended and she sagged weakly against the bowl, her moist forehead pressed to the cool porcelain.

"I hate you," she chanted over and over, because she wanted to convince herself that she truly hated Franklin.

After resting for a few moments, Morgana rinsed her mouth and splashed cool water on her face before she retreated to her bedroom. After looking through several drawers containing clothes she'd left during previous trips, she slipped into a pair of panties and pulled a T-shirt over her head. She sat down on a rocker in a corner of the bedroom, picked up the phone, and dialed the area code for Washington, D.C.

She and Bernice Miller had been friends for more than half their lives. They'd met as new teachers at a D.C. elementary school, and had bonded quickly. Morgana had taught first grade and Bernice, third. Both had been recent college graduates and newlyweds. Bernice had taught for twenty-five years, ending her career as an assistant principal in the same school where she had begun teaching.

Bernice answered the call after the second ring with her cheery greeting, "Good morning."

Morgana smiled despite her grief. "Good morning, Bernice."

"What's up, girlfriend?"

"I'm in Salvation."

There was a noticeable pause before Bernice said, "Is everything all right?"

Morgana shook her head even though her friend could not see her. "My mother passed away yesterday. My uncle called me last night, and I flew down early this morning."

"Morgana, I'm so sorry. Is there anything you need for me to do? I can close the shop for a few days and come down to help you."

"Thanks for offering, but I think I'll be okay. I'm calling to say that I don't know how long I'm going to be here. I have to take care of my mother's legal affairs."

"Why don't you let Franklin handle that?"

Morgana bit down on her lower lip until she felt a pulse throbbing between her teeth. "I'm leaving Franklin." There came a stunned silence through the earpiece. "He's been sleeping with another woman."

"When did you find this out?" The query came out slowly, as if Bernice had to measure every word.

"Last night. Right after my uncle called me, I called Franklin at the hotel. A woman answered the phone."

"Just because a woman answered, that doesn't mean he was sleeping with her."

"I know my husband, Bernice."

"That may be true, but aren't you being a little paranoid? Didn't you say that whenever he's working on a big case he—"

"I *know* my husband," Morgana interrupted. "The woman said, 'Frank's in the shower.' "

"So?"

"So? Franklin only showers for two reasons: one is before he changes his clothes, and the other is after making love. He'd just showered before we were to go to the TWC dinner-dance. And if he took another shower four hours later it's because he had screwed a woman.

"My husband is nauseated by the smell of stale sex," she continued. "The aversion comes from his childhood. His father used to come home stinking after tomcatting all night with other women. When Franklin had asked his father why he smelled that way, he boasted that it was the smell of pleasure, and held Franklin's head to his crotch, while yelling at him to take a good whiff of what a real man smelled like."

"Damn!"

"He hated his father to his grave, and right now I feel the same way about Franklin. I trusted him, Bernice." There was an audible sob in her voice. "I loved and trusted him, and he repaid my trust by becoming a philandering son of a bitch! If he wanted out of the marriage, why didn't he come to me and say that?"

"Because he doesn't want out of the marriage, Morgana. Franklin loves you."

"Yeah, right."

"I'm not going to argue with you, because you don't need any more stress in your life at this time. I love you like a sister, Morgana, and I want what's best for you. But right now you need to concentrate on burying your mother. Your problem with Franklin isn't going to be an instant fix. You two share more than half your lives, and despite what you believe, you just don't throw away thirty years because he deceived you."

"How about you and Nathan? You left him because he was having an affair."

"I married Nathan on the rebound after Cliff and I split. The truth is I never loved him. I needed a reason to leave him, and he provided me with that reason."

Bernice had divorced her second husband because she hadn't loved him, but Morgana wasn't ready to admit that she hated Franklin enough to divorce him. She'd told Bernice that she was leaving Franklin, but the truth was that she *had* left him. She'd come to Salvation to bury her mother, and she didn't know when or if she would return to Maryland. And if she decided not to, then she would give Bernice her share of The Registry and begin life anew. She was forty-nine, educated, in good health, and solvent. She could go anywhere and start a new life.

"Don't worry about coming back until you're ready," Bernice said firmly. "Mrs. Butterfield has been asking to work more hours, so I'm going to call her after I hang up with you and have her come on full-time until you get back."

Morgana smiled. "Thanks."

"Hey, girlfriend. There's no need to thank me. I know you would do the same for me."

"You're right, girlfriend." Less than thirty seconds later she rang off.

She left the rocker and lay across the bed, falling asleep within minutes of her head touching the pillow.

Julian waited on the front porch of his house for Morgana. She'd called to tell him that Johnson Funeral Home was in possession of Katherine's body and she planned to meet with the director to finalize the arrangements. She hadn't asked, but he volunteered to accompany her—he didn't want her to go alone.

Seeing a familiar navy blue Chevrolet, he made his way down the porch as Morgana maneuvered her late mother's car into the driveway. He opened the passenger-side door and slipped onto the seat beside her.

"You look better."

She smiled. "Thank you. I feel a lot better."

Closing his eyes, he pressed the back of his head against the headrest. It did not take the intelligence quotient of a nuclear physicist to know that his niece's marriage was in trouble. She hadn't known Franklin's whereabouts, wasn't wearing a ring and had flown to Georgia—alone. Morgana, Franklin and Sandra had visited Salvation for Easter, and everyone had appeared happy at that time. Or were they?

Julian opened his eyes, staring out the windshield as Morgana put the car in reverse. "Your husband called me a little after one."

"What did he want?"

Julian ignored her harsh, flat query, saying, "He's flying in tonight with your children. He said he and Sandra would have been here sooner, but they decided to wait for Justin."

Morgana thought it odd Franklin would call her uncle's

house. Was he trying to avoid her because she'd hung up abruptly? "What time are they arriving?"

"Around ten-thirty. He said there's no need to meet their flight because he will rent a car at the airport."

Nodding, she said, "I can't wait to see them." She managed to mask her inner turmoil with a deceptive calmness.

She hadn't lied to her uncle. She needed her children's love and support. Reuniting with them would give her the emotional strength she needed to come face-to-face with Franklin.

Her emotions had vacillated between love and hate when she'd searched through Katherine's closet for a dress to take to the funeral home. How could she hate a man she'd loved for thirty years, had been married to for twenty-eight, and had had his children?

And if she did hate Franklin it wasn't because of his infidelity as much as it was his deceit. She'd taken pride that her marriage wasn't just based on love but trust; as a realist she'd known too many couples who had fallen in and out of love.

"Morgan, the light is green."

Julian's soft voice broke into her musings. Stepping on the gas, she drove through the intersection. There were five cars behind hers. A wry smile curved her mouth. It was rush hour in downtown Salvation.

Each time she returned to Salvation, Morgana felt as if she had stepped back in time, because seemingly nothing had changed in thirty years. It was Poole's Hardware instead of Home Depot, Collins's Pharmacy, not CVS or Walgreens, and Gallagher's Office Supply instead of Staples. A few of the stores sported new awnings, but that's where the revitalization began and ended. The population of a little more than twelve hundred had remained relatively constant over the years, new births offsetting deaths.

A well-kept, white, one-story Colonial-style structure came into view. A gold-lettered sign affixed to a post on a manicured lawn identified it as Johnson Funeral Home. Although Johnson Funeral Home, Johnson Real Estate and Johnson Insurance were no longer owned or managed by anyone who claimed Johnson blood, the names had remained.

Morgana pulled into the parking area, turned off the engine and waited for Julian to get out and come around to open the door for her. As a young girl he'd admonished her sternly when she'd jumped out of his car before he could assist her. His statement: *A man of any worth always opens a door for a lady, seats her and rises to his feet whenever she enters a room,* was imprinted on her brain. She'd thought the ritual archaic, but as she matured she'd come to appreciate the custom.

She smiled up at Julian as he opened her door. "Thank you."

Julian returned her smile, the gesture softening the lines in his angular face and making Morgana aware that her elderly uncle was still a very handsome man. Tall, slender and elegant, he'd aged beautifully like the most expensive wine, with a feathering of fine lines fanning out around his deep-set, penetrating eyes.

Of the four Johnson brothers Julian had been the most educated of the quartet, but he had also been the only one who hadn't married or fathered a child.

Opening the rear door, she reached for the garment bag resting on the backseat. Julian took the bag from her. "I've decided to hold a graveside service. If anyone wants to come, they're welcome."

Nodding, Julian followed her across the parking lot to the

entrance. He opened the door to the funeral home Randolph had established more than fifty years before, waiting until his eyes adjusted to the dimness. He noticed the frown settling between Morgana's eyes. Even though she'd buried her father, death was still a stranger to her. For him the cycle of birth and death was as familiar to him as the face that stared back at him in the morning. He was quickly approaching eighty, and there were times when he doubted whether he would wake up to greet a new day, but it was obvious God wasn't ready to reclaim the breath given him at birth.

Morgana sat with Julian and the funeral director in a cool, dimly lit office, talking quietly. If she hadn't been there to make arrangements for her mother's funeral she would've found the scene hilarious. George Turner was involved in a business wherein his *customers* were not bothered by either bright lights or loud voices.

Leaning forward, she stared at the short, light-skinned man with a receding hairline. His attempt at camouflaging his hair loss with a straightened comb-over style was almost comical given the half dozen strands pasted to his moist scalp.

"Mr. Turner, I'd like a private graveside service early Tuesday morning. There is to be no wake or public viewing. These were my mother's wishes."

The director placed a manicured hand on his chest, inclining his head. "Mrs. Wells, Johnson Funeral has continued the tradition established by your father. No detail or request will be overlooked or denied. I am here to see to your family's comfort."

She smiled. "Thank you, Mr. Turner." Unzipping the garment bag lying across her knees, she removed a dress, which had been one of Katherine's favorites. The pearl-gray silk garment was wrapped in plastic. "Please put this on my mother." She handed the funeral director the dress.

"How would you like for us to style your mother's hair?"

"No curls. Just brush it to frame her face. I don't want a lot of makeup. Only a hint of rose-pink lipstick and blush."

Katherine Johnson hadn't cut her hair after her husband's accident, and over the next twenty-three years it had grown long enough to reach her hips. A month after Randolph Johnson died, she went to a local beauty parlor and had it cut above her shoulders. She'd worn the modified pageboy style until her sixtieth birthday, then celebrated this milestone year with a short pixie style that had showed off the delicate bones of her face and the brilliance of her large, light-gray eyes to their best advantage. In the ensuing years the red hair faded, becoming a shiny gray that was a flattering contrast to her complexion. Rising to her feet, Morgana extended her hand, thanking the director for his patience and understanding.

She drove Julian back to his house, the trip accomplished in complete silence. She sat waiting and watching as he made his way up the steps to his front door. Just before he opened and closed the door behind him, he raised a hand in a wave.

She had wanted to invite Julian to share dinner with her, but didn't. There was an obvious profound sadness in the older man that made her want to weep for him. Julian Johnson was her oldest surviving relative. Her parents, grandparents, paternal and maternal aunts and uncles were all gone. Besides her West Coast cousins, whom she hadn't heard from in years, there was only her uncle Julian. And she had to decide before she left Salvation what she wanted to do with him. At seventy-nine, the retired family practitioner lived alone and was able to care for his day-to-day needs—but for how much longer?

Morgana returned to her mother's house and went directly to her parents' bedroom. Walking into the room, she pulled a handmade quilt off the foot of the bed, folding it neatly before she stripped the bed of a lightweight cotton blanket, followed by a set of floral sheets. She put them into a large wicker laundry basket, taking it downstairs to a laundry room off the kitchen. She spent the next two hours putting up several loads of wash, dusting the surfaces of bedside tables, a triple dresser, lingerie chest, armoire, and vacuuming the floor in her mother's bedroom.

She remade the bed, and then sat in an armchair in a corner, listening to the soft beating of her heart. Everything was quiet, still. The sun had set, taking with it the intense daytime heat, and she wanted to open the windows to let in the nocturnal sounds serenading the countryside. A wry smile curved her mouth. Katherine was right about living in an artificially cooled environment. Not opening windows was like existing in a silent tomb.

Nightfall had blanketed the countryside by the time she walked down the winding staircase to the expansive wraparound porch; she sat on a cushioned rocker, watching the sweep of headlights in the distance light up the countryside. The house was dark except for the table lamp in the entryway and one in her bedroom. Sitting in the dark had always been a balm for her. It masked the familiar and permitted her to fantasize about what wasn't and what could be.

She watched the spray of stars littering the nighttime sky, telling herself she should get up and prepare something to eat, but loathed moving. Closing her eyes, Morgana pressed the back of her head to the rocker's cushioned softness and smiled. Her smile was one that had captured the rapt attention of an aspiring young lawyer thirty years before.

FOUR

It was the spring semester of 1974 and most major U.S. newspapers' lead article covered a federal grand jury's conclusion that President Nixon had joined in a conspiracy to cover up White House involvement in the Watergate break-in at Democratic Party offices. The finding that Nixon was a co-conspirator in the Watergate cover-up was contained in a sealed report, but this held little or no interest for Morgana Johnson because she had fallen under the sensual spell of a fellow student.

Finals were less than three weeks away, and she looked forward to completing her sophomore year at Howard University. An A student, she had earned a near-perfect grade point average, but in the romance department she was running a D average and had given up hope of ever finding someone who she would find compatible. As a freshman her on-again, off-again liaison with an upperclassman had left her in an emotional tailspin, yet somehow she'd found the courage and strength to walk away from him. She hadn't dated anyone in more than five months, even though she'd been asked out several times.

Sitting in a coffee shop several blocks from the Howard University campus, eating lunch while reviewing for a psychology final, she did not know her life was about to change.

Franklin Wells sat at a nearby table with five other students reading aloud from the lead article in *The Washington Post.* There was a strange silence in the place as everyone listened to his sonorous Southern drawl. And it was his voice that had captured Morgana's rapt attention even before she noticed his face. Its timbre was as soft and smooth as whipped cream.

Glancing up from the open textbook beside her plate, she stared at the face that went along with the velvet voice. The sound of forks hitting plates was the only accompaniment as he finished the article, folded the paper neatly, and raised his head, his gaze meeting and fusing with hers.

She felt a shiver of awareness settle in the pit of her stomach when he smiled at her. The shape of his strong mouth, the flecks of liquid gold in his expressive eyes and the sharp angle of high cheekbones above a short black beard were imprinted on her brain within seconds. Waves of heat washed over her as she tried recalling what she'd just spent the last half hour reading, realizing the exercise had been futile She berated herself for coming to the restaurant to study instead of going to the library.

Morgana returned his bold stare, her mouth softening in a sensual smile before she lowered her gaze. The next quarter of an hour passed with her watching him through her lashes as he broke off pieces of a thick slice of cornbread while taking sips of sweet tea. His dining partners continued to filled their mouths with forkfuls of greens, smothered cabbage, candied sweet potatoes and crispy fried chicken, fish or spicy spareribs until their plates held the remains of bones and crumbs.

Franklin Wells angled his head close to a slender girl sitting next to him sporting a natural hairstyle and a colorful orange and yellow dashiki and whispered in her ear. Reaching into the pocket of his jeans, he handed her a coin. Nodding, she got up and dropped a quarter into a jukebox in a corner. He also rose to his feet. Seconds later the distinctive voice of Roberta Flack singing "The First Time Ever I Saw Your Face," floated from the speakers.

Morgana's head came up again, her eyes widening at the significance of the song title. She was tempted to jump up and run out of the restaurant when the man with the mellifluous voice made his way over to her table.

Smiling broadly, he extended his hand, introducing himself. "Franklin Wells."

She stared at his large, well-formed hand before she shook it. "Morgana Johnson."

"May I join you?"

She flashed a friendly smile. "Sure, but only if you let me have my hand back."

He loosened his grip, but did not release her fingers. His thumb rested on the underside of her wrist, and she was certain he could feel the runaway beating of her pulse. A knowing smile tilted the corners of his mouth upward. "Do I frighten you?"

Morgana jerked her hand away, a slight frown marring her smooth forehead. "Should I be frightened of you?"

Pulling over a chair, Franklin sat down, his knees bumping hers under the small round table. His gaze moved slowly over her face. Morgana was exquisite. Even without makeup he'd found her stunning. Her reddish curly hair was pulled off her deeply tanned golden-brown face in a single braid that fell over one breast. Her eyes were hypnotic. They were a sooty gray with pinpoints of dark green, reminding him of a cat's.

He decided then and there that he liked Morgana, her cool looks and her poise. Lowering his eyelids, Franklin offered her his most winning smile.

"No, Miss Johnson. You have no need to be frightened or suspicious of me."

She studied him for a full minute, silently admiring his smooth brown skin and his neatly barbered hair. His hair wasn't close-cropped, and yet it wasn't long enough to be considered an Afro. He wore the attire affected by many students: a loose-fitting dashiki and bell-bottom slacks or jeans.

"So goes the refrain of undercover government agents posing as students to identify radicals and subversives on college campuses."

His smile faded quickly. "You think I'd inform on my people?"

She lifted an eyebrow. "You wouldn't be the first."

It was his turn to frown. "I came to Howard to learn how to defend our people, not rat them out, *my sister.*"

"Are you a law student, *my brother?*"

Nodding, he said, "Pre-law." He glanced over at her open textbook. "Psychology or social work?"

"Neither. Early-childhood education."

His light brown eyes glittered with excitement. "Wonderful choice. Our people need teachers to teach, lawyers to protect, and doctors to heal."

"Social workers to advocate," she countered.

"Ministers to help heal the spirit."

"Writers to inspire."

Franklin nodded, smiling. "Singers and dancers to entertain."

They continued enumerating occupations and professions until they exhausted their lists. Meanwhile the students at Franklin's table had settled their bill and were filing out the door.

"Aren't you going with your friends?"

"Nope." He picked up her fork and speared a portion of the macaroni and cheese she'd barely touched.

"Don't you have a class?" she asked.

"Nope," he said, after he'd chewed and swallowed the flavorful side dish. What he should've done was head home after his last class instead of coming to the restaurant with his friends. He'd planned to study for several hours before going to sleep. At ten he would get up and then prepare to go to work.

"The mac and cheese isn't bad."

She glanced at her watch, knowing she had to leave in another twenty minutes, or she would be late for a class. And her professor was demanding about beginning his lecture on time. He'd warned that three tardies would result in a full letter grade reduction. Getting anything less than a B would jeopardize her remaining on the dean's list. Closing the textbook, she placed it atop several spiral notebooks.

"I have to go. I have a class."

Franklin placed his left hand over her right. "Will I see you again?"

"Maybe."

He smiled. "Is that a yes or no?"

Running her tongue over her lower lip, Morgana gave him

a seductive sidelong glance. "It's a yes." She'd said yes when no was poised on the tip of her tongue.

"When?"

"Tomorrow."

"Where?"

"Here."

"What time?" Franklin asked, continuing his questioning.

The next day was Friday and Morgana had an English lit class at ten. "Three." Meeting him at three was not what she considered an actual date. And meeting him at that time would give her enough time to return to her apartment to shower and change her clothes.

"Make it two and you're on."

Her lids lowered as she glanced up at him through her lashes, unaware of the blatant seductiveness of the gesture. "Then two it is."

Franklin stood up, pulling back her chair. "I've got it," he said when she opened her wallet to pay her bill.

She shook her head. "That's all right."

"No," he insisted. "I'll take care of it this time."

"Only if you permit me to pay the next time."

He smiled. "Okay."

Franklin waited until Morgana left the restaurant, and then reached into his pocket, berating himself for offering to pay for her meal. He had barely enough money left to pay for his own side order of cornbread and iced tea. And he wasn't due to get paid again until the following Friday.

Shrugging a broad shoulder, he picked up the receipt and walked over to the counter. It wouldn't be the first time he'd found himself nearly broke. He'd come to Howard on a full academic scholarship. The award included tuition, but not room and board. That meant he had to work.

Within his first week as a Howard University student he found a night job cleaning offices, working the eleven-to-seven A.M. shift, while negotiating with the building's management to let him use one of the executive bathrooms to shower before he left for his first class. He'd also used what would become his masterful power of persuasion to barter eating at the building's employee cafeteria in lieu of a raise. This arrangement had worked well for him his first two years at the college even though he worked hard, studied even harder and had forfeited a social life because he had neither the money nor the time.

But something told him that was going to change. Something about Morgana Johnson had touched him the way no other woman had. There was the physical attraction, but it didn't stop there. It was as if he knew intuitively that she would become a part of his life and his future as he would hers. They would become the perfect couple.

The morning had passed at a snail's pace for Morgana as she daydreamed through her morning class. She hadn't heard a word of the lecture as the youthful-looking professor extolled the creative genius of Melville's *Billy Budd.* The allegorical novella had held no appeal for her as the powerful image of Franklin Wells lingered with her. The lecture ended and she raced out of the building instead of lingering as many of the young women did who always flirted shamelessly with their brilliant professor when given the opportunity. It would be another year before they all groaned in unison as the news of his sexual predilection was whispered about around the campus.

Morgana walked the four blocks to where she'd parked her orange Volkswagen Bug and drove home. She'd accomplished the trip in record time, staying barely under the speed limit. Her spacious studio apartment was on the top floor of a well-maintained brownstone building along a street that had managed to escape the rapid deterioration of a once upscale neighborhood. She preferred walking the many steps in lieu of having someone stomping over her head at the most inopportune hours.

Unlocking the door, she walked into the sunny space, dropping her books and handbag on a gossip bench. Seconds after the self-locking door closed, she made her way to the bathroom. She kicked off her sandals and jeans, and pulled a loose-fitting peasant blouse over her head. Her panties and bra followed.

Turning on the shower, she adjusted the water temperature, stepped into the tub and closed the glass enclosure. She undid the single plait falling down her back, shampooed and conditioned her hair.

Her thoughts drifted to the young man who was bold and confident—so much so that he'd approached a stranger to introduce himself. She could have called him arrogant when he'd asked to see her again, but instead of rejecting his offer she'd agreed to meet him. She had asked herself over and over why Franklin Wells and not some of the other male students who'd openly made it known that they were quite interested in her.

Turning off the faucets, she slid back the glass doors, reaching for a towel. She dried and moisturized her body with a scented cream. Using a wide-tooth comb, she combed the heavy strands until they flowed around her shoulders and halfway down her back. Whenever she moved her head corkscrew spirals bounced, taking on a life of their own.

Her thoughts returned to Franklin. There was just something about him that touched her core like no other man had done before. She'd had a boyfriend in high school, but their relationship never went beyond chaste kisses or hand-holding. It wasn't until she entered college that she felt she was mature enough to handle a physical relationship. Fortified with an ample supply of birth control pills she'd slept with a student at the end of her freshman year. Despite the fact that he was more experienced than she was, he still lacked the patience or sensitivity necessary for her to achieve sexual fulfillment. Most times she lay motionless, waiting for him to finish. Never—not once—had he ever asked if she enjoyed it. She *never* enjoyed sleeping with him, and in the end it was she who'd ended what had become an unfulfilling, lackluster liaison.

She selected what she would wear, placing the garments on the sofa, which converted to a queen-size bed. After changing her top twice, she finally settled on a slim black linen gabardine midi-length skirt, a black ribbed tank top and a multicolored patchwork silk bolero jacket. The shocking pinks, oranges and reds were a vivid contrast to the somber black. Pushing her bare feet into a pair of black suede sandals with a sporty wedge heel, she stared at her reflection in the full-length mirror on the back of the bathroom door. At first she'd decided not to wear makeup, but changed her mind. Smoke-gray eyeliner, shadow and a coat of mascara accented the gray in her eyes, while a rose-red lipstick brought out the richness of her deep tan.

She changed her purse from a large leather saddlebag to a smaller crocheted one with a shoulder strap. Making certain she had her keys, driver's license and an extra twenty-dollar bill, she left her apartment to return to the restaurant where she'd met Franklin the day before.

Franklin was waiting in front of the restaurant when she arrived. She was twenty minutes early. She tapped the horn lightly to get his attention. He walked toward her car, bending slightly to make certain he knew who was honking at him.

Turning off the engine, Morgana got out of the small car, dangling the keys in front of her. "Hi there. Would you like to drive?"

Franklin's eyes lit up when he saw her, and he flashed a broad smile. "Hi yourself." He took the keys, then lowered his head and kissed her cheek. Cupping her elbow in his hand, he led her around to the passenger side, opening the door and waiting until she was seated before he sat behind the wheel. Pushing back the seat to accommodate his longer legs, he adjusted the rearview mirror, put the key into the ignition, shifted into gear, and smoothly pulled away from the curb.

Stopping at a red light, he gave Morgana a sidelong glance. "You look beautiful."

He wanted to tell her that she also smelled wonderful. It was the first thing he'd noticed about her other than her incredible face. The perfume she wore had a soft almond fragrance he found hypnotic. And after seeing her again he knew at a glance that Morgana Johnson wasn't an impoverished student struggling to make ends meet. The cut of her clothes and the fact that she had her own car indicated he was not in her economic class.

She smiled at him. "Thank you. You look very nice, too." Franklin wore a cream-colored cotton pullover V-neck sweater with a pair of tan slacks and brown oxfords.

Nodding, he acknowledged her compliment as he concentrated on his driving. He didn't have Friday classes, which meant he could come home from work and sleep. He'd gotten up at noon, shaved and showered in the communal bathroom on the floor where he rented a furnished room. After selecting what he would wear for his afternoon outing with Morgana, he set out to walk from his apartment to the restaurant. Walking the three miles saved him the cost of taking the bus.

"Do you want to go anywhere special?" he asked as he drove along Sixth Street, passing the School of Engineering and Architecture and Planning.

"Have you had lunch?"

He lifted an eyebrow. "No. Have you?"

Morgana shook her head, curls bouncing over her forehead and around her face. "I know a place in Baltimore that offers the best soft-shell crabs I've ever tasted. It'll be my treat."

Downshifting, he maneuvered off the road and parked. He put the Volkswagen in neutral while his right foot covered the brake. Turning to the right, he laid an arm over the back of her seat, his fingers touching her unbound hair.

"I'd like to clear the air before you decide whether you want to spend the afternoon with me."

She gave him a startled look, her mind reeling in confusion. Mixed feelings surged through her. Had she said or done something wrong? "What?" The single word came out harsher than she'd intended.

"I don't have much money. No, let me rectify that statement. I don't have *any* extra money. Not until I get paid next Friday. And that translates into my not being able to treat you to dinner or a movie until that time."

Morgana folded a hand on her hip. "Did I ask you to treat me to dinner or a movie?"

"I asked to see you."

"Exactly. And now you see me. And what I want to do is eat. Now either you drive on, Franklin Wells, or get the hell out of my car. Right here, right now!"

He recoiled as if she had struck him. Her cool exterior was a deceptive foil for a quick red-hot temper. Everything within Franklin told him to get out of the car and walk away—walk away and never look back. But he couldn't as waves of rage shimmered through him, making it virtually impossible for him to move.

Swallowing what was left of his fragile pride, he glared at Morgana. "This is the first and last time I'm going to permit you to talk to me like you just did. I'm merely trying to explain that I'm broke right now. And when I take a girl out I usually do the paying. And there's one thing I'm not and that is a *pimp.*" He spat out the word.

"I didn't call you a pimp, Franklin." Her tone had changed, becoming softer and more conciliatory. "You paid for my food yesterday, so I'm merely returning the favor. Remember, I told you I'd let you pay if you permitted me to pay the next time. Well, today is the next time."

He studied her thoughtfully for a long moment before his lips parted in a smile. "You're right, Morgana."

She returned his smile with a smug one of her own. "I know I'm right. Franklin, please. I need to eat or I'm going to faint on you."

His right hand moved up, fingers catching in the wealth of dark brown curls with shocks of red highlights running through them. "Where in Baltimore?"

"It's between Cathedral Street and Park Avenue."

Franklin nodded. "Once we get into the city you'll have to show me how to get there."

Leaning over, Morgana kissed his clean-shaven cheek. "I'm sorry I snapped at you."

He turned his head slightly, his mouth brushing hers. "Apology accepted."

They arrived at the Crab Shack, took a table in a corner and ordered soft-shell crabs with side orders of fried onion rings and cole slaw. After the waitress set the plates on the table they stared at the mounds of food. The portions were large enough for four people.

They ate all of the crabs and half the sides, both admitting to eating too much, and opted for a walk before returning to the car for the drive back to D.C.

It was a few minutes after seven when Franklin parked the Volkswagen in front of Morgana's brownstone. They sat in the car discussing the impeachment proceedings against President Nixon. Franklin was particularly pleased that Congressman John Conyers, Jr. and Texas Congresswoman Barbara Jordan were among the predominately white members of the House Judiciary Committee. The topic segued from politics to sports, and finally to movies and music.

Franklin glanced at the dependable Timex on his wrist. It was after ten. He couldn't believe he and Morgana had spent the past three hours talking.

"I have to leave now, or I'm going to be late for work."

"I'll drive you."

He shook his head. "That's okay. You've done enough for me today."

Morgana gave him a long, penetrating stare. "You're not always going to be a struggling student, Franklin. One of these days I'm going to open a newspaper and read about you winning a case that will have everyone beating a path to your door for you to represent them."

His expression was impassive. "Do you really believe that?"

"Yes, I do."

Franklin stared at her lush mouth—a mouth he longed to kiss passionately. Her lips had just verbalized what he'd prayed for, because he wanted to be the brightest and the best. He wanted better for himself and for his suffering, hardworking mother. It pained him that his sisters were adding to their mother's woes. Two had had babies out of wedlock, while the third had become addicted to heroin.

"I pray you're right, Mo."

She touched his cheek, her hand soft and cool against the smooth warm flesh. "I know I'm right, Franklin."

Morgana rested her forehead on his solid shoulder. "You're the first man I've met who can carry on an intelligent conversation without talking about himself."

Franklin nuzzled her ear. "You don't want to hear about me."

"Oh, but I do, Franklin Wells," she said, chuckling softly.

Pulling back, he ran a forefinger down the length of her nose. "The next time I'll bare my soul to you."

"Is that a promise?"

"Yes, it is, Miss Morgana Johnson."

She sat back on her seat. "Let's go if you want to get to work on time."

He drove to downtown Washington, parking in front of a towering office building. As he moved to get out of the car, Morgana's fingers curled around his right wrist.

"If you're not doing anything Sunday, why don't you come by for dinner."

He smiled at her. "I'd like that very much."

"How's four?"

"Four it is."

Franklin opened the driver's side door and came around the car to help Morgana out. She offered her hand and he pulled her smoothly to her feet. They stood on the sidewalk staring at each other. Without touching her, Franklin lowered his head and brushed his mouth over hers.

"Good night, Mo."

She smiled. "Good night, Franklin."

He returned her smile. "Get home safe."

"I will."

"I want to see you drive away before I go in."

She got into the car, and moments later drove away. The image of Franklin standing on the sidewalk outside the office building where he worked the graveyard shift, waving at her, was imprinted on her brain.

He was so handsome, intelligent and so very proud. She hadn't known him twenty-four hours, but an inner voice whispered to her that he would become the perfect husband and father for the children she hoped to have.

After their first date Morgana and Franklin saw each whenever they had a free moment. She drove him to work and picked him up before they began their first class of the day. They studied together at the library, shared Sunday dinners and occasionally took in a movie. Despite her protests, he insisted on picking up the expenses for their dates.

He hadn't asked to sleep with her and Morgana was relieved because she felt becoming intimate with Franklin would ruin their easygoing relationship. But all of that changed three days before she was scheduled to leave Washington to return to Georgia for the summer.

They sat in the dining area of her studio apartment, drinking coffee and eating slices of homemade pound cake. "I'm leaving Monday."

Franklin's head jerked up and he stared at Morgana in shock. "Where are you going?"

"Home."

"But . . . but you never said anything about going home."

The semester had ended three weeks before and she'd delayed returning to Salvation because she hadn't wanted to leave Franklin. She'd called her mother telling her she had a few things to take care of and not to expect her back until June tenth. Katherine's tone was coolly disapproving when she told Morgana that she'd had a surprise for her—someone she'd wanted her to meet. And no matter how much she pleaded or cajoled, Katherine refused to tell her who the person was.

"I usually go home right after finals."

Franklin closed his eyes briefly. "When are you coming back?"

"A week before classes begin."

He quickly calculated how long it would be before he saw Morgana again. Eight weeks. Two months. Placing his fork beside his plate, he pushed back his chair and rounded the small table. Pulling her up into a close embrace, he kissed her hair.

"How am I going to make it through the summer without you?"

She inhaled the lingering scent of the cologne clinging to his shirt. Her arms tightened around his slim waist. "You, Franklin. What about me?"

"I love you, Mo." He felt her body stiffen before it relaxed again, going pliant. "I've never said that to another woman."

Tilting her head back, she peered at his face. His brows were drawn together in an agonized expression. Her eyes filled with tears. "I love you, too." And she did love him. She didn't know how it had happened so quickly, easily.

He kissed her tenderly at first, then his mouth slanted over hers, seemingly trying to absorb her into himself.

A swath of heat swept over Morgana, settling between her thighs. The pulsing increased until she thought she was losing her mind. This was what her girlfriends talked about when they said a man got them *hot.* She was more than hot; she was on fire.

Franklin's hands moved under her blouse, his fingers sweeping over her breasts and squeezing her nipples until they were hard as pebbles. One moment she was standing, and then she found herself in his arms as he carried her over to the sofa. He lowered her to the cushions, his body following and permitting her to feel the solid bulge in the front of his jeans.

Morgana stared up at him, love radiating from the depths of her smoky-gray eyes. She was ready—ready for Franklin and more than ready for what they would offer each other.

She was shocked at her own eager response as he methodically undressed her. The buttons to her blouse gave way, revealing her heaving bosom under a white cotton bra. Her jeans followed, then her bra and panties. It was when she lay naked to his gaze that she sought to cover herself.

Franklin captured her hands, holding them in a firm grip. "No, Mo. Let me look at you."

He stared, awed, at the perfection of her body. Her pale breasts were full, tipped by light brown nipples. Her waist was small enough for him to circle with his hands, and her hips were slim, much slimmer than they appeared when she was fully clothed.

Leaning over, his lips touched a nipple, tantalizing it until he heard Morgana's soft moan. His lips teased one nipple, then the other, while she shook like a fragile leaf in the wind.

He wanted her—had wanted her—since first seeing her in

the restaurant. He usually slept with a woman by their third date, but he knew Morgana was special. She wasn't a woman he wanted to sleep with then discard whenever he tired of her. She was a woman to whom men declared their love and married.

His tongue traced a path down her ribs to her stomach, and still lower to the damp, tangled curls between her thighs. She arched, gasping in shock. His hand moved between her trembling thighs, finding her wet, throbbing, and ready.

Moving off the sofa, he undressed, leaving his clothes in a pile on the floor. He reached down and eased Morgana to her feet. It took him less than a minute to remove the seat cushions and pull out the convertible sofa bed. Pulling back the top sheet, he picked Morgana up and placed her in the middle of the bed.

He lay down beside her, threading his fingers with hers. "We can never go back to the way we were."

Closing her eyes, she nodded. "I know." The two words were a hushed whisper.

Shifting, he faced her, marveling at her unabashed beauty. Tendrils of reddish hair curled around her dewy face. Her lips were red and slightly swollen from his rapacious kisses. There was a lethal calmness in his eyes as he stared at Morgana.

"I can't afford to get you pregnant—at least not now."

She cradled his face between her hands. "And you won't. I'm on the Pill."

A satisfied light came into his eyes. He longed to tell her that he wanted her to have his children, but only after he'd graduated law school. He didn't want to start a family until he could afford to take care of them financially.

Morgana kissed Franklin, finding his lips warm and intoxicatingly sweet. His smell wafted in her nostrils as she curled into the curve of his hard, slender body.

His hands and mouth explored her body, short-circuiting her senses. There wasn't one inch of her flesh he didn't taste, and when he finally eased his hardness into her throbbing flesh Morgana sobbed with the exquisite ecstasy tearing her asunder.

She climaxed, frightened by the sensations hurtling her to another dimension. The first climax was followed by a second—this one stronger and longer than the first. A third ensued, shattering her into a million pieces as love flowed through her like warm honey. She lay drowning in pleasure so exquisite she felt herself slipping away from reality.

Franklin buried his face between Morgana's neck and shoulder, gritting his teeth and swallowing the moans struggling to erupt from his constricted throat. He tried concentrating on anything but the wet, hot flesh squeezing his rock-hard penis. Never had he ever remembered being this hard. He reached for her legs, pulling them up around his waist, the position allowing for deeper penetration. Seconds later he exploded as her pulsing flesh milked him until he lay heavily on her slender body, struggling for breath. He found the strength to move off her slight frame. Swinging his legs over the bed, he made it to the bathroom on trembling legs to shower, struggling not to gag from the lingering scent of their lovemaking.

Morgana opened her eyes and smiled the smile of a satisfied woman. It was the first time she'd experienced what it meant to be born female. She slipped from the bed and joined Franklin in the shower. They made love a second time, staring into each other's eyes when their passions peaked simultaneously.

A quarter of an hour after Morgana walked through the door after driving from Washington, D.C. to Salvation, Georgia, her mother handed her a padded envelope addressed to her that had come in the mail earlier that morning. Recognizing Franklin's handwriting, she opened the package to find an audiocassette. It was The Temptations' "Hey Girl (I Like Your Style)." She played it over and over during that summer, and two years later it became their wedding song.

FIVE

"Wake up, Mo."

Morgana heard the familiar male voice and straightened, startled. She had fallen asleep. Hunkered down in front of her was the man who had been the subject of an erotic dream that left the area between her legs pulsing with a lingering passion she hadn't felt in a while.

Franklin curved a hand around his wife's neck. "How long have you been sitting out here?"

Her eyes blazed fire. "Don't touch me."

Leaning forward, he tightened his grip. "Mo, don't. The kids don't need to get involved in our business."

Her gaze shifted as she spied her son, daughter, and future son-in-law unloading the trunk of the rental car. "They're not kids, Franklin. In case you haven't noticed lately, they *are* adults."

"Morgana—"

"Take your hand off me!"

"Dad! Do as she says." Their son Justin stood on the lower step of the porch, dressed in a Navy uniform and holding a large dark blue canvas bag with the United States Navy insignia emblazoned on its sides. Franklin's hand fell away as he rose to his feet. "Just let her be," Justin continued in a softer tone.

Franklin watched his wife rise to her feet and walk down the four steps to her firstborn. Pain squeezed his heart as Justin cradled Morgana to his broad chest. In that instant he knew it should've been him consoling his wife, not their son. Sandra walked over to her mother and brother, and the three hugged one another, offering comfort and support.

Morgana broke down completely, sobbing uncontrollably. She cried for her father who'd spent almost twenty-five years confined to a wheelchair; she cried for her mother who'd sacrificed her young life to care for an older invalid husband; she cried for her uncle, the last surviving Salvation Johnson. But she would not cry for herself. She had no intention of dissolving into an abyss of self-pity. She should've recognized the signs that her marriage was in trouble. All of the signals were there, yet she'd denied anything was wrong.

Justin dropped his bag and swung his mother up in his arms when her knees buckled, carrying her up the porch steps and into the house. Sandra turned to her fiancé, burying her face against his neck as he cradled her to his chest.

"Mom's hysterical." Her voice broke.

Kenneth rubbed Sandra's back in a comforting gesture. "Get her into bed and I'll give her something to calm her down."

Sandra nodded, pulling a crumpled tissue from the pocket

of her slacks and dabbing her eyes. She eased out of Kenneth's embrace, walked up to the porch and offered her hand to her father. "Come on, Daddy. It's time you get some sleep, too. You look like crap."

Franklin had to smile. His daughter had always been brutally honest—a trait he'd always admired until now. "Thanks for the compliment."

"Well, it's true. I can't remember the last time I've seen you unshaven."

Wrapping an arm around his daughter's waist, he hugged her. "Losing your grandmother is a wake-up call that I'm not going to have my mother forever."

"Just love her, Daddy. That's all you can do."

He nodded, following Sandra into the house.

Kenneth walked into the living room, cradling several bags under his arms. "Where should I put your luggage?"

Franklin stared at Kenneth. He wasn't the man he'd wanted his daughter to marry, but who was he to tell Sandra whom she should fall in love with. He was pleased she had chosen a doctor, but felt life would be a lot easier for Sandra if she'd planned to marry a black man. Kenneth was tall and lanky with a mane of wavy black hair and vibrant blue eyes. He and Sandra had met at a Baltimore Raven's game. They'd dated for a year before announcing their engagement Christmas Eve. They planned to marry the following September.

"Leave it here." Franklin flopped down to a plush armchair while running a hand over his stubbly chin. "I could use a drink right about now. How about you, Doc?"

Kenneth dropped the suede bag; it landed with a soft thud. "I think it's about time you stopped calling me Doc. I do happen to have a name."

Franklin's head jerked up, meeting a pair of blue eyes

shooting off angry sparks. He regarded the younger man with an impassive coldness that mirrored his disapproval. He hadn't found fault with Kenneth Allen except that he was white.

But then he had to ask himself whether the man's race was really an issue. Or was it he didn't want to lose his daughter to another man? He loved his son, but somehow along the way he had come to the conclusion that he loved his daughter more.

It was he she'd come to whenever she hurt herself. He had been the one to dry her tears after her first boyfriend broke her heart when he reneged on his promise to take her to her senior prom and had taken another girl.

He stood up, walked over to the cardiologist and offered his hand. "You're right, Kenneth. I know it's a little late, but I'd like to welcome you to *my* family."

Kenneth ignored the proffered hand as he hugged Franklin, thumping his back gently. "Better late than never, Franklin."

Franklin pulled him closer. "You're right. Just don't mess over my baby girl."

Easing back, Kenneth met Franklin's cold stare. "What are you going to do? Shoot me?" Franklin's jaw dropped. "Sandra told me how you planned to shoot that boy who stood her up at her senior prom."

Franklin managed to look contrite. "Damn. We made a solemn promise never to repeat that story."

Amusement flickered in the blue eyes. "She told me about the incident the night I proposed to her."

"Now that I look back, I know I really wouldn't have shot that kid. I just wanted to scare the hell out of him. The gun was for his father, who happened to stand about six-seven and weighed in around three hundred pounds."

Kenneth smiled. "I'm certain when Sandra and I have children I'll probably react the same way. The only difference will be that I'll use a scalpel instead of a gun. It's quiet and a lot more deadly when you hit the right spot."

"Shame on you both," Sandra chided, walking into the living room. "How can you talk about killing people at a time like this?"

"How's your mother?" Franklin asked, ignoring the admonishment.

"She's in bed talking to Justin."

"She needs to sleep," Kenneth said.

"I agree," Sandra concurred. "I've never seen her so upset."

Franklin stared at Kenneth. "Can't you give her a sedative?"

He nodded. "Let me get my bag and I'll check her vitals. Have that drink ready for me when I come down."

Sandra waited until her fiancé took a small leather case from his luggage and climbed the staircase to the second floor before she turned to her father. "You finally bonding with my future husband?"

Cradling Sandra's hands in his, Franklin smiled at her. She looked enough like Morgana to have been her younger sister. She eclipsed her mother's five-eight height by an inch, and had inherited her slender body, curly hair, and gray eyes. Justin resembled him, with the exception of his eye color. They were a peculiar shade of amber and green.

"Life is too short to hold grudges. Especially about something we have no control over."

Sandra squeezed his fingers. "I'm sorry it's taken Grandma Katherine's death to make you come to your senses."

Your grandmother's death, and the possibility that your mother may divorce me. The inner voice was talking to Franklin again. His conscience—the voice of reason—had tortured him during the flight from Baltimore to Savannah. He probably would have broken down and started babbling and slobbering like an idiot if Sandra and Justin hadn't come with him. Having his children in attendance would act as a buffer between him and Morgana.

He loved her too much to give her up without a fight. The drive and determination he'd employed to become a successful criminal attorney was what he would draw on to try to save his marriage.

"Do you want a drink, baby girl?"

Sandra smiled, nodding her head. "You make the drinks while I check the refrigerator. Airline peanuts and soft drinks don't top my favorite food list."

Franklin walked into the paneled library. Everything in the large room reeked of elegance, from the heavy mahogany chairs covered with the finest brocade, to the priceless imported Turkish rugs, to the rosewood desk with a dark green, gold-veined marble surface and the fully leaded bases of a quartet of table lamps. The mantel over the ornate fireplace made of Mexican limestone held a collection of Chinese jade figurines in colors ranging from ivory to black. A series of photographs of Katherine Graham-Johnson's family crowded a drop-leaf table and a matching table against the opposite wall held photographs of Randolph Johnson's family.

Peering closely at his late mother-in-law's parents he noticed the paleness of their skin for the first time. How had he missed it before? He studied another sepia-tone photograph. Katherine's grandparents were fair enough to pass for white. How could he reject Kenneth as a son-in-law when his own children had inherited the genes of their white ancestors? Morgana's coloring—curly hair and gray eyes were the most obvious physical characteristics—had been passed along to her own daughter.

Franklin opened an armoire to reveal a well-stocked bar. Crystal decanters filled with rum, rye, scotch, vodka and bourbon were identified with sterling pendants hanging from their gracefully curved necks. He'd just slid three goblets off a built-in rack when Justin, Kenneth and Sandra entered the library.

Justin had changed out of his uniform into a pair of jeans, a navy-blue T-shirt and a pair of running shoes. At twenty-five he was as physically fit as he had ever been in his life. Lean with a tightly coiled, muscled body, the young lieutenant commander presented a handsome figure.

"Mom's sleeping. Kenneth gave her something to help relax her. However, she said she wants someone to look in on Uncle Julian."

Sandra took a glass from Franklin, handing it to Kenneth, and then took another for herself. Her brother refused to drink anything alcoholic. "After we eat, Kenneth and I will go over to his place. We'll probably spend the night with him."

"That's a good idea," Franklin said. "It's not good for him to be alone right now. What are you drinking, Kenneth?"

"Scotch neat."

"I'll have vodka with orange juice," Sandra announced. "I found steaks in the freezer and potatoes and salad fixings in the vegetable bin."

Justin walked over to the armoire, opening a refrigerator built into a lower portion of the ornately carved cabinet. "I'll fix the drinks. Dad, give me your glass."

Sandra put her glass on a mahogany credenza. "I'll come back for mine. I'm going to defrost the steaks in the microwave."

It was exactly midnight when Franklin, Justin, Sandra and Kenneth sat at the table in Katherine's spacious kitchen to eat. Everyone concentrated on eating, while the soft sounds of contemporary jazz came through the speakers of a radio on the countertop.

Franklin dropped his fork. There was complete silence except for the sound of an updated version of a Marvin Gaye hit. The song brought back memories for Franklin of a passionate weekend he had spent with Morgana when they'd sat up all night playing albums of their favorite recording artists. He preferred Isaac Hayes and Barry White, and Morgana, Marvin Gaye and Gladys Knight and The Pips.

Three pairs of eyes were fixed on Franklin when he did not pick up the fork. His steak was broiled the way he used to eat it, yet he couldn't bring himself to swallow more than one small piece. He hadn't eaten meat—red meat in particular—in months, but he hadn't had the heart to tell Sandra that.

Justin touched the corners of his mouth with a napkin. "Why don't you turn in, Dad?"

Franklin closed his eyes. "I don't want to go to bed."

"Well, you should," Justin countered. "You look like shit."

He opened his eyes, glaring at Justin across the table, his mouth twisted into a sneer. "When did I get such disrespectful children? My daughter tells me I look like crap, while my esteemed son says I look like *shit!*"

Justin's eyes narrowed. "Dad, don't start—"

"Stop it!" Sandra screamed, pounding her fist on the table. "Neither of you have any respect for my mother or my grandmother." Her eyes were brimming with unshed tears. "How can you carry on at a time like this?"

Franklin's angry gaze swung to Sandra. "Your mother's hurting and I can't help her. She won't even let me talk to her."

Justin and Sandra stared at each other, understanding dawning. Morgana refused to share her grief with her husband, preferring instead to drown in her own pain alone.

"Give her time, Dad. She'll open up to you."

"Justin's right, Daddy."

Pushing back his chair, Franklin mumbled a curse. "I'm going upstairs."

Waiting until his father walked out of the kitchen, Justin looked at Kenneth. "Do you think you should sedate him, too?"

Kenneth shook his head. "No."

"He's always taken care of Mom," Sandra said, "but now that she doesn't want him to take care of her he feels as if he's failed her. He also fears losing his mother. Grammy's at least ten years older than Grandma Katherine."

Sandra and Justin hadn't bonded with their paternal grandmother as they had with Katherine. Their father had tried enticing Erna Wells to leave Birmingham when he'd offered to buy her house in Maryland or Washington, D.C., but the elderly woman refused to leave Alabama. Knowing she would never move, Franklin paid a contractor to renovate the house where he and his three sisters had grown up. Two more bedrooms were added to accommodate his oldest sister's grandchildren whenever they came for an extended visit.

Sandra pushed a cherry tomato around her salad plate with her fork. "Instead of going back to Baltimore I think I'm going down to Birmingham to visit Grammy."

"How long do you plan to stay?" Justin asked.

"I don't know. Probably no more than a week."

"Maybe I'll come with you." He'd been granted an official two-week leave.

Sandra smiled at her brother. "Thanks. I could use the company."

Kenneth stared down at his plate, schooling his expression not to reveal his rising annoyance. If he and Sandra were living together and were to marry then he thought she should've at least consulted with him before making plans not to return to Baltimore. He planned to talk to her about it, but only after her grandmother's funeral.

Sandra picked up her plate. "If everyone's finished, then I'll do the dishes."

"Leave them," Justin insisted. "I'll clean up the kitchen. If you two are going to Uncle Julian's, then you'd better get going."

Sandra stood up and kissed her brother. "I'll see you in the morning."

He nodded, then rose to clear the table. The clock above the sink in the kitchen chimed one o'clock when Justin locked the front door, extinguished the lamps on the first level and climbed the staircase to the second floor. Walking into the bedroom he usually occupied when coming to Salvation, he stopped short. His father was sprawled across the bed, asleep.

Closing the door, he made his way to another bedroom at the far end of the hall. The light from a full moon lit up the space like daylight. He stripped off his clothes and slipped between the cool sheets and lay staring up at the ceiling until sleep claimed him.

Morgana woke feeling as if her mouth were filled with cotton. Blinking against the brilliant sunlight pouring into her bedroom, she lifted her arm to look at her watch. It was after nine. She hadn't slept that late in years.

She rose on an elbow and threw back the sheet, then went completely still. Franklin sat on the rocking chair, staring at her. She had to admit to herself that he looked better this morning than he had last night. He'd shaved, and he was meticulously dressed in a pair of taupe slacks and a short-sleeve, white silk shirt.

Ignoring him, she slipped off the bed and headed for the bathroom. At that moment brushing her teeth to rid her mouth of the acrid taste and taking a shower were much more important to her than anything Franklin wanted to say.

She reentered the bedroom twenty minutes later, a towel wrapped around her body. Franklin hadn't moved from his sitting position. He sat motionless, only the blinking of his eyes indicating he was alive and breathing.

Bracing her hands on her hips, Morgana stared at him. "Please leave."

Franklin shook his head back and forth. "No, Mo. I'm not leaving until you listen to what I have to say."

"You have nothing to say. I suggest you save your words for a judge."

His expression changed and his gold-flecked eyes hardened like brilliant stones. "You're not leaving me, Mo."

"Don't tell me what I can or cannot do." The veins in her neck bulged. "I am not one of your clients, Franklin."

He stood up, his hands rolled into tight fists. "And I have a right to be heard."

"You have no rights—not with me, Franklin Wells. Whatever rights you had you forfeited the moment you slept with *that* woman." Her eyes narrowed. "Just looking at you sickens me."

"Mo—"

"Get the hell out of here!" she shouted, cutting off whatever he'd planned to say. He took a step toward her, glaring, then turned and walked out of the bedroom, closing the door softly behind him.

Franklin made his way down the wide carpeted hallway, coming face-to-face with his son. "Good morning." The greeting was barely audible.

Justin noted his father's strained expression. "You all right, Dad?"

"I'm fine," he lied smoothly. "Your mother still won't talk to me."

Justin dropped an arm over Franklin's shoulders. "Give her time. She'll come around. What's important is that we're all here for her."

Franklin forced a smile. "You're right about that."

"I came up to get you and Mom because Sandra, Kenneth, and Uncle Julian just arrived. We need to decide whether we're going out for breakfast or eating here."

"Your mother's up and getting dressed right now. Why don't we wait for her?"

"Okay." Still holding on to his father, Justin led Franklin down the staircase. "I just put up a pot of coffee. I figured everyone could use a cup right about now."

Franklin savored the warmth and strength of his son's arm around his shoulders. He may have lost his wife temporarily but he still had their children. And he didn't know what he would do if he lost them, too.

~

The sound of animated voices and the fragrant aroma of brewing coffee greeted Morgana as she walked into the sun-filled kitchen. Sandra noticed her first.

"Good morning, Mom. How are you feeling?" She came over to Morgana and kissed her cheek.

"A lot better than I did yesterday."

Julian, sitting at a table in the breakfast nook, lowered his coffee cup and smiled at her. She headed toward the coffeemaker on a countertop, but Justin curved an arm around her waist, directing her to the breakfast nook.

"Please sit down, Mom. I'll pour your coffee."

Franklin stood up, pulling out the chair next to his. "Sit here."

She sat down, her gaze lingering on those seated at the round oak table. Sandra stood behind Kenneth, both hands braced on his shoulders.

"I want to thank everyone for being here for me, but I also want to reassure you that I'm not going to have an emotional meltdown." Franklin rested a hand on her shoulder and she went completely still, but he did not remove it. "I've made the decision to have a graveside service. My mother had stopped attending New Canaan a long time ago. Therefore, it would be somewhat hypocritical to have her funeral there. If any of you have another suggestion then this is the time to make it known." She stared at Julian. "Uncle Julian?"

He gave his niece a long, penetrating stare before saying, "I'll go along with whatever you propose."

Justin placed a cup of steaming black coffee in front of her; she smiled at him. "Thank you." Franklin was forced to remove his arm when she reached for a pitcher of milk, pouring a liberal amount into the porcelain cup. "If that's the case, then I'll contact Mr. Turner and confirm for early Tuesday morning."

Justin sat down on Morgana's left. "Will Grandma Katherine be laid out for viewing?"

"No. Your grandmother had given me specific instructions

after my father died that she didn't want a wake or public viewing."

"But I'd like to see her."

"So would I," Sandra said, agreeing with her brother.

"Anyone who wants to go can ride with me." Julian's voice was deceptively calm, masking the grief he'd refused to acknowledge.

"Do you want to go with us, Mom?" Sandra asked, hugging her fiancé.

Morgana offered a sad smile. "No. I'll wait and see her Tuesday." She would say good-bye to her mother just before the top of the coffin was closed a final time.

Leaning over, Justin pressed a kiss to his mother's hair. "If you're not going with us, then we'll all eat breakfast here before heading over to the funeral home."

Straightening, Sandra walked over to the refrigerator. "Kenneth and I will make breakfast while the rest of you relax on the sunporch." Kenneth's head came up as he gave Sandra an incredulous look. "All right," she conceded smiling at him. "You can help me cut up the ingredients for omelettes." Exhibiting the take-charge attitude she'd learned from her father, Sandra shooed everyone out of the kitchen.

Morgana busied herself setting the table in a corner of the large space that had been set up as a dining area. Every Sunday morning she and her parents had shared breakfast on the sunporch. Eating in her favorite room in the four-bedroom house had become a ritual she'd waited for all week.

It had been her job to set the table with a starched linen tablecloth, fine china, silver and crystal. By the time she'd celebrated her eighth birthday she was able to set a table for a formal dinner party. It hadn't mattered that her parents no longer entertained, because just sitting down to a beautifully set table had become a very special ritual for Morgana—a ritual she continued after she'd established her own household.

Franklin and Julian passed the time perusing the Sunday edition of the *Atlanta Journal-Constitution* while Justin returned to the kitchen to help his sister.

Sandra appeared forty minutes later, wearing one of her grandmother's aprons around her waist. She held a platter of bacon covered with a paper towel in one hand and a pitcher of chilled orange juice in the other.

"I can't believe how much food Grandma Katherine kept on hand. You'd think she was cooking for an army when there was only herself."

Kenneth and Justin returned with a basket filled with golden-brown biscuits and a platter piled high with omelettes. They spooned omelettes onto everyone's plate.

Sandra noticed Franklin staring down at his plate. "What's the matter, Daddy?"

He looked at the folded omelette with diced onion, ham and red and green peppers. "I've stopped eating meat."

Sandra's eyes narrowed. "Why didn't you say that last night when I broiled a steak for you?"

He managed to look sheepish. "I didn't want to hurt your feelings, baby girl."

Her delicate nostrils flared. "It's not about hurting anyone's feelings, Daddy. It's about being open and honest with those you love."

Morgana's gaze swung to Franklin, a smug smile tugging at the corners of her mouth. Sandra could not have said it better.

He couldn't meet his daughter's direct stare. "I'm sorry, Sandra."

"There's no need to apologize, Daddy. I'll fix you a couple of eggs. You like them scrambled well, don't you?"

Dropping his head in resignation, Franklin nodded. In that instant Morgana felt a wave of compassion for her husband. He looked whipped, defeated. However, the emotion fled as quickly as it had come.

How Franklin Wells felt was no longer her concern. Nothing about him was her concern. He'd shattered the trust she'd had in him. And for Morgana trust in a marriage far exceeded any passionate declaration of love.

After Sandra had scrambled two eggs for Franklin, everyone began eating.

Flanked by her husband and uncle, Morgana sat under the shade of a white canopy at Salvation's Calvary Cemetary. She was so still she could've been carved out of marble. A large weeping willow tree shaded the open grave where Katherine Faith Graham-Johnson would be laid to rest alongside her long-deceased parents. The vacant look in Morgana's eyes reflected a grief that had carved fissures on her heart. She wanted to cry, but couldn't. It was as if the well of life had dried up within her. Julian wept silently beside her.

Sandra gripped her brother's and fiancé's hands as she sobbed softly against Justin's shoulder.

Franklin sat stiffly, eyes closed, lips moving in a silent prayer. He prayed for Katherine's soul and for his own. He prayed for forgiveness and for the return of an inner peace that had eluded him since that fateful telephone call four days before.

The funeral director's sonorous voice led the assembled in two of Katherine's favorite psalms: 17 and 51. The brief service ended with Morgana rising to place a jonquil-yellow rose on the top of Katherine's casket. Then, one by one, the mourners stood and placed a rose on the gleaming bronze casket. The flower had been Katherine's favorite.

In just fifteen minutes it was over—over for Katherine Johnson. But for Morgana it was about to begin.

All of the reasons Randolph and Katherine had given for why she shouldn't marry Franklin Wells came back in vivid clarity. *What if he's like his father? How do you know he won't walk out on you and your children? What if he's inherited his father's proclivity for sleeping with other women?* The what ifs and hows had gone on and on until she had screamed at her mother and father to stop—stop or she would be forced to choose between them and Franklin. And she hadn't had to say she would've chosen Franklin.

How had Katherine known that Franklin would deceive her with another woman? Was it because once women reached a certain age they just knew these things, or was it because Katherine had been deceived at one time in her own life? For the first time Morgana wondered if Randolph Johnson had ever cheated on his wife.

SIX

Morgana stood on the porch watching Justin and Franklin load the trunk of the rental car for their drive to Birmingham, Alabama. Kenneth had flown back to Baltimore the night before. Franklin had decided to join his children for the trip south to visit with his mother and sisters. He'd tried to convince Morgana to join them, but she'd rejected his offer.

Her eyes narrowed behind the lenses of her sunglasses as he made his way back to the porch. She was forced to admire his tall, slender physique. Franklin Wells was as breathtakingly virile now as he'd been thirty years before. He had a distinctive walk she would know anywhere, and a way of angling his head that she'd always found endearing.

He smiled, flashing perfect white teeth. "Are you sure I can't get you to change your mind and go with us?"

Her expression was impassive. "Very sure."

"Do you want me to get someone to help you with the sale of the house?"

After offering the house to Sandra and Kenneth, who had politely declined because of their desire to remain in the D.C./Baltimore area, Morgana decided to sell it. She hadn't bothered to ask Justin because his future plans included making the Navy his career, and he did not know from one year to the next where he would be stationed. But Sandra did agree to accept all of the furnishings for the home she and Kenneth hoped to purchase once she graduated law school.

"No, thank you. It's going to take me some time to catalogue everything before I put the furniture in storage."

Katherine hadn't left a will because she'd given her only child and sole heir power of attorney over all of her legal affairs the day she'd celebrated her seventieth birthday. All financial records, including bank accounts, bore Katherine's and Morgana's names. Katherine had had her lawyer draw up the papers and then forwarded them to her son-in-law for his approval. She had wanted to make certain when she died the state of Georgia would not claim a large portion of her estate for taxes.

Slipping his hands into the pockets of his trousers, Franklin rocked back on his heels. "How long do you think that's going to take?"

Folding her arms under her breasts, Morgana glared at him. "I don't know."

"What about your shop?"

"Bernice will take care of everything."

"But what if she can't?"

Her temper flared. "Why shouldn't she, Franklin? You think because she's a woman she can't run a business? It's apparent you haven't heard a word I've been saying to you about The Registry. We've realized a profit these past two years." She waved a hand, dismissing him. "Please go, Franklin. Your children are waiting for you." Sandra and Justin stood outside the car, staring at their parents.

"When are you coming home?"

"Don't ask me that because you may not like my answer."

A muscle in his jaw quivered. "What's that supposed to mean?"

"I don't know if I'm *ever* coming back." Waving to her son and daughter for the last time, Morgana turned and retreated to the coolness of the house, while Franklin stood rooted to the spot.

Her declaration hit him with the force of a sharp jab to his nose. He'd been in Salvation for five days, and it had taken that long for reality to rock his well-ordered existence. The reality was that his wife was leaving him.

Franklin's knees felt like jelly, his entire body slumped in resignation. Didn't Morgana know she wasn't the only one grieving? He was also grieving for what was and what he knew would never be again. It was the end of something so sacred, something so vital to him that he hadn't known what it was until now: his marriage.

What he refused to accept was that Morgana no longer loved him. Regardless of the road their lives would eventually take, he knew she still loved him and that he would love her with his dying breath.

Perhaps, he prayed, perhaps all they needed was space to reassess all they'd shared for three decades. He would give her the time and space she needed to heal from losing her mother, and then he would return to Salvation. As long as she hadn't mentioned divorce he would come back again and again.

Morgana knew she should begin the task of going through her mother's personal items but loathed moving from her reclining position. She'd flopped down on a chaise on the sunporch and hadn't moved in more than an hour. Streams of sunlight filtered through bamboo slats. The clock on the fireplace mantel chimed once. Shifting, she glanced at it. It was eleven-thirty.

She lay on the chair until the noon hour before she finally pushed off the chaise to retreat to an upstairs bedroom to begin the task of sorting through closets and dresser drawers.

It was after three when the chiming of the doorbell echoed melodiously throughout the house. Morgana went down the staircase to answer it. A smile crinkled her eyes when she saw her uncle smiling at her through the mesh on the screen door. Unlatching the door, she pushed it open.

"You look wonderful, Uncle Julian. Please, come in."

And he did look well. The lines of tension that had ringed his mouth had disappeared. He appeared rested for the first time in days. He'd returned home after the graveside service, pleading a headache. Morgana had called him later that afternoon, inviting him to spend the evening with her. He'd politely declined, saying he wanted to rest.

He smiled. "Thank you."

As Julian walked into the entryway, Morgana turned and stared at him. A lightweight tan suit, starched white shirt and a patterned chocolate and beige tie was the perfect complement to his smooth dark skin. He held an exquisite Panama hat in his right hand. It had been years since she'd seen her uncle wear a hat.

He gave her a shy smile. "I know it's short notice, but I've come to ask my princess if she would join me this afternoon for a drive in the country."

"I'd love to go out with you, sir," she teased, curtsying. It was a game they'd played when she was a young girl. Julian had told her people in Salvation had once treated Randolph like a king and when he'd married her mother, Katherine Graham had become his queen. She had become their princess, and because he was brother to a king, he was considered a prince.

Taking his hand, she led him into the living room. "Please rest yourself while I make myself presentable. May I offer you something cool to drink?"

Deep-set dark eyes sparkled behind the oval lenses. "No, thank you."

"I'll be right back as soon as I take a quick shower and change my clothes."

Julian watched Morgana climb the curving staircase, her fingers trailing along the smooth surface of a banister with intricately carved newel posts. Folding his tall frame down onto a loveseat, he crossed one knee over the other and placed his hat on his lap.

He'd deliberately stayed away because he knew it wasn't often that the Wellses were all together in one place at the same time. His niece, her husband and daughter had come to Georgia for Easter, but the last time he'd seen Justin had been at his graduation from the naval academy.

Closing his eyes, he leaned his head back against the cushioned loveseat, willing the hot tears welling behind his eyelids not to fall. Since Katherine's passing he felt old for the first time in his life. She'd been so vibrant and full of life that she'd kept him young—much younger than seventy-nine.

Despite the fact he'd never married he hadn't lived a monastic life. There were women—not so many he couldn't remember who they were. But he had always been discriminating and discreet. Salvation was too small, its inhabitants much too nosy for him to conduct an open affair with a woman. That meant he'd lived more than half his life in secret. And like many others who lived in small towns he would take his secrets with him to the grave.

A familiar fragrance wafted in his nostrils, and Julian stood up quickly, his eyes widening in shock. It was Katherine's perfume, but the person wearing the scent wasn't Katherine, but Morgana. She stood several feet from him.

Noting his strange expression, Morgana asked, "Are you all right, Uncle Julian?"

"I'm just fine. But . . . but you're wearing Katherine's perfume."

A slight frown furrowed her forehead. "Mama and I have always worn the same perfume." Her mother had given her a bottle of Chanel No. 5 perfume as one of her wedding gifts, and it had quickly become her signature fragrance.

"I suppose I never noticed it before."

Winding her arm through Julian's, Morgana stared up at his solemn expression. "Would you prefer I not wear it?" She did not want to compound her uncle's emotional distress of losing his sister-in-law.

Julian patted the hand tucked in the bend of his elbow. "No. It smells as wonderful on you as it did on Katherine." He smiled. "Are you ready, princess?"

"Yes."

Morgana sat beside Julian, staring out the side window at the passing landscape. The weather was perfect for an early summer day. Noontime temperatures were in the low eighties, the humidity moderate, and the sky was filled with white puffy clouds.

"When are you coming to Maryland to spend some time with me?"

Julian did not take his gaze off the road in front of his vintage Mercedes-Benz sedan. "Soon."

She turned her head, staring at his distinctive profile. "You said that at Easter."

"I know I did, but your mother wasn't up to traveling at that time."

"My mother's gone, Uncle Julian."

He inclined his head. "I know that, Morgan."

"And?"

"Soon."

"That's it? Soon?"

"Yes, Morgan, that's it."

When, she thought, had he become so stubborn? There was never a time when she'd ask something of him that he wouldn't comply without hesitating. What had changed? Why had he changed?

"I'll let you know when I'll drive up," he said after a long silence.

"You don't have to drive Uncle Julian. I can always send you a plane ticket."

"I don't like flying."

"Okay," she conceded. "Do you want me to fly down, then we can drive back together?"

Julian glanced at Morgana for the first time since he'd helped her into his car. "Do you think I'm too old to drive from Georgia to Maryland by myself?"

"Of course not, Uncle Julian. Besides, you're not old."

"Hogwash!" he spat out. "I'll be eighty my next birthday. And in my book that's old." He drove past sites where new homes were being built. "If developers keep buying up land

and putting up these large so-called gated communities, pretty soon we're going to look like Atlanta's suburbs."

"People relocate to Atlanta for employment opportunities. What would be the appeal to move to this part of Georgia?"

"Retirement."

That was the last word they exchanged until they sat in a small seafood restaurant half a mile from Savannah's waterfront. It was more of a fish house than a restaurant. It was aptly named The Fish House and had an official seating capacity for thirty.

They sat in a booth covered in bright red Naugahyde. Julian clasped his hands together atop the Formica-topped table. "This place was your mother's favorite restaurant."

Morgana's jaw dropped. "This place? This . . ." Her words trailed off.

He lifted an eyebrow. "Dive?" She nodded, appearing embarrassed that he'd read her mind. "It's not fancy, but the food is excellent."

"When did you first bring her here?"

"It was a month after your father passed away. Katherine had developed a strange habit of sitting in the house in the dark. And whenever I went to see her she refused to open the door. I'd give her a few days, and then return. It went on for about a week before I took matters into my own hands. I wound up kicking in the door. She hadn't washed and had barely eaten enough to keep herself alive."

Julian ignored the soft gasp that escaped Morgana's parted lips. "I undressed her, gave her a bath, combed her hair, telling her that I was taking her out to eat. I'd expected a fight, but she was too weak to anything more than nod. That's when I brought her to The Fish House. She didn't eat much, but it was enough to put some color back in her cheeks."

"Why didn't you tell me this before?"

"Because I didn't want to lose Katherine's friendship. If I'd called you to let you know what was going on Katherine would've shut me out of her life forever."

"But I had a right to know. She was my mother."

He nodded. "You're right about her being your mother, but at that time she'd become my responsibility. I was the one living in Salvation, not you. If I hadn't been able to handle the situation I would have called you."

An unwelcome blush suffused her cheeks. She had no right to chastise her uncle. "I didn't mean to sound ungrateful, Uncle Julian."

Reaching over, he patted her hand. "Hush up now. There's no need to apologize."

"I know my mother could be difficult at times."

Julian smiled, nodding in agreement. "At times."

Katherine was prone to periods of prolonged silence. She'd answer when spoken to, but refused to initiate further conversation. There had been days when Morgana existed in a world of silence when Randolph also elected to stop talking. It was as if she existed in a household with two mute parents. The intermittent silent hostility between her mother and father had prompted her to apply to college out of the state instead of enrolling in Spelman College, Katherine's alma mater.

"Where's your wedding band, Morgan?"

The query was totally unexpected. Morgana attempted to pull her hand from Julian's grasp when he tightened his hold on her fingers. "It's home."

He stared at her, his gaze unwavering. "Do you want to talk about it?"

"There's nothing to talk about."

He angled his head. "Are you sure, Morgan?"

How could she tell her uncle that her husband was cheating on her? That he had been sleeping with another woman? That she couldn't remember the last time she and Franklin had had sex?

"I can't talk about it—at least not right now."

Julian released her hand. "I want you to remember that I'm here for you, princess."

Her eyes filled with moisture again, this time the tears overflowing and staining her cheeks. She swiped at them with the back of her hand. "Isn't it ironic that you're more loyal to me than the father of my children?"

"It's not that ironic. You and Franklin are husband and wife, while you and I share a common bloodline. That accounts for the old adage that blood is thicker than water."

She smiled through her tears. "How true." Seconds later she turned her attention to the plastic covered menu in front of her. "How are the catfish fritters?"

"Excellent." Julian studied the menu even though he knew every selection. "I think I'm going to order the salmon croquettes."

Raising her gaze, Morgana studied his lean face. "Are you on a diet? You look as if you've lost weight."

"Only a few pounds. I've been getting up early and walking at least three or four times a week." What he didn't tell Morgana was that he'd tried to convince Katherine to join him, but she refused to leave her bed at sunrise. Julian had asked himself over and over would Katherine still be alive if she had exercised?

A waiter approached the booth and took their orders. Twenty minutes later a plate piled high with strips of spicy fried catfish and another with flaky salmon croquettes in a black bean sauce and accompanying sides covered the table's surface.

Julian noted Morgana's stunned expression. "Everyone leaves with a take-out bag."

"That's apparent by the size of the servings."

Both managed to eat only a small portion of what they'd ordered and when the waiter came over to their booth again, he was carrying plastic containers and small shopping bags with the establishment's name and logo stamped on its sides.

Julian drove back to Salvation, taking the longer route. He'd asked Morgana about her shop and she told him about the long hours she spent going over items prospective brides wanted listed in their registries.

"Some change their minds two and sometimes three times before they're able to narrow their choice for a china pattern."

"I don't know what the big fuss is all about when the design is hidden under the food."

Morgana laughed softly. "You wouldn't understand because you're not a woman."

"Thank the Lord for that."

The topic of conversation changed to a lighter note. Julian related stories about some of the patients he'd treated during the forty years he'd been Salvation's family practitioner, refusing to name names when she pleaded with him to tell her about whom he was talking.

Their afternoon ended as he walked her to the door with a promise they would share breakfast at his house. Kissing his cheek, Morgana told him she would see him at eight the following morning.

SEVEN

The week following Katherine's funeral found Morgana sharing breakfast and dinner with her uncle. They alternated preparing the meals—breakfast at Julian's and dinner with her. Sandra had called to tell her that she was back in Baltimore, and that Justin had returned to his base in Colorado the day before she and Franklin left Birmingham. She hadn't asked about Franklin, and Sandra hadn't mentioned her father.

It was over dinner one Thursday evening that Morgana felt comfortable enough to reveal what lay in her heart. Staring down at the salad in front of her, she said softly, "Franklin is sleeping with another woman."

The ensuing silence was punctuated by the sound of music coming from the radio on the kitchen countertop. His fork halted in midair, Julian stared across the table at the pained expression on his niece's face.

"Is or was?"

Her eyelids fluttered wildly. "Please, Uncle Julian, don't intellectualize this. Only minutes after I returned your call I called Franklin's hotel suite and a woman answered the phone. She said—no, let me get this right: 'Frank's in the shower. Would you like to leave a message?' "

Julian placed his fork beside his plate. His eyes behind the lenses were hooded like those of a hawk. "Are you certain that's all he was doing? Just taking a shower?"

"I've slept with Franklin Albert Wells for thirty years, and there aren't too many things I don't know about him."

Julian studied her intently. "Has he admitted sleeping with another woman?"

"He didn't have to."

"Could it be you've accused him unjustly?"

"I haven't said a word to him, because I didn't have to."

"You didn't let him explain?"

"What was there to explain? My husband is sleeping with another woman, or maybe even women, and you want me to listen to his lame-ass, inane explanation as to why he feels the need to sleep around."

"There has to be a reason why he would be unfaithful to you. And the reason could have nothing to do with you."

Throwing down her napkin, Morgana pushed back her chair, rising to her feet at the same moment Julian stood up. "Franklin cheats because his father cheated on his mother. As much as he claims he hated his father for his infidelity he's just like him. However, I'm nothing like his mother, because I'm going to wait around for him to walk out on me."

"Are you going to divorce him?"

"I'm seriously thinking about it," she spat out.

"Talk to him, Morgan. Even a guilty man is entitled to his day in court."

She gave the older man a long, penetrating look. "I'll think about it."

"Morgan?"

"I said, I'll think about it. Let's take our coffee on the sunporch."

Julian studied the lethal calmness in Morgana's eyes. Her expression was one he'd seen Katherine exhibit at a very critical time in her life. Not only did Morgana look like her late mother, but she'd also inherited her stubborn streak. Once Katherine set her mind to something no amount of pleading would get her to change it. The only exception had been when he'd convinced Katherine to accept Franklin as her son-in-law. He'd risked everything he'd shared with Katherine up to that point in their lives when he continued to meddle in a situation in which he had no right. He'd told Katherine to consider either gaining a son or losing her daughter. Three days later Randolph and Katherine Johnson announced the upcoming nuptials of their daughter to Franklin Albert Wells.

Morgana left her bed at dawn the following morning, showered and pulled on one of a half dozen dresses she'd left at her mother's during prior trips. Saturday would mark two weeks since she'd left Maryland, and she knew it was time to replenish her wardrobe.

Squeezing a small amount of gel onto her palm, she rubbed her hands together, and then massaged it into her short hair. She couldn't remember the last time she'd missed having her hair washed and coiffed at a salon, but it felt good to just brush her curly hair off her face and not have to worry whether anyone saw her without makeup or her hair mussed.

Slipping her feet into a pair of leather thongs, she made her way down the staircase. She had spent so much time indoors that she felt as if the walls were beginning to close in on her.

It had been years since she'd visited a nearby lake. The last time had been when Katherine told her she no longer opposed Morgana's decision to marry Franklin.

The lake had always been a special place for Morgana and Katherine—a fairy-tale setting where they went whenever they felt the need to confide in each other. It was a place where families gathered to picnic on Sundays or sail on the water's clear placid surface. It was also a place for lovers to lie under the sweeping branches of the many weeping willow trees and declare their undying love for each other.

Morgana drove her mother's car the short distance to the lake and maneuvered into the designated parking area. There was one other car parked at the far end of the field. The heat from the rising sun poured through the windshield as she turned off the ignition. The raucous chatter of birds filled the air as she left the car and made her way toward the water.

Slowing her steps, she noticed the figure of a man sitting on the grass, holding a camera in both hands. He moved with the speed and grace of a cat as he stood up and snapped pictures of the surrounding landscape. She sat down under a tree to watch him.

Suddenly he turned in her direction and a shaft of sunlight swept over his face, causing Morgana to stop breathing for several seconds. The golden light turned him into a statue of gold.

It picked up the yellow undertones in his medium brown skin—a complexion that reminded her of the inside of a yam—and added fire to his stark white shirt. His hair was a heavy mass of shoulder-length twists. It wasn't as dark as she'd originally thought but a reddish-brown. She felt a shiver of uneasiness as he walked over to her.

He hunkered down, staring at her face. Raising the camera, he snapped the shutter again. "Incredible." The single word spoke volumes as he snapped three more frames in rapid succession. "Your eyes are magnificent."

Instead of being flattered by the compliment Morgana was annoyed. She'd come to the lake to be alone, not to be photographed. "Do you make it a habit of taking pictures of strangers?"

"Only those with interesting faces." He folded his lithe body down beside her. "May I sit?"

She lifted an eyebrow. "You ask permission after you sit?"

He sprang up, extending his right hand. "Erick Wilson."

Morgana stared at the hand with the long slender fingers.

She would question herself later, but said, "Sit down, Mr. Wilson."

"Thank you, Ms. . . ."

Turning her head, she stared out at a lone duck swimming across the lake to join others on the opposite bank. "There's no need for you to know my name."

Erick leaned closer, his mint-scented breath sweeping over her ear. "Oh, but I do, Miss. How am I going to get your photographs to you?"

"I don't want them."

Erick's gaze lingered on the curve of her long neck, the slope of her shoulders under the delicate fabric of her dress. The curly hair brushed off her forehead allowed for an unfettered view of her fine-boned face. He studied her with the trained eye of an artist, finding her a perfect subject.

"But I want you to have them." Morgana shifted, rising to her feet, but his hand stopped her. The strength in his slender hand was deceiving. "Please, don't leave."

She glared at him. "I came here at this time because I thought I'd be alone."

Erick flashed a slow smile, his eyes crinkling attractively. "That's the same reason I come here most days. I don't want to be distracted when I study my subject."

"Your subject?"

"The lake and the surrounding landscape."

She attempted to extract herself from his grip. "If you let go of my hand I'll leave."

"Please don't," he said. "I've gotten what I need." He released her hand, stood up and walked away. Just before he turned off onto the path leading to the parking area, he glanced over his shoulder to find her gray-green eyes watching his retreat.

Morgana's gaze met and fused with his and a shiver of heat raced down her back. There was something about the brash young photographer that was charming and familiar. He reminded her of a younger Franklin Wells. The only difference was his hair. She glanced away, and when she turned to look at where he'd stood the space was empty.

Pulling her legs up to her chest, she rested her chin on her knees. She closed her eyes and rocked in a side to side motion.

She'd left her home and business to bury her mother—and she had. But she had chosen to stay in Salvation because she did not want to return to a lifestyle that other women envied only because she was Mrs. Franklin Wells.

She was mistress of a residence that had become a showplace rather than a home. The man she'd married had become a celebrity in his own right because of his unbroken string of legal victories. She and Franklin were listed as one of the country's leading African-American power couples, but little did anyone know that she would willingly relinquish all of the material possessions they'd amassed over the years to go back to the way it was. Back before the status cars; countless rings, bracelets, necklaces and earrings set with precious stones that were hidden away in a drawer in her armoire; before Franklin had amassed a small fortune when he began buying apartment buildings and renovating them; before he expanded his practice to include partners; and before the firm leased a suite of rooms at a hotel. Franklin's rationale was that the firm would write it off as a business expense.

She couldn't remember the last time they'd gone to a movie together; taken a drive and stopped at a motel to have mad, mind-blowing sex. It had been years since they'd lain in bed beyond sunrise holding hands and talking, or prepared a meal together. They hadn't taken a vacation in three years. The last one had been a cruise in a sloop down to the Caribbean to celebrate their twenty-fifth wedding anniversary. And in another two days she would celebrate her twenty-eighth, while now she sat contemplating whether to divorce the only man she'd ever loved.

Walking back to where she'd parked her car, she found a business card under the wiper blades. Plucking it off the windshield, Morgana read the embossed letters: ERICK WILSON, ARTIST-IN-RESIDENCE, Savannah College of Art and Design, Savannah, Georgia. Turning the card over she noted a handwritten telephone number. Below the number he had written: *call me to retrieve your photographs. EW.*

So, she thought, he was an artist, wondering if he was as

talented as he was persistent. Reaching into her purse, she retrieved her cell phone and dialed the number on the card. It rang twice before an answering machine was activated, requesting the caller leave a detailed message.

"This is Ms. Johnson. You can mail the photographs to me." She gave him her mother's address before ending the call. If it was so important that he give her the photographs, then she'd just made it easy for him. She was curious to see what image he'd captured with his camera. It had been a long time since anyone had taken a candid pose of her. Recent photos always revealed a coiffed, poised, confident middle-aged woman on the arm of Franklin Wells as they stared adoringly into the other's eyes.

Dropping the card and phone into her bag, she opened the car door and slipped in behind the wheel and drove to Julian's house for breakfast.

When Morgana walked into Julian's house, she found him sitting at his kitchen table, his face streaked with tears. His glasses lay on the table next to a glass of water. Rushing into the room, she sat down and wound her arm through his.

"What's the matter, Uncle Julian?" Her heart ached to see him this way.

"I miss her, princess. I miss her so much. She was my very best friend."

"I miss her, too," she whispered as tears welled in her eyes.

Reaching into a back pocket of his slacks, Julian pulled out a handkerchief, handing it to Morgana, who blotted her tears before she handed it back to him. He wiped angrily at his face. She picked up his glasses, setting them on the bridge of his nose.

Smiling, she kissed his cheek. "Feel better?"

He lowered his head. "I'm sorry, Morgan."

"About what?"

"For upsetting you."

"Hush. Now, you're talking foolish."

He flashed a sad smile. "I feel foolish."

"Why?"

"I didn't want you to see me crying."

"Why?" she asked again.

"My daddy always lectured his sons never to cry in front of women or they would think we were weak."

"That's archaic. Nowadays men who cry aren't thought of as weak but sensitive. And most women look for sensitivity in a man."

Staring at his hands, Julian let out a sigh. "Remember the fun times we used to have whenever the carnival came to town? Your mother wouldn't go on any of the rides except for the carousel. And when you got old enough to sit on a horse by yourself, it, too, became your favorite. I liked the Ferris wheel and roller coaster."

Morgana smiled. "Remember the time you took me on the Ferris wheel without Mama's permission?" Julian nodded. Her riding the Ferris wheel had remained their secret.

"Remember the time you came to my house instead of going home after you and that fast little gal Cissy Winters sampled her granddaddy's moonshine?"

Morgana grimaced. "Please don't remind me. I didn't know what was worse. Getting drunk or the medicine you gave me to clean me out."

Julian chuckled. "The laxative was the lesser of the two evils, especially if your folks had found out."

"I learned my lesson well. The next time I had anything alcoholic was ten years later at my wedding reception. Thank you for keeping my secrets."

"Anything for my princess," Julian said softly.

She recalled the times she had gone to her uncle rather than her parents because she had always trusted him to remain objective. "What if I take you out for breakfast this morning?"

Julian gave her a startled look. "But I usually fix breakfast for you."

"We're going to break tradition just for today because I want to go to the real estate office. It's time I listed the house."

He nodded. "Okay, but I'm driving."

EIGHT

Morgana celebrated her twenty-eighth wedding anniversary dusting and vacuuming her mother's house so it would look its best when the realtor arrived. She had just finished showering and dressing when the realtor rang the doorbell. Morgana greeted her at the door and led the real estate agent up the winding staircase to the second floor.

"There are four bedrooms, two with adjoining baths, and a full bathroom on this level. The master bedroom also has a sitting and dressing area."

Eileen Madsen, a petite birdlike woman, made notations on a pad as she followed Morgana along a carpeted hallway. "What do you plan to do with the rugs?"

"I'm keeping them." The handmade Turkish rugs in the library, formal living and dining rooms would one day cover the floors in Sandra's home.

She'd listed the house with a realtor at Johnson Realty, another local business that had been owned by a Johnson brother. Once the house was sold her only connection to Salvation, Georgia, would be her uncle.

The image of him sitting at the table sobbing was a blatant reminder that he was the last of the Salvation Johnsons. She wasn't certain whether she would ever return to her house in Chevy Chase, but she was certain wherever she went she would take her uncle with her.

It took another quarter of an hour for Eileen to survey the bedrooms. She pointed to a staircase leading to another level. "Do you have an attic?"

"Yes, but it's not finished. We only use it for storage."

The agent stuck her pen into an upsweep of pinkish cotton candy-colored hair. "May I see it?"

Morgana climbed the six steps, opened the door to the attic and flipped a light switch on the wall. A bulb in a ceiling fixture illuminated a space filled with two steamer trunks, boxes labeled with books, china, glasses, record albums, odd chairs, lamps and a bright pink dollhouse covered with a sheet of clear plastic.

She smiled, her gaze settling on the dollhouse. It had taken her, with her mother's assistance, six months to put the house together. By the time it was completed, Morgana had lost interest in it.

Eileen pulled a small but powerful flashlight from her shoulder purse, directing the stream of light on the overhead beams. "Very good. No leaks."

"The roof is only three years old, and has been guaranteed to last for twenty."

"Your mother's house is one of the finest maintained structures I've seen in years. I'm certain if you let me sell the house with the piano along with all of the furnishings I can get you a phenomenal price."

Shaking her head, Morgana said, "No."

"But, you can get—"

"This is not about money," she interrupted. "I'll leave the appliances and nothing else." There was a hard edge to her voice that indicated it was no longer a topic for discussion.

The tour of the interior of the house completed, Morgana showed the surrounding grounds, which included an outdoor patio, flower garden, and an orchard with a quartet of pear and peach trees. Randolph Johnson had built his home on ten acres of prime property that had appreciated dramatically in value since the early 1940s.

After touring the grounds, Eileen thanked Morgana, and assured her that the property would be listed within a week. Retrieving her car, she backed out of the driveway seconds before a van maneuvered into the space where she'd parked.

Shading her eyes with her hand, Morgana squinted at the lettering on the vehicle's door: Meade's Flowers. She stood on the porch, watching the van driver as he stepped out of the vehicle, slid back a door, and picked up a large vase filled with an enormous bouquet of flowers. A large red bow was tied around the mouth of the glass urn.

The lanky young man bounded up the walk, smiling. "I have a delivery for a Mrs. Wells."

Morgana lowered her hand. "I'm Mrs. Wells."

"Then these are for you, ma'am. It's heavy, so I'll carry it into the house for you. I'm going to need you to sign for it."

She held the door open, instructing him to place the vase on the table in the entryway next to another vase of fresh flowers. Morgana had continued her mother's tradition of placing a welcoming bouquet of fresh flowers near the front door.

During colder weather when her garden no longer bloomed, Katherine had always bought seasonal bouquets from a local florist.

Morgana scrawled her signature across the receipt. "If you'll wait I'll get you a tip."

The driver shook his head, pushing the receipt into the breast pocket of his jumpsuit. "That's okay, Mrs. Wells. The tip has been taken care of."

The screen door had opened and closed with a soft click. She didn't have to be a psychic to know the flowers were from Franklin. He had called her twice, leaving brief messages on the answering machine and asking that she return his call. As soon as she heard the messages she promptly erased them.

She didn't want to talk to him. In fact, they had nothing to talk about, because she wasn't ready to bring up the topic of his infidelity. She did not want to hear the lies, excuses or his rationale for sleeping with another woman. And more important, she did not trust herself not to say something she would regret for the rest of her life. For if Franklin tried to blame her for his adultery she would then say the dreaded D-word.

She pulled the card off the ribbon and slipped it into the back pocket of her jeans. Showing Eileen Madsen the attic had sparked her curiosity. It had been years since she'd ventured into the storage area. Walking across the living room, she climbed the staircase to the upper level and opened the door to the attic. The space was hot and had the musky smell associated with attics. She turned on the light and walked over to one of two steamer trunks.

Smiling, she fingered the lock. It was the trunk she had taken with her to college. Pulling her hand back, she stared at her fingertips. They were coated with a layer of dust. Ignoring the dust, she slid the catch on the lock until it sprang open. Kneeling, she pushed open the top, a wide grin on her face. The trunk was filled with dolls and toys from her childhood. She picked up a threadbare Raggedy Ann. It had been one of her favorites. Her mother had not understood why she preferred rag dolls to the more glamorous ones with the painted porcelain faces and stiffly curled hair. Replacing the doll in the space where it had been resting for years, she closed the top.

Opening the second trunk proved more of a challenge. The lock wouldn't budge. She found a rusting toolbox filled with screwdrivers, a hammer, and pliers in a corner. One blow with the hammer and the lock gave. She pushed back the cover and sat staring at dozens of cloth-bound notebooks wrapped in oilcloth.

Picking up one of the books, she unwrapped it as carefully as an archaeologist dusting off a relic at a dig. The oilcloth had preserved the cloth fabric. However, the muskiness had penetrated the protective covering.

She sat on the bare floor, flipping pages. Every page was dated and filled with her mother's neat slanting script. The word *love* jumped at her.

Morgana's hands were trembling when she realized she was reading her mother's diary. The steamer trunk was filled with books chronicling her most intimate thoughts.

Her heart racing with excitement, Morgana gathered up as many books as she could carry, carefully making her way down the staircase to her bedroom. It took three trips before she finally emptied the trunk. She removed the protective oilcloth coverings and stacked the diaries on a table in the corner of the room, in four piles. There were six books in each pile, which meant there were twenty-four volumes.

She opened one. The date at the top of the page read *February 3, 1953.* "That's a year before I was born," she whispered to the silent room. Quickly, she opened each book, putting them in chronological order. The first entry in the first book was dated *May 20, 1952*—exactly a month before her mother and father were married.

Sitting back in the chair, Morgana quickly calculated her mother's age. She'd been twenty-two when she'd begun keeping a diary. Her eyes quickly scanned the page, lingering on a name: Randolph Johnson. Katherine had underlined his name and had drawn a tiny heart next to it.

Closing the book, she pressed it to her breasts. A gamut of perplexing emotions swept over her. She was holding part of her mother in her hands. The words on the pages were certain to reveal who Katherine actually was and who she would become.

Strange and disquieting thoughts raced through her mind. Did she really want to know her mother that well? Could she read Katherine's thoughts, desires, and yearnings without prejudice?

The woman she had known and loved was soft-spoken, gentle, and generous. But she'd also found her moody and secretive. Katherine would leave the house, announcing she was going out, and return several hours later without explaining her whereabouts. Those were the times when she appeared more like a stranger than her mother.

The final entry in the last volume was dated *Easter Sunday, 2002.* It was the last time Morgana had seen her mother alive, and it had been a joyous occasion. Sandra had proudly shown her grandmother her engagement ring. Katherine had hugged and kissed her granddaughter while telling her she didn't want to wait until she was ninety to become a great-grandmother.

Justin, who was on a secret training mission, hadn't been able to make the celebration, but had sent a bouquet of flowers and a fruit basket.

Remembering the flowers, Morgana reached into the back pocket of her jeans and removed the card from the envelope. Her brow furrowed. Franklin hadn't sent the flowers. Her gaze raced over Sandra's precise print: *Happy Anniversary. Kenneth and I pray our marriage will be as perfect as yours and Daddy's. Love, Sandra and Kenneth. P.S. Daddy got the same bouquet and card.*

"It's not perfect, sweetheart," she whispered.

She picked up the phone, dialing the number to her daughter's fiancé's apartment. It rang four times before she heard the generic greeting from their answering machine.

"I want to thank you guys for the beautiful flowers. And, Sandra, thanks for remembering." She paused, closing her eyes. "I love you." She replaced the receiver on its cradle, then made her way into the bathroom to shower and change her clothes.

Morgana started when she returned downstairs and saw Julian standing in the kitchen, a stack of mail in one hand and a bottle of champagne in the other. Placing both hands over her chest, she exhaled audibly.

"You frightened me." Her voice came out in a breathless sigh.

He placed the mail and wine on a counter at the cooking island. "I'm sorry. The door was open, so I just walked in."

Wiping her hands on a towel, she smiled at her uncle. "I don't know why I bother to lock it anyway. No one ever comes out this way."

"Salvation has changed. Gone are the days when you could go to sleep and not lock your front door or your car."

"It's still safer than Baltimore or D.C." Morgana pointed to the bottle of champagne. "What are we celebrating?"

Angling his head to the left, he stared at her. "Your anniversary."

A wave of heat darkened her cheeks. "You remembered?"

"Of course," he said smoothly, with no expression on his face. "How could I forget walking you down the aisle and giving you away to a man you defied your parents to marry."

A smile trembled over her lush mouth. She had been ready to disassociate herself from her mother and father if they hadn't accepted Franklin. And despite their disapproval, she was glad neither was around to say "I told you so."

Glancing at the clock over the sink, she said, "We should sit down to eat in about fifteen minutes."

Julian removed his jacket, placing it on the back of a tall stool. "Do you need any help?"

"No, thanks. I have everything under control." She'd even set the table, a task she usually left for Julian.

He opened the side-by-side refrigerator-freezer, placing the bottle of champagne on a shelf. Closing the door, he walked back to the cooking island. "You know you don't have to cook for me."

Morgana stopped squeezing the juice from a lemon. She'd decided to make lemon chicken. "I like cooking for you."

"Every night?"

"Why not? I have to eat, too."

"You may have to eat, but you don't have to cook every night."

She folded a hand on her hip. "What are you saying?"

Julian stared at Morgana until she dropped her gaze. "I can eat leftovers. In fact, I like leftovers."

"You don't want me to cook?"

"Not every night."

"Oh . . . kay." It came out like two words. She went back to squeezing the lemon.

"Have I upset you?"

"No."

He smiled. "You're not a very good liar."

Picking up the other half of the lemon, she clutched it tightly, squeezing out the juice into a small bowl. "Why would you say that?"

"You're mutilating that poor lemon."

It's a good thing it's not Franklin's neck, she thought. The doorbell chimed, startling Morgana and Julian as they stared at each other.

"Are you expecting company?"

She shook her head. "No."

"I'll see who it is."

Morgana poured the lemon juice and a cup of dry white cooking wine into a skillet, and then added a teaspoon of black pepper and a tablespoon of capers. Stirring the mixture until it was heated, she poured it over a serving dish of chicken cutlets delicately seasoned with minced garlic.

"Hello, Mo."

The skillet slipped from her hand, landing with a dull thud on the countertop. Franklin stood under the arched entrance to the kitchen. Her eyes widened until the dark green pupils were clearly visible. "What the hell are you doing here?" Her voice, low and raspy, trembled with repressed rage.

Franklin smiled, extending his right hand, offering her a small blue shopping bag. There was no doubt it contained a piece of jewelry from Tiffany's. "Happy anniversary, darling."

"Whatever it is, you can give it to your whore!"

Lowering his arm, his face suddenly went grim. "I'm sorry, Morgana!" he shouted. "Is *that* what you want to hear? I'm sorry I slept with *that woman.*"

Folding her hands on her hips, she said, "You're not sorry you *fucked* her! What you're sorry about is that you got caught!"

Julian pushed by Franklin, walking into the kitchen. "Morgan!" It was the first time he'd ever heard her utter a profanity.

"Dammit, Uncle Julian. Mind your business." The veins in her neck were visible.

He recoiled as if she'd slapped him. Reaching for his jacket on the back of the stool, he slipped his arms into the sleeves. Shaking his head, he looked at her before turning and walking out of the kitchen.

Franklin glared at his enraged wife. "There was no need for you to talk to him like that."

Morgana was beyond being reasonable. "If you don't leave I'm going to call the police and have you arrested for trespassing."

"No, you're not," Franklin stated confidently. "You're going to stand right there and listen to what I have to say."

"Wrong, Franklin. What I should've done was listen to my mother and father twenty-eight years ago when they told me not to marry you." He came toward her like a stalking cat, but Morgana did not move, not even to blink.

He threw the bag across the kitchen and slammed his hand down on the butcher-block counter, rattling dishes and serving pieces. "Are you saying what we have, what we've shared all of these years means nothing to you?"

"Apparently it meant nothing to you when you decided to

whore around. The only worthwhile things to come from our marriage are *my* children."

"If that's the case, then you've been lying to me all these years, saying that you love me."

"I'm trying not to hate you, Franklin."

She picked up the platter of chicken and dumped it into the garbage. Everything she'd prepared also went into the garbage. She moved around the kitchen as if she were the only one there, while Franklin stared at his wife as if she were a stranger.

And she had become a stranger. A woman he recognized, but did not really know. She'd shocked him with her unbridled rage.

After rinsing and putting the pots and pans into the dishwasher, she turned to Franklin. "Go back to Maryland and get some help for your problem."

"I don't have a problem."

"You're deluding yourself if you think you don't. Get help or you're going to wind up just like your father."

"What are you implying?"

"I *ain't implyin' nuttin',"* she said, lapsing into dialect. "Your father was a whoremaster, and you're just like him." A warning cloud settled into his features. "That's right, you've become your father. A man you claimed you despised." Throwing a dish towel into the sink, she said, "I'm going out. Please don't be here when I get back." She picked up her handbag off a stool in a corner, and stalked out of the house.

Morgana hadn't realized how much her hands were shaking until she tried putting the car key into the ignition. It took two attempts before the engine turned over. Counting slowly to ten, she drove away, not seeing her husband standing on the porch watching the taillights until they disappeared from his line of sight.

Hypocrite.

The single word played over and over in her head as she drove. Just when she'd come to grips that her husband was an adulterer, he sought to minimize it by pretending they would go on with their lives as if nothing had happened. Did he really believe that because he'd offered her an expensive bauble that all would be forgiven?

A shadow crossed the road and Morgana slammed her foot on the brake, causing her to lose control of the car and skid off the road. She ended up on the shoulder, her heart pounding painfully in her chest. Lowering her head to the steering wheel, she mumbled a prayer of thanks. She was lucky there hadn't been a car in back of her.

Once she had recovered from the shock that Franklin had been unfaithful, she knew she would have considered attending marital counseling sessions with him. She'd worked too hard to make her marriage a success to throw it away without trying to salvage a small piece of it. But for Franklin to just show up at her mother's home and expect her to fall into his arms because he offered a trinket was ludicrous. Had he expected her to say all is forgiven and believe that he would not do it again?

Stay away from me, Franklin, before I grow to hate you, her inner voice shouted silently.

Waves of guilt attacked her as she maneuvered off the grassy surface and back onto the road. She'd screamed—no, cursed—at her uncle, and she didn't think she would ever forget the pain in his eyes. Julian did not deserve her wrath.

Was she losing her mind? Becoming a madwoman?

NINE

Morgana drove around Salvation several times before deciding to go to the lake. She maneuvered the car into the parking lot at the lake, turned off the ignition, and sat in the car, staring out the windshield. After a few moments, she rested her head on the steering wheel and closed her eyes. The image of Katherine's face surfaced without warning and the tears flowed.

"Mama," she sobbed. "Oh, Mama, why did you have to leave me now? I'm so confused and I need you so much." She knew she sounded selfish, but she couldn't help herself. She was alone and lonely. She needed and wanted her mother's touch and advice.

The minutes ticked, and Morgana cried until spent. She left the car and walked down to the lake. Trailing her fingers in the water, she splashed her face. It was cold, refreshing and cleansing. She wanted to wash away the confusion and uncertainty that held her in a punishing grip and refused to release her so that she could move on with her life.

She sat on the grass until the sun sank beyond the horizon, taking with it the intense heat. A sprinkling of stars had covered the nighttime sky by the time she stood up and walked back to the parking lot and her car.

An audible sigh of relief escaped her lips as she pulled into the driveway to her mother's house. Franklin's rental car wasn't there. She entered the house, washed her hands, and took a small container of sliced honeydew melon and strawberries from the refrigerator.

Sitting on a stool at the cooking island, she ate the fruit and sorted through the mail Julian had left on the countertop. She picked up a large manila envelope, studying her name and address written in a precise calligraphy. A slight frown creased her forehead. There was no return address. She opened the envelope, shaking out its contents.

She went completely still. The images staring back at Morgana made her breath catch in her throat. They were the photographs taken by Erick Wilson. The fact that the prints were black-and-white did not shock her as much as the haunted eyes staring out at the camera.

It was as if she were looking at her mother's face. It was the same nose, mouth, and cheekbones. Only the shape and color of the eyes was different. Hers were a darker gray and deep-set, while Katherine's had been a clear gray and round, giving her the appearance of being slightly surprised whenever she glanced at someone.

Erick had captured the essence of her emptiness—an emptiness that she'd been feeling for a long time. It was as if he could see the hollowness in her soul. Had others seen what he saw that day?

Reaching for her purse, she searched for his card. Trancelike, she dialed his number.

"Hello." She hadn't remembered his voice being that deep. "Hello?" he repeated.

"Hello." Her voice came from somewhere deep in her throat. "Is this Erick Wilson?"

"Who's asking?"

"Ms. Johnson. Morgana Johnson."

"Ah, Ms. Johnson. I take it you saw your photographs."

She smiled. "Yes, I did."

"Do you like them?"

She could picture him smiling. "Yes and no."

"Can you explain the yes and the no?"

"Yes, because I think you're very talented."

"Thank you. And the no."

"I looked so sad."

There was a pause before his voice came through the line. "Did you have a reason to be sad?"

"Yes. I lost my mother a couple of weeks ago."

There was another pause. "I'm sorry. I take it you were very close."

"More than close. She was my very best friend. There were times when I believed I loved her more than my own children."

"Does that bother you?"

"Look, Mr. Wilson, I didn't mean to disturb you. It's just that I want to thank you for helping me to see who I have become."

"Do you like what you've become, Ms. Johnson?"

"No. I've taken up enough of your time. Thank you again—"

"Where are you?" he asked, cutting her off.

"I'm in Salvation."

"How about we meet for drinks? You choose the place."

"I'm afraid I can't drink anything until I've eaten. I can't tolerate alcohol on an empty stomach."

"Then we'll eat before we drink. Shall I come and pick you up?"

"No."

"Look, Ms. Johnson, I don't want to get in your business, but it sounds as if you don't need to be alone right now. After dinner, a drink and a few laughs I promise you'll feel better."

She had to smile at his arrogance. "Can you guarantee that, Mr. Wilson?"

"The only way you'll know is if you let me take you out."

She knew she would later question her decision, but said, "Okay." She gave him the directions to her mother's house.

"I'll see you in half an hour."

She ended the call and covered her face with her hands. What was wrong with her? She'd just set up a date with a total stranger. A strange man who'd taken her photograph, a man who could possibly be a psychopath. She'd hadn't been that irresponsible when she was nineteen. Why now at forty-nine?

She didn't want to ask herself why she'd called him or had agreed to meet him for a late dinner and drinks. She didn't want to ask because she knew the answer to her own question—loneliness.

How had she permitted all of it to happen? Instead of demanding Franklin spend more time with her, she'd opened a business. It was as if she'd silently given her husband permission to seek out another woman's bed. And it was all because of a long-ago promise they'd made to each other: she would support Franklin in his quest to become the very best he could be, and vice versa.

Erick Wilson stared at Morgana's hauntingly beautiful eyes unable to believe she could improve on perfection. She looked different than she had at the lake—more confident, sophisticated. She wore a pair of taupe-colored linen slacks with an off-white silk, classic man-tailored blouse. A narrow brown lizard skin belt around her trim waist matched a pair of wedge-heel sandals.

He studied her face, a slow smile tilting the corners of his mouth. The day he'd met her at the lake she hadn't worn any makeup. He'd found the spray of freckles over her delicate nose and cheeks enchanting. Everything about Morgana Johnson was enchanting—from the top of her curly head to her expensively shod feet.

Morgana's smile was dazzling when she saw Erick in the brightly lit entryway. He had the most graceful body language of any man she'd ever seen in her life. She realized he was much taller than she'd remembered. But then again, maybe his slimness made him appear taller.

He looked every inch the artist dressed all in black: black banded-collar shirt, loose-fitting linen jacket with a shawl collar, matching slacks. A pair of highly polished low-heel boots completed his Bohemian look.

"Hello again."

He returned her smile. "Hello. May I call you Morgana?"

"Only if I can call you Erick."

Lowering his head, he stared at her with a pair of eyes so dark she couldn't see the centers. "Of course you may," he replied, winking at her. "What do you feel like eating?"

She shrugged. "Anything."

He lifted his eyebrows. "Possum? Squirrel?"

Shuddering, Morgana grimaced. "Please, no."

Erick chuckled softly deep in his throat. "You did say anything." Amusement shimmered in his dark eyes. "I'd like to take you to a restaurant on St. Simons Island. The menu is varied, the dishes prepared to perfection, but the only drawback is it's not fancy."

She smiled up at him. "Who needs ambience when the food is good and one's dining partner is interesting."

Resting a hand on the small of her back, Erick escorted her out of the house and down the porch to his late-model black truck. "You should reserve comment on how interesting you may think I am. I just might bore you to tears."

She gave him a sidelong glance, admiring his sharply defined profile. He had a long, angular face with high flat cheekbones that made him appear foreign, exotic. There was something about the shape of his face and features that made him look Ethiopian.

"And if you do, then I'll be certain to let you know."

Erick turned and looked down at her, an expression of surprise lifting his dark silky eyebrows. "You don't bite your tongue, do you?"

"I don't have to. Not when I'm going to turn fifty my next birthday."

He stopped and Morgana bumped into him. Reaching out with his free hand, he held her waist to steady her. "You're how old?"

Tilting her head, she smiled up at him under the soft glow of a pair of spotlights over the garage. "Forty-nine."

Erick was momentarily speechless with surprise. "I really don't know if there are criteria for how a forty-nine-year-old woman is supposed to look, but I think you're incredibly beautiful."

"Are you flirting with me, Erick?"

He shook his head and a profusion of twists brushed his wide shoulders. "No, ma'am."

She laughed. "Now I'm a ma'am. What happened to you calling me Morgana?"

He wound an arm around her waist, the gesture as natural as if he had executed it many times before. "Let's go before I wind up putting my foot in my mouth." He pressed a button on a remote device, unlocking the doors to a truck with California plates.

"Where do you live in California?" she asked after Erick seated her and then took his own seat behind the wheel.

He started up the vehicle, and the soft strains of classical music flowed from the truck's speakers. "I'm from the San Diego area."

"You've come all the way from California to teach in Georgia?"

He nodded. "I'm a visiting artist-in-residence."

"How many courses do you teach?"

"Three. Studio drawing, landscapes, and still-life."

He drove through Salvation and headed for Savannah and the Interstate. Traffic along I-95 was light, which meant he could drive to the island in record time.

"Which one do you prefer?" she asked, continuing her questioning.

Erick gave her a quick smile. "All of them. However, my true passion lies with photography. That's what I was doing the other morning when I met you. I've spent the past year photographing Savannah and most towns within a twenty- to thirty-mile radius. One of these days I'd like to complete a series of black-and-white photos of this region."

Morgana was intrigued with Erick. "Why black-and-white and not color?"

"I believe the true test of an artist is working in black-and-white."

She nodded. "I do have a preference for black-and-white films."

Erick smiled. *"Citizen Kane."*

"Who's Afraid of Virginia Woolf?" she countered.

"The original *Les Miserables* with Fredric March and Charles Laughton," Erick added.

Morgana nodded again. "What a masterpiece."

"On The Waterfront," they said in unison, laughing because they'd thought of the same film.

The soft strains of a classical composition swelled to a crescendo, then faded with the lonely haunting sound of an oboe as Morgana and Erick talked about the films of Alfred Hitchcock. Time seemed to slip by and Morgana was disappointed when he pulled into the parking lot next to a small restaurant several blocks from the ocean.

Erick stepped out of the truck, came around, and opened the passenger-side door. Extending his arms, his fingers closed around her waist, lifting her and setting her gently to her feet until she stood beside him. Reaching for her right hand, he held it in his protective warmth. It was a gesture she'd missed. He closed the door with a solid slam, locked the truck with a remote device, released her hand, then wound his arm around her waist, fingertips burning her flesh through the delicate fabric of the silk blouse.

She was barely able to control the shiver that raced along her nerve endings, telling herself that Erick was too young to elicit a craving of desire. She doubted he was much older than her son.

The restaurant he had chosen was small, almost rustic in appearance. Long wooden tables and benches were set up for family dining and smaller round tables with seating for two or four. And despite the late hour, most of the tables were occupied.

"The food's wonderful," Erick said close to her ear. "The bartender is a friend of mine, and he's made quite a reputation of concocting the most outrageous drinks on the island."

She gave him a skeptical look. "I hope not so outrageous that I'm going to have to become the designated driver tonight."

He smiled, and distinctive lines fanned out around his expressive eyes. Seeing the lines deepen forced Morgana to reassess her opinion that Erick was only a few years older than Justin. In that instant she knew he was not a boy-man, but a man—mature and erudite.

"If anyone's going to be the designated driver, then it'll be me. After all, I did promise you dinner and a drink."

Morgana wanted to remind Erick that he'd initially offered to share a drink with her, but it was she who'd mentioned dinner. She followed him to a corner and a table for two.

Waiters and waitresses, costumed like pirates and serving wenches, worked quietly and efficiently, and twenty minutes after sitting Erick and Morgana were eating an appetizer of steamed mussels in a lemon-garlic sauce. At Erick's recommendation, she'd ordered a Bermuda Triangle and after two sips of the icy-cold fruity concoction she began to relax.

"Why did you decide you wanted to become an artist?"

"I can't remember when I did not want to be an artist. As an only child I spent a lot time by myself, so whenever I was bored I began tracing objects in books. Once I entered grade school I realized I could draw freehand. The year I turned sixteen I was taking private lessons from a very successful artist who at one time had lived in the Bay Area. It was during this time that I developed what would eventually become what I saw as my style for drawing."

Morgana chewed and swallowed a tender mussel. "Have you ever had a showing?"

He nodded. "Once."

"Was it successful?"

Shrugging a broad shoulder, Erick stared at Morgana, memorizing her face. Again, he found himself transfixed by the shape and color of her eyes. "Somewhat."

"Is that a yes or no?"

Leaning back on his chair, he smiled. "I'd managed to sell every piece, but I wound up losing money because after I paid the gallery their commission and factored in the time it had taken me to complete the paintings and the cost of my supplies I was in the red."

"At least you got to sell your work."

He nodded. "That was my only consolation. I'd become a legitimate artist."

"The card you left for me indicated you're an artist-in-residence at SCAD." Almost everyone in Savannah called the Savannah College of Art and Design by its acronym.

Erick took a sip of his drink. He didn't want to eat because he preferred staring at his beautiful dining partner. After seeing her again, he had to admit to himself that he was attracted to Morgana Johnson. Not as an artist relating to a subject as he initially thought, but as a man to a woman. She was older than he was by twelve years but he did not see that as a problem, because he'd always been attracted to older women. His ex-wife had been five years his senior.

"My tenure at SCAD ends August eighth."

She arched an eyebrow at this disclosure. "Where will you go next?"

"Back to California. I'm on sabbatical from an art school near L.A. What about you, Morgana?"

"What about me?"

"What do you do?"

"I have my own business."

"Where?"

"In Maryland."

Leaning closer, he placed his hand over hers. "Just a business?"

Morgana did not drop her gaze or attempt to pull her hand away. "And a house."

"A house, but not a home."

A slight smile softened her mouth. "Am I that transparent?"

He shook his head and a profusion of coiled, twisted hair moved over his shoulders and back. "No. I've been there."

"You're divorced?" Her voice was a breathless whisper.

"Three years."

"Was it painful for you?"

"For me—no. Losing my son—yes."

"How old is he?"

"Nine."

"Where does he live?"

"He lives with his mother and stepfather in Denver. He usually gets to spend all of his school holidays and the summer with me, but this year is the exception. I'd thought about not accepting the position to become an artist-in-residence because I would forfeit spending time with Jamal, but that decision was taken out of my hands when he told me he wanted to spend time with his new baby brother. Tell me about your business." He smoothly changed the topic.

"The Registry is a gift shop that caters to brides-to-be.

We offer china, stemware, and silver patterns, along with the elegant little items that make a home comfortable and unique."

"It sounds very nice." There was admiration in his voice.

"It is nice."

Morgana drank less than half of the Bermuda Triangle, but managed to finish a delicious Caesar salad with popcorn shrimp. Erick had ordered Maryland crab cakes with a spicy mayonnaise and a small spinach salad. It was minutes before midnight, and closing time, when he settled the bill.

Holding her hand firmly within his grasp, he led the way out to the parking lot and his truck. "Thank you, Erick, for dinner and your company."

He squeezed her fingers. "You're quite welcome. But I'd also like to thank you for your company. Perhaps we can do it again."

Morgana decided she liked Erick. He was talented, intelligent and a good listener. The fact that she found him attractive added to the total package. "Perhaps we can."

He moved closer without actually taking a step. "When?"

Standing this close to him made her aware that he was at least six-two or -three. "I'll call you."

He lowered his chin and she felt the warm moisture of his breath sweep over her mouth. "May I call you?"

She shook her head. "No. I'll call you."

His dark eyes smoldered in the lights of the restaurant's parking lot. "Okay."

The drive back to Salvation was made in complete silence with only the soft sounds of classical music as a backdrop. Erick dropped Morgana off at her mother's house, waiting until she unlocked the door.

He stood with his hands pushed into the pockets of his

slacks, smiling. His smile widened when she returned it with a sensual one that made his pulse race a little faster. She stepped into the house and closed the door.

He stared at the door, then turned and walked back to his truck. He felt good knowing the sadness he'd captured in his camera lens was no longer there. He didn't know whether he had anything to do with the change in Morgana, but what he did know was that spending time with her had changed him. He hadn't painted in more than three years—not since his divorce. And now he wanted to paint. He wanted to paint Morgana Johnson.

Morgana closed and locked the front door behind her and headed to the upstairs bathroom to prepare for bed. She brushed her teeth, washed her face, patted it dry and applied a moisturizer. She smiled at her reflection in the bathroom mirror. Sharing dinner with Erick had lifted her dark mood.

She walked into her bedroom, undressed and slipped into bed. As she turned off the lamp on the bedside table she realized that she had celebrated her twenty-eighth wedding anniversary with a man who was not her husband.

Morgana settled against the pillows and within seconds she fell into a deep sleep for the first time in weeks. She slept undisturbed throughout the night.

When Morgana woke the next morning, her gaze lingered on the piles of cloth-covered books on the table in the corner of the room. Pushing back the sheet, she went downstairs to prepare a cup of instant coffee, and when she returned to her bedroom she walked over to the rocking chair.

Shifting the tattered teddy bear in the chair, she sat, sipping coffee. Bright sunlight poured through the sheer curtains on the windows. She wondered what the diaries would tell her about her mother, and perhaps about herself.

Opening the oldest book, she read the inscription on the front cover: *This Book Is the Property of Katherine Faith Graham.*

Morgana turned to the first page.

TEN

May 20, 1952

In exactly one month I will become Mrs. Randolph Johnson. I am thrilled at the prospect of becoming his wife, yet at the same time I am somewhat frightened. What bothers me most is that I do not know what I am frightened of. The fact that Randolph is fifteen years older than I am is of little or no consequence to me. I have spoken to Mother of my fear, but she says I should not be concerned. She says it is just premarital jitters. She spoke to me about what a husband expects from his wife in the bedroom, and while I managed to keep a straight face Mother blushed the entire time. I had once thought my mother a modern woman, but I was mistaken. I sat without saying a word when she talked about how babies are made. I now believe the girls at Spelman—even the ones who are vir-

gins—know more than my mother. I hear voices downstairs, so I must stop. Randolph is expected for dinner. I am not afraid to admit that I have fallen madly in love with him. I know I am the luckiest woman if not in the world, then in Salvation.

Katherine closed her diary, stood up and slipped it under the cushion on the rocker. She went into the bathroom, examining her face in the mirror on the back of the door. Anticipation had darkened her gray eyes and added a soft rose-pink hue to her cheeks. She'd brushed her shoulder-length, wavy auburn hair until it shimmered with bright copper highlights before tying it back with a black velvet ribbon.

At first she'd thought about letting it flow over her shoulders, then changed her mind. She hadn't wanted to appear too loose or too wanton for her fiancé, because there had never been a time when he hadn't been proper with her. And she could now refer to Randolph as her fiancé, since he had given her a ring as a sign of their betrothal the day she graduated from college.

Smoothing down the front of her white cotton blouse over her breasts, she made it certain it was neatly tucked into the waistband of her slim black skirt. Peering over her shoulder, she checked the seams of her stockings. They were straight. Confident she was presentable, Katherine went downstairs to greet the man to whom she had pledged her future.

Randolph Johnson stood in the middle of the living room with Edward Graham, barely listening to the man's rambling conversation. His gaze was fixed on the tall, slender figure of the woman descending the winding staircase. Her gaze met his as a mysterious smile curved her lush lips.

You've done it again, Randolph. He had to congratulate not only himself, but also Edward. The man had come through on his promise to let him court and marry his daughter.

And in one month he would claim Katherine as his wife. He would take her to his bed, and sire strong, handsome sons and daughters who would be certain to inherit some, if not all, of his wife's delicate characteristics.

Randolph headed for the staircase, taking the hand Katherine presented to him. Lowering his head, he raised her hand and kissed her cool fingertips. "You look lovely, Katherine."

She smiled up at him, her eyes gleaming like polished silver. "Thank you, Randolph." Moving closer, she kissed his cheek, her breasts brushing his chest. He jumped as if she'd burned him with a red-hot poker. "If you'll excuse me, I'm going to see if Mother needs help in the kitchen." Randolph nodded, his gaze watching her retreat.

Edward, already on his third drink, weaved unsteadily on his feet. "Sheese lovely, isn't she?" His speech had begun to slur.

Randolph turned, glaring at Edward. Taking three steps, he closed the distance between them, and pried the glass filled with scotch from his fingers. "You've had enough of these for one day. You don't want your daughter to see you in your cups, do you?"

Edward flopped down to a nearby chair. "Why should you care how much I drink? Are you afraid I'm going to tell her about our deal?"

Randolph's right hand shot out, his fingers tightening around his future father-in-law's throat. "If you ever speak of that night I'll strangle you with my bare hands." He loosened his grip when the man's face turned a deep purple. "You've made out well from our arrangement. I've forgiven your gambling debts, and you're handling all of my legal business. In my book I'd say we're even." He released his throat.

Edward's chest shuddered as he tried to regain his composure. Even though he gambled and drank heavily, he was still a very good lawyer. There had been a time when he had to turn away clients until he hired an assistant.

He had a thriving law practice, his daughter had graduated college and had secured a teaching position with a private school for colored children in Savannah, and now she was planning her marriage to Salvation's most prominent businessman. He should've been happy, but he wasn't. He had offered his only child up like a sacrificial lamb to pay off his gambling debts, and she unknowingly had walked into the trap her father had set for her.

Katherine took the wooden spoon from her mother. "Let me make the gravy."

Wisps of silver-streaked red hair had escaped the elaborate twist at the back of Lauretta Graham's head, clinging to the nape of her neck. She had labored most of the morning and afternoon to prepare a special meal. It was to be the first time Randolph would dine under her roof as her daughter's fiancé, and she wanted to make certain this dinner was exceptional.

"Just make certain there are no lumps in it."

Katherine smiled. "I've never made gravy with lumps."

Lauretta stood at the stove, watching carefully as Katherine poured measured amounts of cold water into the pan with turkey giblets and drippings. She smiled and tiny lines deepened around her blue-gray eyes. "Very good."

Katherine glanced at her mother. "I learned from the best."

Curving an arm around Katherine's narrow waist, Lauretta hugged her daughter, whose height eclipsed hers by four inches. No one would ever say they weren't mother and daughter. Both had dark red hair, and where Lauretta's eyes changed from blue to gray, depending on her mood, Katherine's were a clear sliver-gray.

"You're going to be a wonderful hostess for the parties you and Randolph will host in that grand house of his."

"Don't forget, Mother, that when I marry Randolph it's going to be my house, too."

"You're right." She noted the thickening gravy. "I believe everything's ready now. I'm going to get the men."

Katherine poured the giblet mixture into a gravy boat. Wrapping it in a towel, she held the handle tightly and walked into the dining room. The oak table was set with a damask tablecloth, napkins, china, silver and delicate stemware. The light from an overhead chandelier shimmered like diamonds. She set the gravy boat down next to a serving dish filled with collard greens.

Katherine had wanted to invite the entire Johnson clan to dinner to celebrate her engagement, but Lauretta had protested, saying there would be time for everyone to get together during the rehearsal dinner.

She had already met Randolph's parents, two of his brothers and their wives and children at several church socials. The only one missing was his youngest brother, Julian, who was completing his medical training in New York. Julian had called to say he wouldn't be able to attend the wedding, but was planning to send a gift to the newlyweds.

Edward entered the dining room, Randolph on his heels. A lopsided smile curved his mouth. "Everything smells wonderful." Weaving slightly, he said to Randolph, "Doesn't it, my boy?"

Randolph's expression did not reveal his revulsion at Edward's inability to hold his liquor. "Why don't you sit down? I'll seat the ladies." He seated Lauretta at one end of the table, then pulled out a chair for Katherine. The delicate fragrance of her perfume lingered in his nostrils even after he'd taken his own seat.

Lauretta glanced across the table at her husband. "Edward, will you please do us the honor of saying grace?"

Although intoxicated, Edward spoke eloquently, thanking God for life, good health and blessings for his loved ones and the food placed before them.

Katherine peered up through her lashes at her father and fiancé, realizing how different the two men were. Both were tall, over six feet in height, but that was where the similarity ended. Her father was fair in coloring with hazel eyes and straight light-brown graying hair. Edward's late mother had been light enough to pass for a white woman, but she had always made it clear that she was a Negro.

Once she'd turned twenty-one, Randolph had kissed her on the mouth for the first time. He'd touched his lips to hers, permitting her to inhale the lingering scent of tobacco on his breath. What she loved about being close to him was his masculine smell. She liked his kisses, but craved his touch more. No matter how much she'd begged him to touch her, he wouldn't, declaring he wanted to wait until they were married.

He came to the Graham house every Sunday when she was home for school recess and holidays, and the more she saw him the more she had wanted to see him.

Platters and serving bowls filled with turkey, baked yams,

collard greens, rice, and thick slices of buttered cornbread were passed around the table. Randolph poured gravy over his rice and slices of turkey breast. "If my Katherine can cook half as good as her mother, then I'm in for a real treat."

Lauretta lifted a dark eyebrow. "Katherine is a fabulous cook. She will do you proud."

He smiled at Lauretta, his white teeth showing brightly beneath a clipped mustache. "I'm more than certain she will. And I hope to make her proud that she has chosen me to become her husband." He turned his intense stare on Katherine. She nodded and smiled.

Lauretta touched her napkin to the corners of her mouth. "I hope everyone will save room for dessert. The strawberry shortcake Katherine made will go very well with Randolph's gift of a bottle of champagne." Edward licked his lips at the mention of champagne.

"I'll get the dessert from the refrigerator," Katherine announced softly, rising to her feet.

Randolph stood, quickly rounding the table to pull back her chair. "I'll help you."

He felt a tightening in his groin when she smiled at him over her shoulder. It had not been easy to keep his hands off her, especially when she'd begged him to touch her. He'd refused because he wanted her pure; he wanted her to be a virgin bride. He had been with enough women to recognize passion even before he took them to his bed. And Katherine Graham had enough passion for two women.

He followed her, his gaze fixed on her back as she headed toward the kitchen. All he wanted to do was grab her hips and hold her against the bulge in the front of his trousers. He wanted her to know how much she excited him. But he would not take her—not until their wedding night. There was another woman who would assuage the throbbing between his legs and he would continue to sleep with her until he married Katherine. Then, and only then, would he become a faithful husband.

After dinner, Katherine walked Randolph outside and stood with him next to his car, holding hands. The brilliance of a full moon lit up the countryside in an eerie silvery light.

"What are your plans for tomorrow?"

Closing her eyes, she smiled. A dreamy expression crossed her delicate features. "Mother and I are going shopping for my trousseau."

"True what?"

She opened her eyes. "Trousseau. It's a French word for personal items a bride will need. It can be anything from linens to nightgowns or even little things for her house."

"I have everything you'll need for the house."

"That may be true, but I'd like to add my personal touch."

"There's nothing wrong with my house."

"There's no need to take offense, Randolph. There is nothing wrong with your house, but when it becomes our house I'd like the option of making a few changes. Of course I'll always confer with you first."

Randolph registered a hint of censure in her voice. In the past she had never challenged him. There was one thing he did not intend to become, and that was a petticoat man. His mother had found fault in everything his father ever did. She always corrected him because she had had more schooling, and there were times when he saw his father hold back tears rather than argue with his wife.

"You're right about that. We will talk about it first."

Leaning over, he brushed a light kiss over her lips, tasting the sweetness of the strawberries and champagne they'd had with their dinner. He pulled her against his chest, deepening their chaste, closed-mouth kiss. Reluctantly he pulled away. "Good night, Katherine. I'll call you tomorrow."

"Are we still going to Bessie's Place tomorrow night?"

He nodded. "Yes."

Katherine had asked him to take her to Bessie's, a restaurant that had earned a reputation for serving the best fried chicken and biscuits in south Georgia. Bessie's had also become renowned for its live music. Some of Bessie's performers had gone on to signing recording contracts with major record labels.

She smiled. "Good night, Randolph."

Katherine waited for him to get into his car and drive away before she turned and walked back into the house.

A muscle in Randolph's jaw quivered as he drove past his house. He knew he shouldn't be seeking out a woman while another wore his ring, but this was one night he did not want to be alone. Half a mile later, he maneuvered his car behind a small one-story frame house. Lenora Hazelton's modest home was far enough from her closest neighbor that his comings and goings weren't that obvious. And he never came to her during the day. It was always at night, under the cover of darkness. Just like their decade-long liaison.

He had been sharing Lenora Hazelton's bed for years, knowing he would never marry her because she'd given herself to him too freely. Anytime he called, she opened her door to him. And if he stayed away for months she still accepted him. Even if she knew he had been with another woman, she still opened her arms and her legs to him. He would continue to sleep with Lenora until he married Katherine.

Lenora opened the door at his knock, pulling him into a dimly lit parlor. She was dressed for bed, her full breasts spilled over the lacy bodice of her nightgown.

Her right hand went to his crotch while her left was busy pulling his jacket off his shoulders. "You're heavy tonight, Daddy. What do you have for me?" Her raspy voice grated against his ear. Too many cigarettes had changed the timbre of her voice so much there were times when she sounded like a man.

"I have two days' worth." Lowering his head, he caught her earlobe between his teeth. "Stop talking and take care of me."

"Ouch. So you want it rough. Come on, Lenora's going to take good care of you tonight."

He ripped off his tie while Lenora unbuttoned his shirt. One reason he slept with her was because he did not have to use a rubber. She had had an operation in her late teens in which a doctor had removed her uterus. She'd almost bled to death from a botched abortion, and the attending doctor's only alternative was a partial hysterectomy to save her life. The hospital's records listed the surgical procedure as a spontaneous rather than an illegal abortion. She had told him stories of young colored girls who had found themselves pregnant, concealed it from their families, and then delivered their babies in hospitals in another city. Most times they walked away, leaving their infants a ward of the state. The thirty-four-year-old nurse had mentioned marriage several times, but Randolph had no intention of marrying her because she had two strikes against her: she was too dark *and* she was barren.

Lenora crawled over Randolph like a cat in heat. He had

barely stepped out of his pants and underwear when she curved her arms around his neck and pulled herself up until her legs encircled his waist. His erect penis grazed her pubic mound, bouncing against the split in her firm, rounded behind as he carried her toward her bedroom.

She fell across the bed, he following and landing heavily on her. Lenora wasn't tall, but her body was voluptuous. Her legs were beautifully formed, her feet small and slender. She was dark, nearly blue-black in coloring. The lushness of her body paled in comparison to her face. Tiny, delicate doll-like features had most men gaping whenever they looked at her. She was smart, beautiful, and was skillful enough in bed to make most men forget their names in the throes of passion.

Raising his hips, Randolph guided his penis into Lenora's body, but she scooted out from under him. Easing him onto his back, she straddled him. There was enough light from the table lamp for him to see her expression. Her slanting eyes and tiny pointed teeth made her look catlike.

"Do you want me to taste your candy, Daddy?"

Closing his eyes, he grunted his approval, girding himself for what was to come. The first time Lenora had put her mouth on him he felt as if he was losing his mind. He was used to being in control, and Lenora's power over him had been a surprise. It was another six months before he permitted her to do it again. Now, he looked forward to it.

Lenora ran the tip of her tongue around the head of his penis, inhaling the fragrance of his sex. The odor was strong and musky. It was an odor she craved. She licked and suckled him until he rose off the mattress, writhing and groaning as if in pain. Just when she felt him ready to explode, she changed position and rhythm.

Randolph, tiring of her teasing, jerked her head up.

Seconds later he had her on her back and drove into her, wanting to split her in two. The harder he pounded, the more she taunted him.

"Come on, Daddy. Do it! Do it harder. Is that all you got?"

Rage and passion were inseparable as he battered her body until she screamed and moaned. Her fingernails bit into the tender flesh over his ribs as she shuddered once, twice, three times. He lost count as he felt the dizzying rush and then felt his seed explode inside the hot, wet walls convulsing around his flesh. He collapsed heavily on her chest. They lay joined, their breaths coming in labored gasps.

"Daddy?"

"Yes?" His face was buried between her neck and shoulder.

"Why don't we do this every night?"

"We can't."

Lenora opened her eyes. "Why can't we? If we were married we could."

Randolph rolled off his paramour, knowing he had to tell her about Katherine. "I can't marry you, Lenora."

She sat up, staring down at his moist face. "Why not? We've been together for almost ten years."

Throwing an arm over his forehead, he closed his eyes. "That may be true, but I'm getting married next month."

Her eyes widened until they were round as silver dollars. "To who?"

He lowered his arm and sat up. "Katherine Graham."

"The lawyer's wench?"

"She's a lady, Lenora. She graduated Spelman last week and accepted my proposal to become my wife."

Lenora blinked back tears. "When? How long have you known her?"

"I've known her family a long time." His voice was soft, almost comforting. "We started courting four years ago. It was expected that we marry."

"Four years! You've been coming to me for the past four years all the while you were thinking of marrying that yellow, gray-eyed bitch."

Reaching out, he touched her cheek. "Watch your mouth, Lenora. You're talking about my future wife. I want children, and you can't give me a child."

She fell against him, her arms clinging to his neck. "We can adopt."

He forcibly pushed her away. "I want my own child, not someone else's castoff." The tears filling her eyes fell, sliding down her velvety cheeks. Randolph caught the moisture on the tip of a forefinger. "I'm not going to abandon you, Lenny," he crooned, using his pet name for her. "I know you want a larger house. I'm going to give you enough money so that you can buy the house you want."

Lenora wanted to tell him to go to hell, but quickly changed her mind. She sniffled. "No strings attached?"

He shook his head. "None."

"The deed will be in my name?"

He smiled at her childlike expression. "Yes, Lenny. It will be in your name."

Placing her hand on the middle of his chest, she let her fingers trail down over his flat belly to his flaccid penis cradled between his powerful thighs. "Will you let Lenny thank you properly, Daddy?"

He kissed her tenderly on her parted lips. "Yes. But let me take a nap first."

Reaching over, Lenora turned off the lamp, then moved into Randolph's warm embrace. She trusted him to follow through on his promise to buy her a bigger house because he had bought this one for her.

"Will I see you after you get married?"

There came a pregnant silence. "No."

The excitement of his promise to provide her with a larger house vanished like a streak of lightning crossing the summer sky. In that instant Lenora Esther Hazelton hated Randolph Johnson as much as she loved him. A sly smile curved her mouth as she considered a plan that was certain to *fix* him.

He'd only slept with her because he knew she could never accuse him of getting her pregnant. Now he was marrying because he wanted babies—babies she would never be able to give him. She couldn't have a child, and her revenge for his betrayal would be to make certain he would never father one.

Just before dawn they made love again, and this time Lenora let Randolph ejaculate into her mouth. While he lay on his back regaining his breath, she went to the bathroom, searching through her hamper for a pair of Randolph's drawers. Finding them, she spat the semen into the cotton garment. Folding it neatly, she returned it to the hamper under a pile of sheets and towels.

Making her way over to the sink she rinsed her mouth, splashed water on her face, and then patted it dry. When she returned to the bedroom she found Randolph pulling on his clothes.

"Aren't you going to take a shower before you leave?"

"No, Lenny." Reaching for his shirt, he slipped his arms into the sleeves.

"Would you like me to fix you breakfast?"

His dark gaze swept over her naked body. "No, thank you." Closing the distance between them, he kissed the top of her head. "I'll clean up and eat at home. I'll see you in a few days."

She forced a smile. "I'll be here."

Waiting until the door closed behind him, Lenora sank down to the floor and began laughing. The sound escalated until she sounded like someone crazed. Suddenly the laughter stopped, followed by a wave of sobbing.

She cried for the innocent teenager she'd been, for trusting a man when he had told her she wouldn't get pregnant if he didn't pull out. She cried for the moment she discovered she was pregnant; cried for when her mother took her to a woman who'd promised to get rid of the *mistake* in her womb; cried for the pain and bleeding that wouldn't stop until a doctor removed her uterus, leaving her barren. And now she cried because the only man she had ever loved had discarded her like the newspaper people scaled their fish on. He wanted babies and she couldn't give him babies.

She stopped crying long enough to curse her lover. She vowed that before the sun rose again she would make certain Randolph would never father a child.

Lenora stood up, made her way to the bathtub and turned on the faucets. While the tub filled with water, she brushed her teeth. Stepping into the tepid water, she sat down and washed away the scent of Randolph's cologne and their lovemaking. Twin emotions of love and hate swirled through her as she bathed. She had fallen in love with Randolph because of his passion and generosity, but now hated him for his deceit.

She dressed quickly, got into her car and drove a mile to a small house near a copse of trees bordering a swamp. The front door opened as soon as she rang the bell.

A tiny dark-skinned woman stood in the doorway. "The spirit told me you would show up here today."

"I hope it was a good spirit, Miss Mamie."

Mamie Edmonds shook her head and opened the door

wider. "What I saw disturbs me." She beckoned to Lenora. "Come in."

Lenora followed Mamie into a small room off the parlor. The heat from dozens of burning candles in various colors made the room stifling. She averted her gaze from the pile of bleached bones from small birds and animals on the table in a corner. Most people in Salvation referred to Mamie as a "conjurer" and "root worker." Lenora hadn't known what they had meant until she was older. It was usually under the cover of darkness that most women and sometimes men came to see Mamie about their love affairs. There had been occasions when someone sought victory in a court case, and others to secure a job position.

"Sit down."

Lenora sat down at a table across from Mamie. She glanced down at the water in a large clear bowl instead of meeting the knowing gaze of the old woman staring at her.

Mamie inhaled, then sighed audibly. "He's leaving you. I see him marrying another woman."

Lenora leaned forward on her chair, whispering softly. "I don't want him to make any babies."

Mamie did not blink. "Did you bring me something to work with?"

She handed the woman a bag with Randolph's semen-stained underwear. "Everything you need is in here."

"He's a powerful man, so it's going to cost you."

"How much?"

The woman quoted a price, eliciting a smile from Lenora. Reaching into her purse, she counted out enough money to pay in full for the work required to render Randolph Johnson sterile. Long, slender fingers took the bills, and within seconds they disappeared into her bosom.

"I work with phases of the moon. When is he getting married?"

"Next month."

"Good. That gives me enough time to work. Don't worry. You will get your wish. Not only will he be childless, but he and his wife will grow to hate each other."

Lenora stood up. "That suits me just fine." Leaning over she kissed the older woman's cheek. "Thanks for everything, Miss Mamic."

Large, dark, alert eyes crinkled into a smile. "You're welcome, baby. I got him to give you a house. You know I could have gotten him to marry you, too."

Lenora shook her head. "I refuse to root-work a man to make him marry me."

"How do you know that yeller wench didn't put a root on him?"

"We will find out soon enough, won't we?"

"Yes, we will, baby. Yes, we will indeed."

ELEVEN

Katherine felt her pulse quicken as she mounted the steps to Bessie's Place with Randolph. The sound of blues floated through the open windows. She had grown up hearing people talk about Bessie's not being the place for a proper young lady to visit. There were rumors of an occasional shooting or knifing, but most times they remained rumors because Bessie's was crowded to capacity every night of the week with the exception of Sunday. Bessie Taylor, who had inherited the eating establishment from her namesake grandmother, declared that she did no work on the Sabbath.

Katherine moved closer to Randolph as they entered the dimly lit, smoke-filled restaurant. A spotlight created a halo around a quintet playing "Midnight Special." Couples were up on the floor swaying to the soulful sound of a tenor sax and tinkling piano. The tempo changed as the band segued into the upbeat "Drinking Wine Spo-Dee-O-Dee." She watched the hemlines of skirts and dresses flare out around the thighs of women as they were spun around and around by their partners. Bessie's wasn't fancy, but everyone seemed to be having fun.

A waitress passed them carrying a tray filled with bottles of cold beer. She nodded to Randolph and Katherine. "Find a seat and I'll be with you directly."

Randolph curved an arm around Katherine's waist, steering her to a small table in a far corner. From where they sat they wouldn't be able to see the band, but they played loud enough to be heard over the laughter of customers and waitresses shouting orders to those working in the kitchen.

Randolph had brought Katherine to Bessie's because she said she was curious to see what made the restaurant so popular. He had agreed only because he had wanted to please her.

Katherine stared at the unadorned plank walls and uneven floorboards darkened by smoke and the pounding of thousands of feet. The tables, chairs and benches, hewed from Georgia pine trees, were smooth from constant use.

Randolph placed a hand over Katherine's. She turned her head and met his gaze. "What do you think?"

"I thought it would be a little . . ." Her words trailed off.

He lifted an eyebrow. "Fancier?" She nodded. Tightening his grip, he gently squeezed her fingers. "If you want fancy, then you have to go to Savannah or Atlanta. Bessie's hasn't changed in half a century except for indoor plumbing and electricity." He smiled. "Are you hungry?"

She returned his smile. "Starved."

Leaning closer to his right, he kissed her cheek. "If you're disappointed with the decor, then I guarantee you won't be with the food."

Her nose grazed his ear. "How often do you come here?"

Randolph shrugged a shoulder. "No more than a couple of times a year."

Releasing her hand, he touched her hair and combed his fingers through the heavy waves floating around her shoulders. "I like your hair when you leave it loose."

A blush darkened Katherine's cheeks at his compliment. The heat in her face spread to her chest, settling in her breasts. Her gaze followed the direction of Randolph's. The outline of her distended nipples clearly showed through her voile shirtwaist dress.

"Can you please go get me something to drink," she said quickly.

Randolph did not move or blink. "What do you want?"

"Something that's not too strong."

Pushing back his chair, he stood up and made his way to the bar. Katherine hadn't realized she had been holding her breath until he had put some distance between them.

When, she asked herself, would she ever feel completely comfortable with him? They hadn't dated in the traditional sense, and she thought if she asked him to take her out to places in and around Salvation they would be given the opportunity to spend more time together.

Randolph returned with two glasses, placing one in front of Katherine. He sat down. "Let me know if you like it."

She plucked the cherry from the glass and popped it into her mouth. "What is it?"

Randolph stared at her over the rim of his glass filled with scotch and soda. "It's a sloe gin fizz."

Katherine sipped the tart liquid through a straw, her eyes widening in surprise. "It's good." She took another swallow, feeling the effects of the drink within seconds. Its icy coldness slid down the back of her throat, then detonated into a ball of fire in her chest.

The waitress approached their table, pencil and pad in hand. "What ya'll eatin' tonight?"

Katherine found it odd that they weren't given menus. She glanced at Randolph, and when he didn't ask for a menu, she said, "Fried chicken, potato salad, and smothered cabbage."

Randolph noted the high color in Katherine's cheeks. He turned his attention to the waitress. "I'll have the fried porgy with potato salad and collard greens."

The woman wrote down their orders. "How about drinks?"

"Sweet tea," Katherine and Randolph said in unison.

The quintet launched into a slow number and Katherine smiled at Randolph. "Come, dance with me." He stood and pulled back her chair. Holding her hand, he led her to the area set aside for dancing.

Randolph cradled Katherine to his body, her breasts burning his chest through layers of fabric. She moved closer, resting her head on his shoulder. Everything about her was imprinted on his brain: her smell, the soft curves of her body, the silkiness of her hair brushing against his chin and jaw.

Raising her head, Katherine stared up at her fiancé staring down at her. "I love you," she whispered.

The simplicity of the three spoken words filled Randolph with an emotion that he had never experienced before. He forgot about the deal he had made with Edward, and his reason for wanting to marry the man's daughter. Katherine loved him, and he knew he loved her—unconditionally.

"I love you, too, Katherine."

Lowering his head, he buried his nose in her hair, inhaling the floral fragrance clinging to the strands. He had been a patient man, waiting seven years for the woman in his arms, and his patience had paid off because in less than a month she would become his wife. The song ended, and Randolph escorted Katherine back to their table.

Minutes later the waitress placed their selections in front of them, along with a plate filled with golden-brown biscuits. She smiled and light glinted off her two front teeth ringed in gold. "If ya'll need somethin' else, *jest holler.*"

Katherine inhaled the aroma from the crispy fried chicken. "It smells wonderful." Picking up a knife and fork, she cut a small portion of the breast and bit into it. Rolling her eyes, she shook her head. "It's delicious."

Randolph uncapped a bottle of hot sauce, shaking the red liquid over his fish and greens. "Bessie's serves the best food in the state."

They spent the next two hours eating, drinking, and watching couples gyrate to live music. One couple's actions were so risqué that others hooted them off the dance floor, shouting at them to leave that nasty stuff home.

On the drive back to her parents' house, Katherine moved closer to Randolph and rested her head on his shoulder. Her second sloe gin fizz had left her head spinning.

Randolph parked his car behind Edward's. He helped Katherine out, supporting her sagging body as she attempted to stand. "Can you walk on your own?"

She giggled like a little girl. "I think I can." She giggled again. "I believe I'm drunk."

"You're not drunk, Katherine. You're just not used to drinking." She took a step and stumbled. He caught her and swung her up in his arms.

Pounding his chest, Katherine said, "Put me down. I can walk."

He tightened his grip under her knees. "Do you want to fall on your face?"

"I'm not going to fall."

Bending slightly, Randolph lowered her until her shoes touched the concrete. He watched as Katherine concentrated on putting one foot in front of the other until she made it to the front door without his assistance. She unlocked the door, then turned and smiled at him.

"Would you like to come in?"

Closing the distance between them, he brushed a light kiss over her lips. "Not tonight, sweetheart." He winked at her. "I'll call you tomorrow."

She flashed a lopsided grin. "Thank you for taking me to Bessie's. I had a wonderful time."

"So did I." He kissed her again. "Good night."

Katherine leaned against the door frame. "Good night."

She closed the door, locked it and then stumbled into the parlor where she lay across a loveseat and waited for the room to stop spinning. It did stop, but only when she fell asleep. She awoke at dawn and made her way up the staircase to the bathroom.

Slipping out of her clothes, she brushed her teeth, rinsed her mouth, and for the first time in her life she took a cold shower. Her teeth were chattering and her lips had taken on a blue hue when she turned off the water.

She wrapped her wet body in a towel and padded on bare feet to her bedroom. She fell across her bed, falling asleep as soon as her head touched the pillow. When she awoke the second time that day the sun was high in the sky.

June 20, 1952

Today is my wedding day. The sun is shining, the birds are singing and I am ready to exchange wedding vows with Randolph.

Last night we had the wedding rehearsal, followed by an informal gathering at Charles and Belinda's house. Charles, a year younger than Randolph, has been married for ten years and is the father of four children. His two youngest girls have been recruited to be flower girls.

Caroline arrived earlier in the week, and we have spent every minute together talking about everything.

The wedding ceremony will be held at New Canaan Baptist Church at 3 o' clock. Mother has planned a reception on the lawn, beginning at 4. The tent, tables and chairs were set up yesterday. All that remains is for the delivery of the flowers and food. Mother paid Mrs. Bennett to do the cooking. Although she is the best cook in the county, I have to be careful not to eat too much or I will burst the seams on my dress.

Speaking of my dress—IT IS BEAUTIFUL!!! The bodice is covered with what appears to be thousands of pearls. Mother gave me several gifts last night: a strand of pearls, matching earrings, and a bottle of Chanel No. 5 perfume, soap and dusting powder. The scent is simply divine.

Randolph and I will not take a honeymoon until later in the year. He just started up a new business—insurance. He has promised me we will take a week off during my Christmas recess and go to Atlanta. I keep hoping it will be New York, but he said he would like to wait until next summer before we travel that far.

It is now 7:15 and I must get up and ready myself for my big day.

Katherine closed the book and put it in its usual place under the cushion of the rocker. She planned to leave it there until she could find an adequate hiding place in her new home. She'd visited the house two days before, making mental notes on what she wanted to change. If she was to become mistress of Randolph's house, then she intended to run and decorate it to her liking.

The morning passed quickly, and Katherine could not remember what she had eaten or said. She did remember sitting under a dryer at the beauty parlor while a manicurist filed and polished her nails. After returning home, she took a bath rather than a shower to preserve her upswept hairdo.

Her mother applied her makeup while Caroline, her college roommate and maid of honor, helped her into her gown. There came a sharp rap on the bedroom door, and the three women turned to find Edward standing in the doorway.

His jaw dropped as he stared at Katherine sitting on a stool in front of a vanity in her wedding gown. "You look so beautiful."

Her eyelids fluttered. "Thank you, Daddy."

Edward pulled back his shoulders. "It's two-thirty. If we don't leave now we're going to be late."

Lauretta smiled at her husband. "We're finished."

Katherine stood, holding the skirt of her dress above the floor as she slowly made her way out of her bedroom, down the staircase and out to a gleaming new Cadillac. She laughed uncontrollably as she tried getting into the car. Yards and yards of tulle and satin billowed up around her face as she sat on the backseat beside Edward.

Her laughter faded as New Canaan Baptist Church came into view, replaced by an anxiousness that made her stomach roil. Closing her eyes, she whispered a prayer that she would not faint.

Edward stepped out of the car, extending his hand to his

daughter. "Come, Katherine. It's time you meet the man who will make you his wife."

Placing her gloved hand in her father's protective grasp, she stared up at him, seeing moisture in his eyes. "I love you, Daddy."

Pulling her gently to his chest, Edward kissed her cheek before he lowered her veil. "I love you, too." Cradling her hand in the bend of his elbow, he led her up the path and to the entrance of the church.

Lauretta was escorted to her seat by Randolph's oldest nephew, and seconds later the haunting sounds of an organ filled the church. Katherine stared straight ahead, her gaze fixed on the bright yellow streamers on the back of Caroline's headpiece. Her bouquet of yellow and white roses trembled and she sought to steady her hands. Soon the distinctive notes of the wedding march filled the church and she bit down on her lower lip.

Her legs moved on their own. One minute she was standing in the back of the church, and the next she was standing beside Randolph. Peering up at him through the veil of tulle, she caught her breath. She had never seen him look so handsome. His black hair glistened from the sheen of hair pomade. His clean-shaven jaw was so smooth it looked like dark brown velvet. The warmth of his larger hand cradling her gloved one added heat to her chilled limbs.

The pastor began the ceremony, retelling the story of Jesus' first miracle at the wedding in Cana. He spoke of the responsibility of a husband to his wife and the responsibility of a wife to her husband. Randolph cleared his throat softly, and the pastor stared at him. Both men exchanged a smile. He recited the marriage vows and Randolph's voice was strong and emphatic as he promised to love and honor his wife through sickness and health, till death parted them. Katherine repeated her vows, her soft voice carrying easily over the hushed assembly. She, too, promised to love, honor and obey her lawfully wedded husband as they slipped plain gold bands on the third fingers of their left hands.

Slowly, Randolph raised her veil to seal their troth. Katherine's trembling fingers grazed the lapels of his white jacket as his arms encircled her waist, one hand on the small of her back. He lowered his head and brushed a gentle kiss across her lips. They drew apart and turned to face the people lining the pews of the historic church.

"I love you, Katherine." Randolph's voice was low and sensual. And at the moment he did love her. He loved all that she was.

"I love you, too," she whispered, angling her head closer to his. The radiant smile on her face was captured for an eternity when a photographer snapped a picture of the newlyweds.

Flashbulbs followed them as Randolph led Katherine down the aisle and out to the steps of the seventy-year-old church. Curving an arm around her waist, he smiled at her upturned face while their guests snapped photographs. Pride welled up in him as he turned to face friends, family members and business associates who had come to witness his marriage to Katherine.

The Grahams' announcement that Katherine was engaged to marry Randolph shocked the residents of Salvation, including Randolph's family. Everyone's shock was short-lived as invitations were mailed to those who considered themselves Salvation's privileged.

Randolph pressed his mouth to Katherine's ear. "Let's get back to the house."

Holding up the skirt of her dress with both hands, she leaned against Randolph as he led her to the car that would drive them back to her parents' home. She and Lauretta had decided holding the reception on the lawn was preferable to a catering hall.

Randolph sat down beside his wife in the car and laughed. "I feel as if I'm drowning in lace."

She pushed down a layer of tulle. "This doesn't work well in small spaces."

He took her left hand, threading his fingers through hers. His gaze moved slowly over her flushed face. "I didn't think you could improve on perfection, but you have, Katherine."

Her eyes crinkled in a smile. "Thank you."

He nuzzled her neck. "No, my darling. Thank you. I swear to you that I'm going to spend the rest of my life trying to make you happy."

Her fingertips touched his lips. "Don't swear, my love. And you don't have to try, because I am happy, Randolph. I'm the happiest woman in the whole wide world."

The wedding party drove back to the Grahams' stately Colonial home where they posed on the lawn for photographs for their wedding album. Somehow Katherine managed to appear cool, composed and fresh despite the sweltering Georgia heat.

Large white satin bows held together by yellow streamers fluttered from the poles holding up the large white tent, while baskets of white and yellow roses on each cloth-covered table served as centerpieces.

The caterer Mrs. Bennett had had her people set up trays for the food and the warm air was redolent of roasted meats and accompanying side dishes. The bartender was doing a brisk business as everyone lined up to order beverages to cool their parched throats.

Katherine had wanted a small wedding with only family

and close friends, but Randolph overrode her protests when he insisted on having many of his business associates attend their nuptials. Therefore, most of the well-dressed people sitting at the dozen round tables were strangers.

Once the picture-taking was concluded, Katherine removed her veil and white gloves and gained her seat at a table set up for the wedding party. The parents of the bride and groom, Edward and Lauretta Graham, and Randolph Sr. and Mattie Johnson, sat together at a nearby table.

Mattie smiled at Lauretta. "You've outdone yourself, Lauretta. Everything is so beautiful."

Lauretta smiled. Her blue-gray silk suit was the perfect match for her eyes. "Thank you, Mattie."

"I'm glad you decided to hold the reception on your lawn instead of in a stuffy old catering hall."

"Having the reception here was Katherine's idea," Lauretta said.

"It looks as if my son married himself a real smart woman," Randolph Sr. announced proudly.

Mattie frowned at her husband. "Of course she's smart. She graduated college. She's going to be a teacher like her mama." Randolph Sr. compressed his lips at her reprimand.

Edward placed a hand over Lauretta's, and they shared a smile. "Katherine wanted something small, but Randolph kept adding names to the list."

Mattie sat up straighter and glared at Edward. "That's because Randolph is a very important businessman. It wouldn't sit right with his business associates if he did not invite them."

A rush of pink suffused Lauretta's face. "I'll have you know Katherine is a direct descendant of one of Salvation's founding families."

A shadow fell over the table and everyone glanced up to

find Randolph smiling down at them. "I've asked the waiters to bring everyone something cold to drink."

Mattie reached for her son's hand. "Thank you."

Randolph looked at his father. "Are you all right, Papa?"

"I'm fine, son."

Randolph smiled at his mother and father-in-law. "Thank you for *everything.*"

Edward nodded, his gaze fixed on the waiter approaching the table balancing a tray on his shoulder. "Anything for my Katherine."

Randolph kissed his mother's cheek, then rejoined Katherine.

"How are *our* parents getting along?"

He stared at Mattie whispering something to his father. "I'm certain my mother is being her opinionated self."

"I like her, Randolph. She's brutally honest."

He frowned. "Sometimes too honest. Especially with my father."

"They've been married for a very long time. He should be used to her."

Randolph's frown deepened. "Some things you never get used to." Pulling his attention away from his parents, he leaned to his left, his shoulder pressing against Katherine's bare arm. "Can I get you something to drink?"

The off-the-shoulder gown offered him an unobstructed view of her silken throat and shoulders and whenever she inhaled her breasts rose and fell in a deep even rhythm. His hungry eyes drank in the length of her lashes, his nose inhaling the clean freshness of her perfumed skin. He wanted her. Never had he wanted a woman as much as he wanted his *wife.*

Katherine offered Randolph a shy smile. "Yes, please."

Raising his right hand, he signaled to a passing waiter. "Will you please bring *my wife* something cold to drink?"

The waiter bobbed his head. "Of course, Mr. Johnson."

Katherine took furtive sips of an icy-cold punch concoction liberally laced with alcohol. Placing her hand on Randolph's, she said, "It's too strong."

He picked up her glass and took a swallow, grimacing. "It is strong." He handed her his glass. "Take mine."

By the time the first course was served, Katherine had drunk two glasses of punch. She was slightly tipsy, but welcomed the pleasurable sensation because for the first time since Randolph had placed the diamond engagement ring on her finger, she felt daring.

Course after course was offered to the invited guests as a hired band arrived and began setting up. The eight musicians, including a lead singer who resembled and sounded like Big Joe Turner entertained the guests with "One Monkey Don't Stop No Show," "The Chill Is On," and "Chains of Love."

The talented octet took a short break to eat and drink, then returned with a rendition of blues so low-down and dirty that everyone jumped up swaying, bumping and grinding in time to the music.

Katherine danced with Randolph for the first time as his wife, and then with her father. The gaiety continued, everyone drinking, dancing and stopping periodically to toast the bride and groom. There was a lull when Katherine and Randolph cut the three-tiered cake, which was served with premium champagne so dry it was barely discernible on the tongue. Edward and Lauretta had spared no expense for their only child's wedding.

TWELVE

The sun had dipped lower and dusk had settled around the tent when Katherine and Caroline, holding the hems of their dresses above the grass, raced back to the house, up the staircase and into Katherine's bedroom. The two women fell across the bed, holding hands and laughing.

"Well, Miss Kat, this is it."

Katherine stared at Caroline, whose clear brown eyes sparkled in a face tanned a warm gold-brown by the Southern sun. "I'm ready."

"Remember," Caroline said in a quiet voice, "it only hurts for a little while. Relax and everything will go well. Randolph is a lot older than you and much more experienced. Let him handle everything. I know he loves you, so I'm sure he'll try not to hurt you too much."

Placing her hands over her flat belly, Katherine closed her

eyes. "Why didn't I give up my virginity like some of the other girls?"

Caroline touched her shoulder. "Because you're not like those other girls. I only slept with Lloyd because I was curious about sex."

"Don't you want to marry him?"

Caroline sucked her teeth. "Shucks, no. He's all right to fool around with, but I'd never marry him."

Sitting up, Katherine stared at her friend as if she had lost her mind. "But you told me you loved him."

"That was back then. Who I'd really like to marry is a boy my parents would never approve of. His daddy owns a juke joint over on Jekyll Island."

"What's wrong with that?"

Caroline rapped her knuckles softly against Katherine's upswept coiffed hair. "Wake up, Kat. Do you actually think Dr. Marcus and Mrs. Emmaline Gaskin would permit their only daughter to marry a boy with just high schooling?"

"You don't have to get their permission to marry."

"Would you marry without your parents' permission?"

"I would if I was in love."

Caroline stared intently at Katherine. "Do you really love Randolph?"

A dreamy expression softened Katherine's features. "Oh, yes. He's the most—" Her words stopped at a knock on the door. Her eyes widened. "Yes?"

"Katherine, I'm ready to leave."

The two women looked at each other. It was Randolph.

"I'll be down. I'm still changing," Katherine lied smoothly.

"I'll be waiting for you in the library."

"Give me fifteen minutes."

They waited for the sound of retreating footsteps to fade,

then slipped off the bed. Katherine kicked off her white pumps while Caroline unfastened the tiny covered buttons along the back of the gown. It was exactly fifteen minutes later when she walked into the library wearing a pale-gray silk suit and a straw hat in the same shade. A matching veil fell over her forehead. Randolph had also changed out of his formal attire and looked resplendent in a dark blue suit. He held a short-brim straw hat in one hand.

Offering his arm, he smiled. "Let's go home, Mrs. Johnson."

She took his arm and he led her through a door to the back of the house where he'd parked his shiny new Ford Thunderbird. Instead of opening the passenger-side door, Randolph dangled the keys from his thumb and forefinger.

"Why don't you drive, Mrs. Johnson?"

"But . . . but you always drive, Randolph."

He nodded. "That's true. I just thought you'd like to drive your own car just this once."

Her jaw dropped and her heart pounded loudly in her chest. "It's . . . it's mine?"

Reaching for her hand, he placed the keys on her glove-covered palm. "Yes. It's my wedding gift to you."

Tears shimmered in her eyes. She had given him a solid gold cigarette lighter, engraved with his initials as a wedding gift. But that did not compare to a brand new automobile.

Katherine launched herself against his chest, kissing him passionately on the mouth. He went completely still before forcibly pulling her arms down.

"Let's go, Katherine." The command had come out harsher than he had intended, but it was too late to retract it. His wife, however, did not seem to notice as she unlocked the door to the shiny, dark blue car and slipped behind the wheel. He sat next to her, smiling. She was so easy to please. If he could buy his whore a house, then the least he could do was give his wife her own car.

Katherine turned the key in the ignition, and the powerful engine roared to life. Shifting into gear, she stepped cautiously on the gas until she felt herself getting used to the feel of the racy sports car.

The drive ended all too soon as she maneuvered into the driveway behind Randolph's two-year-old Jaguar. He was the first person in Salvation to own a car that hadn't been made in the United States. She waited until he got out of the car and circled around to help her out. They stood staring at each other until Randolph bent slightly and picked her up.

Holding on to his neck, Katherine rested her head on his shoulder as he carried her effortlessly to the house. Mounting the steps to the porch, he shifted her weight, unlocked the front door and carried her over the threshold for the first time as Mrs. Randolph Johnson.

He carried her up the staircase, down the hallway and into the bedroom where he'd slept alone since he'd moved into the house on December 7, 1941. That day would forever be etched in his mind because of the Japanese bombing of Pearl Harbor.

Placing Katherine in the middle of their bed, he smiled at her. "I'm going to change in another bedroom." Leaning over, he brushed a kiss over her cheek. "I'll see you later."

She nodded, not trusting herself to speak because her voice was locked away in the back of her throat. It was about to begin. She was to become Randolph's wife in the biblical sense of the word.

Waiting until he left the room, closing the door quietly

behind him, she sat up. Slipping off the bed, she walked into the dressing room.

Her clothes had been delivered to the house earlier in the week. Randolph's housekeeper had reassured her that she would put everything away for her.

The bedroom was enormous, containing not only a sitting but a dressing room as well. Katherine thought the sitting room was the perfect space in which to begin her day. With its southeast exposure, there was no doubt it would be filled with sunshine and light throughout most of the daytime hours.

She took off her shoes, placing them on a rack with her other shoes in a large walk-in closet, then slipped out of her suit and underwear. Opening the doors to a decoratively carved armoire, she selected a delicate ivory-white nightgown and peignoir from a supply hanging on padded hangers. The frilly garments were gifts from her mother and Caroline. Retreating to the adjoining bathroom, she brushed her teeth and covered her hair with a plastic cap before stepping into the bathtub. Pulling the plastic curtain around the tub, she turned on the faucets, adjusting the water until a stream of lukewarm water sluiced over her naked body.

The scent of Chanel No. 5 wafted in the air as she soaped her body from neck to toes, showering quickly because she wanted to be dressed and in bed before Randolph returned. After patting the moisture from her body and dusting a light film of perfumed powder over her chest, arms and legs, she unpinned her hair and shook out the tight curls. Running her fingertips through her hair, she fluffed it out until it floated around her face like a burnished cloud. Staring at her reflection in the mirror over the sink, she angled her head, tilted her chin, lowered her eyelids while parting her lips, affecting a pose she'd seen actresses perfect for their publicity photographs. With her dark red hair and golden skin she looked like a young Rita Hayworth.

A soft gasp escaped her parted lips when another reflection joined hers in the mirror. Randolph had entered the bathroom without making a sound. He stood less than three feet away, hands thrust into the large pockets of a black silk robe.

Their gazes met in the mirror as he moved closer. Then there was no space between them. Katherine felt the heat of his body, his hardness pressing against her buttocks, and inhaled the scent of his cologne. The fear came rushing back—this time more vivid and frightening than any she had experienced in the past.

She willed herself not to shudder. She did not want her husband to know she feared him. She realized that her fear was not that she couldn't please Randolph in bed. It was because she'd married a man—a stranger she did not know.

"You look beautiful, Katherine."

A nervous smile trembled on her lips. "Thank you."

Lowering his head, he kissed the side of her neck, inhaling the seductive fragrance clinging to her silken skin. "You're perfect. And you're mine," he crooned softly. "You belong to me and only me."

Katherine sagged weakly against his body. His heat seeped into her, eliciting a soft throbbing between her legs. The pleasurable flutters were back.

"I've waited a long time for you," Randolph continued, curving his arms around her waist. "I couldn't believe it when I saw you for the first time. I thought to myself, what a lovely child. But you didn't remain a child very long. I've watched you grow up, and your beauty has exceeded all of my expectations. I came to your house every Sunday just to stare at you, just to convince myself you were real. After a while I realized you had bewitched me."

Closing her eyes, Katherine nodded. Randolph had begun coming to the Graham house for Sunday dinners the year she'd turned sixteen. The moment she'd walked into the parlor to find him sharing a predinner drink with her father she had fallen under Randolph's spell. Tall and impeccably groomed, he'd turned his dark gaze on her, staring intently until her face flamed with heat. There was something in the way he'd looked at her that frightened and fascinated her at the same time.

She'd barely exchanged more than a few words with him over dinner as she watched Randolph interact with her parents. She felt as if she'd been holding her breath once he thanked the Grahams for their hospitality, offering to return the invitation in the very near future. But the invitation never came. He returned to share dinner under the Grahams' roof the following Sunday, and every Sunday thereafter.

"Do you realize how hard it was for me to keep my hands off you? Even when you begged me to touch you I couldn't. I wanted you pure, Katherine. Pure for me."

"I wanted you, Randolph," she whispered. "I wanted you so much. Even before I left to go to college, I wanted you."

Theirs had not been a normal courtship. Randolph continued to come to the Graham house for Sunday dinners. Afterward they'd sit in the parlor talking, or occasionally would walk through Lauretta's garden. It was in the seclusion of the garden that Randolph would tell her of his love for her and that he wanted her to share his life as his wife and the mother of his children.

Randolph rested his hands on Katherine's shoulders, his

fingers tightening on the silk fabric concealing what he had waited so long to view.

Turning around in his loose embrace, Katherine closed her eyes and moved closer to Randolph. The rigid flesh pressing against her thighs made it hard for her to draw a normal breath. "I belong to you, and you belong to me," she whispered, her parted lips mere inches from his.

Randolph wanted to tell her that she was wrong. That he had paid for her. Instead he lowered his head and pressed his mouth to hers. This kiss was different from the one they'd shared to seal their troth. He deepened the kiss, his tongue slipping between her parted lips.

Katherine stiffened, shocked by the rough texture of his invading tongue and the saliva pooling in her mouth. She pushed against Randolph's chest. "Don't. Please."

The entreaty had barely slipped past her lips when she found herself scooped up in her husband's arms as he walked out of the bathroom and into their bedroom.

Randolph dropped Katherine on the bed, his hands going to the belt on his robe. He smiled when he saw the fear in her eyes. She had a right to fear him. He was the most powerful man in Salvation. He could have anything he wanted. Katherine was his prize. He'd set a trap for Edward and all he'd had to do was wait for him to succumb to his vices and fall into it. And what had been so gratifying was that her father had given in, sold her without a fight.

Katherine stared up at Randolph, her eyes fixed on his hands. His belt fell away and the front of the robe parted. Although she'd seen illustrated drawings and statues of the nude male body, nothing had prepared her for what stood before her. Fully aroused, Randolph was huge! There was no way she would be able to take him into her body.

She closed her eyes, recalling Caroline's advice: *It only hurts for a little while. Relax and everything will go well.*

She tried to relax and failed miserably. Randolph had dropped his robe on a chair, turned off the bedside lamp, and joined her on the bed. She counted the seconds as he pushed the hem of her gown and peignoir up her legs, over her knees until he bared her thighs. His breathing had deepened, becoming raspy. His hands moved over her breasts, belly and between her legs.

She felt his weight, his knee parting hers, and then the pain began. He pushed into her body, moaning as he penetrated her virginal flesh. Katherine lay motionless, eyes closed, fingers curled into tight fists, waiting for it to be over. But the pain and burning continued until tears spilled over her cheeks and onto the pillow cradling her head.

It ended with Randolph pulling out, groaning and spilling his seed over her quivering thighs before he collapsed to the mattress, one arm thrown over her waist.

Katherine lay in the dark, crying silently. Her body was bruised and she felt broken, empty.

Waiting until his breathing deepened, she eased out of bed and made her way to the bathroom. Closing the door, she turned on the light. The delicate fabric of her silk nightgown stuck to her thighs and was stained with her blood and the sticky discharge from Randolph's penis. Slowly, as if in a trance, she slipped out of the peignoir and gown, putting them into a hamper. Then she stepped into the tub, sat down and turned on the faucets. The warm water eased the soreness between her thighs and washed away the smell of blood and semen.

She wasn't certain how long she'd sat in the tub, but the water had cooled when she finally stepped out to dry her body.

Wrapping another towel around her herself, she reentered the bedroom and lay down next to her husband. He mumbled in his sleep, calling out the name Lenny.

Katherine lay motionless, listening to the soft sounds that were magnified in the silence: the soft ticking of a clock on the fireplace mantel, the soft snores coming from Randolph and the runaway beating of her own heart.

June 28, 1952

I've been a married woman for 8 days, and this is the first time I've been able to write in my journal as Katherine Johnson. Randolph and I have come to Mother and Daddy's for Sunday dinner.

I am now sitting in my old bedroom, while my husband is downstairs discussing a business matter with Daddy. I don't enjoy having sexual intercourse with Randolph. The moment he touches me I tense up. I try to relax before he comes to bed, but even that does not work. He is gentle with me, and I wonder how long it will be before he loses his patience. Once I told Randolph that I had my monthly period he moved into an adjoining bedroom for my comfort. I am almost ashamed to admit that I don't miss sharing a bed with him.

I have only caught a few glimpses of Mrs. Pitt, our live-in housekeeper. She has an apartment off the kitchen made up of a small bedroom and a private bathroom. A widow, she lost her only child—a son—after he was stabbed to death in an argument over a woman. She came to Randolph asking for work, and he hired her. She has worked for Randolph for nine years. There is not much for me to do around the house. Mrs. Pitt cleans, does the laundry and used to prepare all of Randolph's meals.

That has changed because I have taken over the task of cooking dinner.

Randolph hosted a card game Friday night that was attended by eight other Negro men who live in Salvation, Daddy included. I did not want to welcome them into my home because I really don't hold with gambling of any sort. I did not bite my tongue when I informed Randolph of this fact. He explained that the men had been meeting to play cards for eight years, and he did not intend to end the tradition just because he has taken a wife. After dinner I retreated to the sitting room to read, until I tired and then I readied myself for bed. The next morning I went downstairs to find Mrs. Pitt opening all the windows to let out the stale smell of cigar and cigarette smoke.

I have known Randolph Johnson for six years, yet I truly don't know him. I am hoping all of that will soon change.

Morgana closed the journal, then closed her eyes. The three entries played over and over in her head. First there was the joy of her mother's engagement and impending wedding, followed by the disappointment of what should've been one of the most glorious events in a woman's life: her wedding night.

Opening her eyes, Morgana stared at the smooth painted surface of the bedroom's ceiling. "Mama, how could you marry a stranger?" she whispered.

She did not want to condemn her mother for her trusting innocence. How much could she discern about Randolph over Sunday dinners? Katherine had left Salvation to go to college, spending four years in Atlanta while pledging her heart to a man fifteen years her senior. An older and apparently a much more worldly man as compared to her fragile innocence.

Morgana wanted to read more, but decided it was time to face the day. Pushing off the rocker, she made her way to the bathroom and showered, then slipped into a pair of faded jeans that had seen so many washings they were now soft as velour. A black tank top and running shoes completed her casual look. Reaching for the journal she had left on the rocker, she skipped lightly down the staircase and left the house. She wanted to read as much as she could at the lake before returning to look in on her uncle later in the day.

Traffic was light, given the early hour, and she made it to the lake within ten minutes. There had been times when she and Katherine had walked the distance, but only if the weather had been favorable.

Maneuvering into the parking area, she unconsciously looked for a black truck with California plates. There were two other vehicles, both bearing Georgia plates.

She'd told Erick she would call him, but had changed her mind. It wasn't that she hadn't enjoyed his company, but there was something about him that reminded her a lot of Franklin. And at this moment she did not want to think too much about him.

She walked along a winding path to a stone bench under a towering weeping willow tree. She sat, her gaze sweeping over the idyllic panorama before her. Pinpoints of sunlight glittered off trees, reminding her of the dots of color in the Seurat prints she sold at The Registry. How many colors of green were there? She stared at the placid surface of the lake, smiling.

The sound of birds calling out to one another mingled with the distinctive quacking of ducks swimming fluidly on the water. A smile curved her lips when she spied eight tiny dun-brown ducklings swimming in a wobbly line, following their mother. Waiting until the family of ducks disappeared around a bend, she picked up the journal.

"It's a beautiful morning, isn't it?"

Morgana quickly closed the book, her heart racing at the sound of the familiar deep voice. She glanced up to find Erick stepping over the bench to sit beside her. He'd been so silent that she hadn't heard his approach.

Frowning at him, she said, "What are you trying to do? Give me a heart attack?"

"No."

"Please don't sneak up on me like that."

"I did clear my throat, but I suppose you didn't hear me." He smiled, and tiny lines fanned out around his eyes. "How are you?"

She returned his smile. "Okay."

"Just okay?"

"A little better than okay."

"That's good." Leaning forward, he rested his elbows on his knees and stared out at the lake. "I've been waiting for you to call me."

Morgana stared at the reddish-brown twists falling over the white T-shirt stretching across Erick's broad shoulders. She thought of making up an excuse, but decided against it. There was nothing between her and Erick, so there was no need to spare his feelings.

"I did not call you because I hadn't thought about it."

Erick turned to look at her. "But you said you would call."

"Yes. I know I did."

He schooled his expression to remain impassive. "I wouldn't have minded if you'd told me that you had no intention of ever calling me again. I don't have a problem dealing with rejection. But what I do mind is deceit."

She stiffened as if he'd struck her. "Deceit?" she repeated. "Just because I didn't call as I had promised, you think of me as deceitful?"

"Yes."

Morgana struggled to contain her temper. "Deceit is not a broken promise, Erick. It's a betrayal of trust. Trust that usually takes more than one day's acquaintance to build."

He arched an eyebrow. "What happened between you and your husband, Morgana?"

She wanted to tell him to mind his business, that he had no right to pry into her personal life. That talking about Franklin's infidelity would not permit her to heal or move to the next phase of her life.

Erick placed his left hand over her right, tightening his grip when she attempted to pull away. "You're not the first woman whose husband deceived her, and you won't be the last," he said softly.

Her lower lip trembled and tears filled her eyes. Morgana willed them not to fall. "But he is *my* husband," she whispered.

Releasing her hand, Erick curved an arm around her shoulders. "True, Morgana. He is your husband. But what you fail to realize is that he's not perfect. None of us are perfect."

She smiled through her tears. "I know that."

"If that's the case, then why are you punishing yourself?"

"I'm not punishing myself."

"You think not?"

"I know I'm not."

"If that's true, then I want you to come with me."

Stiffening in Erick's embrace, she pulled away from him. "Why?"

"No questions."

"You expect me to go with you without knowing where I'm going?"

"What do you think I'm going to do to you? If I'd wanted to cause you harm I could've done that the night we drove to St. Simons."

"You think you have all of the answers, don't you?"

"Not all of them. Please, Morgana. Don't make me beg."

"Where are we going?"

"Savannah."

"To do what?"

Erick let out his breath in an audible sigh. She wasn't going to make it easy for him. "Are you always so obstinate?"

"Only when I feel it's necessary."

"Have you eaten breakfast?"

"No. Why?"

"I want you to share breakfast with me—at my place."

"Why?"

His right hand came up, long slender fingers tracing the underside of her left jaw. "Do you always have to ask why, Morgana?"

She forced herself not to pull away. "Yes, Erick."

"It's because I like you."

"You don't know me well enough to like me. In fact, you know nothing about me."

He smiled. "That's true. Sometimes it's better when two people remain strangers. To know too much may shatter the fantasy."

Reaching up, her fingers curled around his wrist, pulling them away from her face. "I am not a fantasy, Erick. I'm a flesh and blood, middle-aged woman who has found herself at a crossroads in her life. I've just buried my last surviving parent, and before the summer is over I have to decide whether I'm going to divorce my husband after twenty-eight years of marriage."

Hesitating, he gave her long, penetrating look. "Is the marriage worth saving?"

"Right now I'd say no."

"But there is a possibility that you may reconcile?"

All of Morgana's loneliness and confusion merged into one strong jolt of yearning. She shrugged her shoulder. "Anything is possible." She gave Erick a long, penetrating stare. "Don't you have to teach a class this morning?"

"It's Saturday, Morgana. I teach Monday through Thursday."

A rush of color darkened her cheeks. It had taken three weeks of inactivity for her to lose track of the days of the week. Days, afternoons and nights had become one. Her once carefully planned daily activities were forgotten the moment she saw her uncle walk into the terminal at the Savannah airport. Every day and most waking hours of her daily planner were filled with an activity.

When was the last time she had taken the time to take a vacation—a real vacation? Why hadn't she come to Salvation to take her mother away for several days wherein they could relive their mother-daughter outings? When was the last time she'd called up Sandra for a mother-daughter luncheon? Why hadn't she insisted Franklin meet her at their favorite D.C. restaurant for dinner and drinks?

The whens and whys attacked her until she wanted to scream at the top of her lungs.

Erick could not pull his gaze away from her face. "You should do that more often."

"What?"

"Blush. It's very becoming on you."

A slow smile trembled over her lips. "Shame on you, Erick. Are you flirting with me again?"

"Guilty as charged. Well, how about breakfast?"

She blinked once. "Okay."

It was his turn to smile as he curved a hand under her elbow. "We won't need two cars. I'll follow you back to your place, then you can ride with me." Morgana reached for the journal as Erick pulled her to her feet.

THIRTEEN

Morgana sat beside Erick, listening to the classical music coming from the truck's powerful speakers. Closing her eyes, she pressed the back of her head against the leather seat.

"You must like classical music."

He nodded, not taking his gaze off the road. "I love it. It inspires me."

"How?"

"It helps me to see pictures in my mind."

She opened her eyes, staring at his profile. "I thought artists paint what they see."

"That's true, but not all artists see an object the same. Take a tree. We recognize it as a tree because it will have a trunk, branches and leaves. However, van Gogh's tree will look different from Tanner's, or Picasso's."

"Is it the same with people?"

"Yes. All you have to do is look at a Modigliani and a Bearden to see the similarities and the distinct differences." There was a comfortable silence before he spoke again. "I'd like to paint you, Morgana."

"Why me?"

Erick turned off the local road, heading for downtown Savannah. "Why not you? You have a wonderful face—especially your eyes. They are filled with secrets that will never be told."

She laughed, the sound low and seductive. "I'm not hiding any secrets."

Erick gave her a quick glance. "That remains to be seen." He stopped at an intersection, waiting for the light to change, his arms resting on the steering wheel. "Well?"

"Well, what?"

"Are you going to let me paint you?"

"I know I should be flattered, but my answer is no."

Erick drove past a college campus and down a residential street where all of the structures were owned by the Savannah College of Art and Design. As part of the faculty, he was housed in a two-bedroom cottage at the end of a street four blocks from the Savannah River.

He stopped in front of the cottage and turned off the engine. Shifting, he placed his right arm over the back of Morgana's seat. "I want you to take a look at some of my work before you turn down my offer to paint you."

Her gaze fused with his. "What if my answer is still no after I see your work?"

He inclined his head. "Then I'll respect your wishes."

Erick withdrew his arm, smiling. Removing the key from the ignition, he pushed open his door, alighted, then came around the truck to open the door for Morgana. Extending his arms, he lifted her easily before he set her on her feet.

Holding her hand, he led her to the front door, and Morgana wondered how many other women he had invited into his home since he'd become an artist-in-residence. There was no doubt Erick Wilson was an attractive man. His photographs of her had proven he was also quite talented as a photographer. She was curious to see if that talent extended to his paintings.

Erick unlocked the door and stepped into the minuscule entryway, bowed gracefully, hands crossed over his heart. "Welcome."

Morgana stepped into the entryway. Cupping her elbow, he led her into a larger room furnished with an assortment of rattan and wicker pieces. A sofa, love seat, and several chairs were covered with cushions in plaids and stripes. The room's predominant colors were dark greens and sunny yellows. The walls were covered with pale yellow wallpaper dotted with sprigs of tiny violets.

"It's not very fancy," he said close to her ear.

Morgana smiled. "It looks comfortable and lived-in."

"That it is. There are times when I wonder how many lived here before me."

"How many rooms do you have?"

"Four. There are two bedrooms. I use the smaller one as my studio. It's not much larger than a walk-in closet." He reached for her hand. "You can look at some of my work while I start breakfast."

"What's for breakfast?"

"A West Coast favorite: tofu, seaweed and raw fish," he said, his expression deadpan.

A frown marred her smooth forehead. "You're kidding, aren't you?"

"Of course I'm kidding." Leaning down, he kissed the end of her nose. "I'm going to prepare an old-fashioned southern breakfast with the works."

"What would a California boy know about an old-fashioned southern breakfast?"

"Plenty. My grandparents left Texas after the Depression, looking for a better way of life in a place that had been touted as a modern-day land of milk, honey and endless sunshine. They fell in love with California but never forgot their humble southern roots."

She followed Erick to the small room he used as a studio. She had to agree with him. It was no larger than the walk-in closet in the master bedroom at her house in Chevy Chase. He flicked a switch on a wall, turning on an overhead light and several table lamps.

Canvases, dozens of them stretched over frames, lay against walls. Several tripods stood in one corner near a table covered with cameras and various lenses. She moved into the space, her gaze lingering on countless framed photographs covering two of the four walls. Like the photographs he had taken of her, these, too, were black-and-white. However, most of them were atmospheric landscapes in sepia-tone.

"These are copies of the photos I've taken of this region."

"How did you get this one to look so dated?" She pointed to a print of ancient live oak trees shrouded in fog overlooking the bank of a swamp.

"There's a special process that produces a sepia-toned, silver gelatin print." He pointed to a photo of the Savannah River. "This one is a platinum print. The process dates back to the 1880s. Even though they're black-and-white images, there's a tonality to them that usually appeals to people who are used to color."

"Do you do your own developing?"

Erick shook his head. "No. But if I had the space I would set up my own darkroom. I used someone who specializes in processing black-and-white prints."

He'd captured the images of flowering trees, an elderly black man sitting on a wooden crate outside a ramshackle house, and one of a young girl holding a small child on her hip.

Moving slowly along the wall, Morgana studied more than a hundred photographs, each one telling a story. She lingered in front of a triptych. Erick had captured the rising sun as it threw different shadows over the landscape. Even though it was in black-and-white she still could feel the heat of the sun and its warming rays.

Her pulse accelerated when she spied the photographs he had taken of her the day she'd met him at the lake for the first time. In the first photograph she clearly looked startled. The second revealed the haunted look in her eyes, while several others depicted her annoyance and disapproval.

She reluctantly pulled her gaze away from the image of her face to look at a canvas perched on an easel. A photograph of a very old black woman sitting on a rocker on a porch was taped to the upper right corner. The photograph was in color. Peering closer, she saw faint pencil markings within a lined grid on the canvas.

Morgana felt the hair on the back of her neck stand up as Erick stepped close behind her. She inhaled the scent of his cologne, and felt the heat of his body pressing against hers.

She closed her eyes, willing her traitorous body not to react to the man who unknowingly had made her aware of herself as a woman with just a glance. It had been a long time since a man had made her feel that way. Not in thirty years—not since she encountered Franklin Wells in a coffee shop.

"Erick?"

"Yes, Morgana." His breath feathered over the nape of her neck.

"You're standing too close to me."

He smiled. "Are you claustrophobic?"

"No." The word was a breathless whisper.

"Then, I'm not too close. In fact, I'm not close enough." Morgana opened her eyes and attempted to turn around, but she was thwarted when he held her arms firmly against her sides. "Don't move," Erick crooned. "Not yet."

"What game are you playing?"

Lowering his head, he buried his face between her neck and bare shoulder. "This is not a game, Morgana."

She took in a lungful of air. "Then what is it, Erick?"

His hands slipped down her arms to cradle her waist. "I don't know what it is. Perhaps you can explain it better than I can."

Morgana shook her head. "No. I can't explain it. I'm here because you invited me to share breakfast with you."

Easing his grip on her waist, he turned her gently until they faced each other. His near-black eyes gave off sparks of laughter. "I told you I wanted to paint you."

Resting her palms on his chest, Morgana gave him a level stare. "Why me?"

"Because I think of you as my muse. This is the first time in more than three years that I've felt the urge to paint."

"What about the photograph of the elderly woman sitting on the rocker?"

He closed his eyes, smiling. "I took that photograph of my grandmother a month before she died. That was almost four years ago. I'd promised myself I would paint it for my parents, but every time I look at it I find myself paralyzed."

"Why's that?"

Erick opened his eyes, shaking his head. "I'm not sure. I've told myself it's because Grandma died the same day I was served with divorce papers, so I had to mourn not once but twice."

Just like me, she thought. Like Erick, her marriage ended the same day her mother died. A rush of pity swept over Morgana and her hands moved up to cradle his face. "Were you expecting the divorce?"

Covering her hands with his, Erick turned his head and kissed her palm. "No. Jean had mentioned she felt trapped, but she hadn't talked about a divorce. It wasn't until a year later when she met the man who was to become her second husband that she told me that she'd never loved me."

"If that's the case, then why did she marry you?"

"She was pregnant with my child," he said quietly. There was no expression on his face.

Morgana lifted an eyebrow. "Oh, I see." She exhaled audibly. "Had you loved her?"

He flashed a sad smile. "Unconditionally."

Leaning closer, she pressed a kiss to his smooth cheek. The gesture was devoid of anything sexual. "I'm certain you'll find another woman who will love you unconditionally."

His smile faded. "I doubt that. The truth is that I'm not looking."

"But . . . but you're young enough to marry again and have more children."

"It has nothing to do with age. I just don't want to marry

again." Angling his head, he stared at her for a full minute. "Once is enough."

Morgana wondered if she would consider remarrying. Did she want to become part of the dating scene again? Did she want to compete with women half her age for men her age?

Once the word was out that Franklin Wells's wife was available, would she be viewed a worthy catch because of a generous divorce settlement? Or would she be seen and treated as a trophy because of her ex's celebrity status? There were so many unanswerable questions.

Focusing again on Erick, Morgana said, "You're extremely talented, Erick. Are your photographs for sale?"

"Which ones do you want?"

She pointed to three depicting the rising sun, then selected several others of a river scene and two of a field of wildflowers. "I'd like several copies in various sizes with mats and frames for my shop."

"You don't want them for yourself?"

A flash of amusement crossed her face. "I'd buy a few for myself, but I'm certain the customers at The Registry would snap them up. How much do you want for them?"

"I'll have to think about it."

"What is there to think about, Erick? I'm willing to pay your price."

His expression stilled, becoming somber. "You can pay me, Morgana. But not with money."

She stood motionless, amazed and disappointed. *Here it comes,* she thought. Here's where he's going to ask me to trade sex for the photographs. And she knew if he did ask her to go to bed with him, then this would be the last time she would agree to see him.

"What do you want?" The words were forced out between clenched teeth.

His expression changed, becoming one of eagerness and tenderness. "Sit for me, Morgana. Let me paint you." Her jaw dropped and her reaction seemed to amuse him.

"That's it?"

Amusement softened his features. "Of course, that's it. Did you think I was going to ask you to sleep with me?"

A wave of color rushed to her cheeks. "Yes."

Pulling her close to his chest, he buried his face in her sweet-smelling hair. "I don't want to ruin what we have by becoming sexually involved with you."

"What is it we have, Erick?"

"Friendship. It's been a long time since I've had a woman as a friend."

It was her turn to smile. "And it's been even longer since I've had a man as a friend." The truth was that she did not have any male friends.

"Come, let's go to the kitchen. After all, I did offer to feed you."

Morgana sat across from Julian, one leg tucked under her as she swung back and forth on a glider. The pitter-patter of an afternoon shower on the veranda's roof was hypnotic and soothing.

Julian stared at his niece, a slow smile curving his mouth. "You're looking well, Morgan."

Her smile widened. "That's because I feel wonderful."

She'd spent the entire morning with Erick. Breakfast had been a gastronomical feast. Diced fresh strawberries and pineapple in their own juices were served over a stack of fluffy pancakes with whipped butter, maple syrup, and grilled breakfast links. She had drunk two cups of brewed coffee with dollops of heavy cream before realizing how many calories she'd ingested in one sitting.

She'd insisted on helping Erick clean up the kitchen before they returned to his studio. It had taken her more than three hours to literally examine hundreds of photographs before she chose eighteen landscapes. Erick told her he'd paid and gotten written releases from all the subjects he'd photographed. She gave him permission to paint her.

Julian nodded, then let out an inaudible sigh as a powerful relief filled him. Morgana's mood swings worried him. A period of mourning and grieving was expected, but her unbridled display of rage at Franklin's visit had been shocking. His niece wasn't the first woman to have a philandering husband. Why, he wanted to ask her, did she believe it couldn't happen to her? Why did she feel as if she were exempt?

"I'm glad to hear that, because I'm going away for a week."

Morgana sat up straighter. "Are you all right, Uncle Julian?"

He offered her a slow smile. "I'm fine. I'm going up to Hilton Head for a reunion with some of my medical school buddies. We always get together once a year to play golf, swim and mostly chew the fat."

He had been one of six young Negro students admitted to the New York University School of Medicine that year, and one of four to graduate. One had dropped out because he hadn't been able to maintain passing grades, and the other transferred to the School of Dentistry after his second year.

"That's wonderful. When are you leaving?"

"Tomorrow morning."

"Are you driving up?"

"Yes. I hope to leave before seven."

"Have you packed?"

Julian shook his head. "I'll do it tonight."

Pushing to her feet, Morgana closed the distance between them. Leaning over, she kissed his cheek. "I'm not going to take up any more of your time. Speaking of packing, I still have to finish the upstairs linen closet."

"How is everything going?"

"Okay. I've boxed up all of Mama's clothes. Someone from a homeless shelter has arranged to pick them up Tuesday morning. The storage company delivered dozens of corrugated boxes for the rest of the stuff, along with inventory forms. I have to catalogue every piece of silver, glass, and piece of furniture."

"How long do you think that's going to take?"

She shook her head. "I really don't know. I'm hoping to have everything done before I get a buyer."

"Have you shown the house?"

"Not yet. The realtor has set up two appointments for next week."

"I doubt if the house will stay on the market beyond the summer."

Morgana nodded in agreement. She did not want to think of that time because once the house was sold then she would have to decide her future.

"You can always hire someone to help you."

Morgana smiled. "I know. But, I'd rather do this myself. Every time I pick up a tablecloth or a serving piece, I'm reminded of a moment from my childhood."

Julian stared out at the falling rain. "Sometimes it's better when you let the past remain the past."

Her gaze narrowing, Morgana studied her uncle, mentally replaying his cryptic statement. What was there in his past he did not want to remember?

Reaching for her fingers, Julian squeezed them gently. "Promise me you're going to continue to take care of yourself."

"I will, Uncle Julian, but only if you promise me that you're going to enjoy yourself and not worry about me."

The seconds ticked off before he said in a quiet voice, "I promise."

FOURTEEN

Morgana plumped up the pillows behind her head, settling into a more comfortable position. The journal lay on her lap. She planned to read, then call Bernice to check in on The Registry.

She'd emptied the linen closet in the upstairs hallway. It had taken more than three hours to unfold, examine, refold, and wrap heirloom sheets, pillowcases, blankets and tablecloths in yards of tissue paper. She'd filled several cartons with bed linens with embroidered monograms belonging to her great-great-grandmother, wondering if Sandra would realize the significance of the centuries-old items.

Opening Katherine's journal, she read the next entry:

July 4, 1952

Randolph and I will host our first social event this afternoon with an Independence Day celebration, even though there are times when I feel Negroes do not have much to celebrate here in the South.

Mrs. Pitt and I spent all of yesterday making potato salad, slicing watermelons, cutting up chickens, spareribs and basting them with a spicy barbecue sauce that is certain to tantalize the most discerning palate. Thankfully, the weather has decided to cooperate. It is hot, but there is a breeze blowing in from the east. Mother, Daddy, Grandma and Grandpa, and, of course, all of Randolph's family are expected to attend.

Julian's wedding gift arrived yesterday. He sent us a pair of exquisite sterling silver candlesticks. The design is modern and delicate, unlike the large heavy ones sitting on Grandma's mantel. I mailed him a thank-you note, despite Randolph's protests, who said I could do that in person by hosting a welcome home party for his brother when he returns to Salvation at the end of August. He's been away for ten years. He left home at 18 as a college freshman, and will return as Dr. Johnson, family doctor. All of the Johnsons are quite proud of him, especially Miss Mattie. Of her four sons, Julian is the only one to graduate college. Miss Mattie went to the 11th grade, but did not finish high school because she was pregnant with her first child.

Katherine walked into the bedroom to find Randolph in bed, his back propped up on several pillows. The glow from a lamp on her side of the bed bathed the space with warm golden light.

Pulling back the sheet, he patted the space beside him. "Come, darling."

She slowed her pace. Tension tightened her belly. There was

only the sound of breathing, punctuated by the brush of her silken nightgown on the crisp laundered sheet as she slipped into the bed. He touched her breasts and she closed her eyes, clenched her teeth, and prayed it would end quickly.

Moving over Katherine, Randolph supported his weight on his elbows. He had missed her. A smile tilted the corners of his mouth.

"Are you ready for me?"

Katherine did not open her eyes. "Yes," she lied. She didn't think she would ever be ready for him.

"Good."

Randolph eased the narrow straps of the gown off her shoulders. Every motion was slow as he bared her body to his heated gaze. He stared at her nude body, stunned. She was beautiful, more beautiful than he had ever imagined she would be. Lowering his head, he brushed his mouth over hers, tasting her. The kiss deepened as she tentatively parted her lips. Her tongue touched his, and Randolph was lost. Moving down her perfumed body, he kissed and suckled her breasts. His hand swept over curves normally hidden by yards of fabric.

He wanted to bury his flesh in her soft body, yearned to feel her softness cradling his hardness. His tongue tasted every inch of her glowing pale flesh. Bracing his hands on her inner thighs, he pushed them apart and buried his face against the silky hair, while inhaling the sweet musk coming from her sex.

Katherine waited for the pain that never came. The pulsing between her thighs grew stronger and stronger until she was unable to swallow the moans building up in her throat. Randolph's tongue was driving her crazy as it moved in and out of her vagina in a measured rhythm that matched her undulating hips. Just when she thought she couldn't take it any longer, she rose off the mattress, screaming with the explosions that rocked her and buffeted her like a tiny boat on a stormy sea.

She lay panting, tears staining her face, as Randolph rolled off her trembling body. Closing his eyes, he stroked his hardened flesh until he, too, climaxed, a rush of semen spilling over on his belly and thighs. Waiting until his pulse resumed a normal rate, he rolled over and pulled Katherine to his chest, her hips pressed to his groin.

He kissed her nape. "Did you enjoy that, baby?"

"Yes," she murmured. She wanted to sleep, not talk.

He smiled. "Good."

July 7, 1952
Randolph and I had our first argument last night.

Katherine brushed her hair until it sparkled like a new penny. A slight frown marred her forehead when Randolph's reflection appeared in the vanity's mirror. She put down the brush and tossed her hair over her shoulders.

Randolph moved closer, pushing her hair aside and curved his fingers around her neck. Lowering his head, he trailed light kisses over her shoulders. "Why is it I can't get enough of you?"

She forced herself to relax. His right hand slipped under the lace on her nightgown and cradled her breasts. "No, Randolph."

Randolph's hand stilled. "No?"

Katherine's gaze met Randolph's in the mirror. "I'm tired."

He withdrew his hand. "Tired, Katherine? You were tired last night."

She frowned. "Is it a crime to be tired?"

"No, Katherine, it isn't. But, what I don't understand is

how can you be so tired when Mrs. Pitt helps you with everything around the house."

"I can't explain it," Katherine lied. She did not want him to touch her.

"Maybe you need to see a doctor."

"I don't need a doctor."

"You don't know what the hell you need."

Her eyes widened. "Don't talk to me like that, Randolph."

"I'll talk to you any way I want."

"Oh no, you won't."

The veins in his neck were visible. "You're *my* wife, Katherine."

"Your wife, Randolph, not your slave. You will respect me."

His fingers circled her throat, tightening slightly. "No, Katherine, you will respect *me.* I will not tolerate you telling me what I can and cannot do with you."

Katherine's heart pounded loudly in her chest and ears. The face in the mirror glaring at her was that of a complete stranger. Someone she truly did not know. In the six years since she had come to know Randolph she never saw this side of him.

"Take your hands off me." His grip tightened and her eyes filled with tears. She was frightened that Randolph would hurt her. "Please." The pressure on her throat increased, then it eased as he released her. The imprint of his fingers was visible on her skin.

"Go see a doctor, Katherine," he ordered in a quiet tone.

She closed her eyes, willing the tears not to fall, and when she opened them she was alone in the dressing room. What Randolph did not understand was that she did not need a doctor for her body, but one for her head. But how could she tell him that she loathed sexual intercourse, that tension made the act painful?

July 8, 1952

I am wearing a scarf around my neck to hide the bruises from Randolph's fingers. He did not sleep with me last night. In fact, I don't know where he slept because when I got up this morning none of the beds in the other bedrooms appeared to be slept in. He could've slept in the library, but at this point I really don't care.

I spent most of today in the sun parlor, reading. I want to call Caroline and tell her everything, but I am too embarrassed. And how could I tell Mother that my husband choked me? Mother and Daddy have had their disagreements, but never has he struck her.

I swear on a stack of Bibles that I will not share a bed with Randolph until he apologizes. And if he doesn't, then we will live apart under the same roof.

Morgana closed the journal. "Oh, no," she whispered, unable to believe her mother had become a victim of domestic abuse. And it was apparent that Katherine and Randolph did share a bed again because he had gotten her pregnant.

She looked at her watch. It was after five, Bernice's dinner hour. She picked up the telephone and dialed the number to The Registry.

"The Registry, Mrs. Butterfield speaking. How may I help you?"

Morgana smiled. "Mrs. Butterfield, it's Morgana."

"Hi, Morgana. Bernice told me about your mother. Please accept my condolences. I sent a sympathy card to your home."

"Thank you, Mrs. Butterfield. May I please speak to Bernice?"

"Sure. I'll get her. You take care of yourself, Morgana."

"I will."

There was a lull before Bernice's voice came through the wire. "How's it going, girlfriend?"

Morgana smiled. "Okay. I'm still packing up my mother's things."

"What are you going to do with the house?"

"I've decided to sell it. I'd offered it to Sandra and Kenneth, but they don't want to leave Baltimore."

"What's with you and Franklin?"

Morgana told her about Franklin coming to Salvation for their anniversary, gift in hand. What she did not tell Bernice was that she'd celebrated her twenty-eighth wedding anniversary sharing dinner with another man.

"Franklin needs to talk things out with a therapist."

"That's what I told him. Right now I'm trying not to give him too much energy."

Bernice offered an update on what was going on with The Registry, adding her colorful anecdotes about their regular customers. Morgana ended the call, smiling. She could always count on Bernice to make her laugh.

She opened the journal again, curious to know how her parents reconciled.

August 28, 1952

I met Julian for the first time this morning. Randolph had picked him up from the railroad station late last night, after he'd spent more than 20 hours on the train traveling from New York City. He is definitely a Johnson, tall, dark and very attractive. He reminds me of a younger Randolph, but with glasses. He is soft-spoken and somewhat shy.

Randolph has insisted Julian live with us until he builds his own home. I probably will not get to see too much of him until the evening meal. I am up early because of my drive to Savannah. I have been assigned to a first grade class, and teaching young children to read and write is the greatest reward for any educator.

I am still unsure of my relationship with Randolph. It took several weeks for him to apologize for choking me in what he calls "a fit of rage." I, in turn, waited two days before I moved back into the bedroom. Although we share a bed, he hasn't touched me again. Most times he gets into bed and turns his back. Perhaps with Julian living with us, things will change between us, become less tense.

Katherine opened the screen door, walked across the porch, and sat down on her favorite chair. She'd just picked up the latest issue of *Ebony* magazine when the soft click of the door opening caught her attention. With eyes wide, she stared at Julian for the first time. He was tall, several inches taller than Randolph, and slimmer. His features were more delicate than any of his brothers', and his rimless glasses made him appear bookish.

He offered her a warm smile. "Good morning." His voice was a soft drawl that identified him as a Southerner. Even after spending ten years in the North he hadn't been able to rid himself of the drawl.

Rising to her feet, Katherine extended her right hand. "Good morning. I'm Katherine."

He cradled her hand, squeezing her fingers gently. "My pleasure, Katherine. Julian."

"I'm surprised you're up so early after your long train trip."

He released her hand, waiting for her to retake her chair before he took a matching one several feet away. "I'm able to function on very little sleep. That's something I learned during my medical training."

Katherine smiled, unaware of the ethereal picture she presented. Red hair, pinned up in a loose chignon, provocatively framed her lightly tanned face.

"Have you had breakfast? If not, then I'll have Mrs. Pitt prepare something for you."

"Please, don't bother. I'll eat later."

She glanced away. "I'd like to thank you for your exquisite wedding gift."

Angling his head, Julian stared directly at her. "You did that already."

She looked at him again. "When?"

"You sent a thank-you note."

A rush of color darkened her cheeks, the contrast highlighting the brilliance of her silvery eyes. "Randolph and I talked about hosting a soiree to celebrate your return."

Crossing one leg over his knee, Julian shook his head. "That's not necessary."

Katherine leaned forward. "But *we* want to. It will give most people in Salvation the opportunity to meet their future family practitioner. After all, these people will become your patients once you open your practice."

Julian wanted to tell his sister-in-law that he came back to practice medicine, not socialize, but did not want to appear ungrateful. After all, she and Randolph were generous enough to open their home to him while he reacquainted himself with his hometown. He knew he could always live with his parents, but had decided against it. He had been on his own for ten years, and living under his parents' roof would not permit him the independence he coveted.

He stared at Katherine, finding her incredibly beautiful. She reminded him of a flower, a delicate hothouse lily. When Randolph had called him to tell him he was engaged to marry a local woman, he never would've imagined Katherine Graham would be so young. And he hadn't connected her to Edward Graham, only because the Grahams were always socially above the Johnsons. At least that was before Randolph began setting up his business ventures.

He had always admired his older brother. Randolph was smart and ambitious. His business acumen equaled the board of any large corporation. He had wanted better for himself and his family.

Julian was indebted to Randolph, who had paid for his medical school education, and had loaned him enough money to build a home and set up a medical practice in Salvation. He was completely loyal to Randolph, unlike Charles and Delano, who'd secretly complained to him about their older brother's dictatorial personality.

The beginning of a smile tipped the corners of his mouth. "I hope you won't mind if I ask to borrow your car for a couple of hours. I'd like to drive over and see my folks."

Katherine returned his smile. "Of course I don't mind. The keys are in an ashtray on the table in the entryway."

She sat on the porch long after Julian drove away, staring out into space. Her thoughts were a jumble of confusion. She didn't know whether she was imagining things, but there was something in her brother-in-law's gaze that indicated he knew things weren't right in her marriage to Randolph. Nagging questions attacked her until she had to ask herself if she had made a mistake. Had she married the wrong man?

FIFTEEN

The next morning found Morgana at the kitchen table, devouring her mother's diary. She'd told herself over and over, just one more, but one more escalated until she couldn't stop reading. The ringing of the telephone shattered the silence, and she closed the journal, reaching for the phone.

"Hello."

"Mom?"

Her pulse quickened at the sob she heard in her daughter's voice. "Sandra? Are you all right?"

"I'm fine, Mom. It's Daddy."

"What about him?" Morgana did not realize her hands were shaking.

"He's here . . ." Her words trailed off.

"He's with you right now?"

"Yes. He's a wreck. He told me everything. About his

cheating on you, and your threat to divorce him. I screamed at him something awful, but he just sat there not saying a word to defend himself. I was so incensed that I called Justin. It was the worst thing I could've done, because he said he's going to kick Daddy's ass. Mama," she wailed, "why didn't you tell us what was going on?"

Morgana closed her eyes, then opened them. "I wanted to, but the time wasn't right. I had to concentrate on burying my mother."

"Are you?"

"Am I what?"

"Are you going to divorce Daddy?"

She sighed audibly. "I don't know."

"Do you still love him?"

"A part of me still does," she admitted truthfully.

"Does this mean you're not going to divorce him?"

"Don't put words in my mouth, Sandra. Right now I'm trying to figure out who I am, and how I want to spend the rest of my life."

There was a pause. "Mom . . . I don't want to take sides—"

"Then don't," Morgana cut in.

"Please, hear me out. I always believed that I had the coolest folks in the world. When my friends were complaining about their mothers and fathers, I thought I was some kind of freak because I loved my parents. And that hasn't changed. I love you and I love Daddy. I'm pissed at him, but that doesn't change the fact that I still love him. He knows he made a mistake, and I believe he's sorry."

"What have you become, his defense attorney?"

"No. I would never condone what he's done to you. You should know that."

"I do know that, Sandra."

"Mom, I'd like for you to promise me one thing."

"What's that?"

"Think about the past twenty-eight years. Then I'd like you to consider a reconciliation."

"I can't promise you that."

"Will you at least think about it?"

"Yes, Sandra, I'll think about it."

"Don't say it just to placate me."

"I think it's time we end this conversation."

There was a long silence, Morgana breathing in shallow, quick gasps. She wanted to hang up, but did not want to end the call with enmity between her and her daughter. There was enough of that between her and Franklin.

"If and when you talk to Justin, tell him that I will handle everything. And I do mean *everything.* And one last thing—take care of your father."

A long sigh came through the wire. "I will. Good-bye, Mom."

"Good-bye," she whispered.

If the situation hadn't been so serious, Morgana would've laughed. She found it hard to fathom proud, arrogant Franklin Wells crying on his daughter's shoulder. She also didn't want to believe that her son had threatened to assault his father.

Justin and Sandra had a right to know that she was estranged from their father, but what she resented was their interference. She would take care of Franklin—in her own time and in her own way.

Morgana opened the door to Erick's ring, finding it impossible to steady her erratic pulse as he stared at her. There was eagerness in his gaze that hadn't been there before. Was he as pleased to see her again as she was to see him?

She had told herself, *he's only a friend.* That was what she wanted to believe when everything she was beginning to feel for him indicated otherwise.

"Good morning. Please come in."

Lowering his head, he brushed his mouth over hers. "Good morning." He handed her a small white shopping bag. "I picked up something to go with the coffee."

She took the bag. "You didn't have to bring anything."

"I know, but I couldn't resist. Sunday morning wouldn't be complete without beignets."

Morgana led the way through the entryway into the spacious living room, then down a wide hallway to the sunporch. She'd invited Erick to Sunday brunch after agreeing to sit for him. He said he wanted to photograph her in a familiar setting with the expectation his lens would be able to capture an image of openness and spontaneity.

The table had been set, and differing aromas wafted from under covered plates in the sunlit space. A carafe of fresh brewed coffee sat on a nearby sideboard. She gestured to a chair. "Please sit down. Everything is ready."

"After you." Erick pulled out a chair, seating Morgana. Rounding the table, he sat down opposite her. Delicate crystal jars with sterling spoons were filled with preserves. "You set a superb table."

"I have to thank my mother for that. She was somewhat pedantic when it came to her table." Erick placed a napkin in his lap, then uncovered his plate. "I hope you like spinach and blue cheese." Morgana had prepared omelettes with fresh spinach and a mild blue cheese. Instead of the usual Sunday morning biscuits, she had baked scones.

Picking up a fork, he winked at her. "You just hit a home run with me."

He savored the delicate taste of the cheese in the fluffy omelette, the thick pulp in the freshly squeezed orange juice, and the raisin and nut scones topped with strawberry jam. After two cups of coffee and beignets, he leaned back and patted his flat belly.

"Hanging out with you is dangerous to my waistline."

Smiling over the rim of her coffee cup, Morgana said, "I could say the same thing about you. I can't remember the last time I put heavy cream in my coffee."

He sobered quickly, his expression impassive. "Tell me about yourself, Morgana."

She lowered her cup, touching her napkin to the corners of her mouth. "There's not much to tell. You know how old I am and how long I've been married." The truth was she knew more about Erick than he did about her.

"That's true. But I want to know more."

"What do you want to know?"

"Where do you live?"

"Maryland."

"Where in Maryland?"

"Why? Do you plan to come visit me?"

He shook his head. "No." He smiled. "Do you have children?"

"Yes. I have a son and a daughter."

"What do they do?"

"Justin is training to be a navy pilot, and Sandra just completed her second year at Georgetown Law."

There was silence before Erick continued his questioning. "What about your husband?"

She glanced away. "He's an attorney."

He digested everything Morgana told him, and he knew who she was. She was among the affluent, the well-to-do African Americans who drove luxury automobiles and lived in upscale communities. They gave back to the community by joining social organizations to help the less fortunate. Most were pretentious and haughty, but they meant well. They were people he was more than familiar with. His ex-wife was one of them.

"Do you have any brothers or sisters?"

Her gaze swung back to his. "No. I'm an only child, as was my mother. My family is very small now. I have cousins who live on the West Coast, but I haven't seen or heard from them in more than twenty years. My uncle and I are the last of the Salvation Johnsons."

"How does that make you feel, Morgana?"

"How am I supposed to feel?"

"Sad? Angry? Lonely?"

A hint of a smile tugged at her mouth. "All of the above." Her expression suddenly brightened. "Let's not get maudlin, Erick. When you immortalize me in your painting I want joy, not sadness, anger or loneliness."

Pushing back his chair, he stood. "I'll help you clear the table, then I'll set up my equipment."

"Let's not waste time. I'll clear the table while you set up." She reached for several dishes as he picked up the half-filled carafe of coffee.

"Four hands work faster than two."

She did not argue with him. Together they cleared the table. She was stacking dishes in the dishwasher when he returned.

"I'd like to try a few outdoor shots first."

"Where?"

"On the porch."

"Is what I'm wearing okay?"

Erick glanced at the white voile shirt tucked into the waistband of her pale-yellow linen slacks. The bodice of a lacy ivory-colored camisole dotted with tiny pearls was visible under the shirt.

"It's perfect." She was perfect. Her world was perfect, only if she took the time to look. Reaching for her hand, he led her out to the porch. "Sit anywhere you feel most comfortable."

Morgana sat on her favorite chair, a love seat covered in a cotton sateen fabric with bright yellow flowers and large green leaves. She watched Erick as he adjusted a tall lamp and flicked on a bright spotlight.

Pulling a small gadget from the pocket of his slacks, he held it close to her face. "It's a light meter." He stared at her until she dropped her gaze. "I want you to close your eyes and think of something that you truly like." She closed her eyes. "Now, take deep breaths. Breathe in through your nose and exhale through your mouth." He watched her breasts rise and fall. "That's it, Morgana. Relax. Breathe in and out. Slowly. Don't open your eyes until I tell you."

Slumping against the back of the cushion, she felt her body go pliant. Her limbs felt weightless.

Erick watched, transfixed at the expression on Morgana's face. He didn't know whether he wanted to paint her with her eyes open or closed. Moving quickly, he picked up a camera and began shooting, the shutter opening and closing and the frames of film advancing in rapid succession.

"Open your eyes and slide down on your side. That's it. Rest your head on your arm while looking at me." He got off a few more shots. "Now, close your eyes." She complied, a secret smile softening her lush mouth.

Erick photographed her on the porch and in the garden before suggesting they go inside. While he gathered his equipment, Morgana went back into the house, up the staircase and into her bedroom.

She lay across her bed, resting her head on an outstretched arm. She watched Erick watching her as he leaned closer. He'd suggested shooting her nude. She had agreed, but only if she could conceal her nakedness with a sheet. He'd felt a sheet was too sterile, and in the end they compromised on draping her body with a large red silk shawl.

His fingertips grazed her cheek. "Look directly at me. That's it," he crooned softly. "Lower your lids just a little." He took a deep breath. "Perfect." She hadn't worn any makeup and the flawlessness of her face was laid bare for the world.

At that moment everything about Erick Wilson seeped into her: his gentle touch, his smell and blatant virility he wore like a badge of honor. Her lips parted of their own volition as she raised her eyelids to stare directly at him.

Erick saw her pupils dilate, the green color deepening until it appeared black. He'd lied to Morgana, lied when he'd told her he didn't want to become sexually involved with her. But it wasn't friendship that had elicited a rush of blood to his groin.

He wanted her.

Moving closer, he brushed his mouth over hers, measuring her response. He was not disappointed when her lips parted. Knowing she was naked under the shawl increased his longing for her. His tongue traced the soft fullness of her lips, leaving teasing kisses at the corners of her mouth.

Holding the shawl over her breasts with one hand, Morgana reached up and stroked Erick's jaw and chin, a fingertip tracing the outline of his goatee. His facial hair was crisp to the touch, exhilarating and masculine.

Opening her mouth wider, she rose off the mattress to meet his kiss. His lips left hers to tease an earlobe before charting a path down the column of her neck to her shoulder.

Staring at him through lowered lids, she whispered, "Erick?" She was shocked at her own eager response to his kisses. She did not recognize her own voice.

He moved back, putting several feet between them. "Don't move. Not even to breathe."

Reaching for his camera, he snapped frame after frame, the shutter opening and closing with rapid-fire action. However, she did move, the silk material covering her breasts slipping lower. Erick's gaze was on the ardent display of skin as he continued to photograph her from every possible angle. He stood over her, dropped to his knees before he scooted away from the bed, snapping pictures continuously.

His heart pumping uncontrollably in his chest, he lowered his hand and the camera fell to the rug with a soft thud. He was finished! He'd gotten what he wanted.

Moving over to the bed, he sat down and covered Morgana's body with his. "Perfect. You were perfect."

She smiled a dreamy expression on her face. "Do you always kiss your subjects to get them in the right mood?"

A smile crinkled his eyes. "Only the ones who have bewitched me."

"How so?"

Lowering his head, he buried his face between her neck and shoulder. "You've cast a spell over me, Morgana. A spell I never want to be freed of."

"You believe I'm a witch?"

He nodded. "A witch or a fantasy. It doesn't matter."

"I'm neither," she crooned, laughing softly.

He raised his head, meeting her amused gaze. "I want you to play out this fantasy with me until we're forced to retreat to the real world."

"What are you saying?"

"You know exactly what I'm saying." He raised himself up on one elbow, waiting. When she remained silent, he moved off the bed, picked up his camera and walked out of the bedroom.

Morgana lay on the bed, staring up at the ceiling. The lump that had settled in her throat at Erick's proposal was still there. Without saying it, she knew he wanted her to sleep with him. And she did want to sleep with him.

She'd lived and slept with the same man for thirty years, but for the past three years she had been alone. What saddened her most was that she'd denied it—for much too long.

Smiling, she closed her eyes. She detected the lingering odor of coconut, the scent reminding her of Erick's hair. He'd thought her a fantasy, a witch, but she was neither. She was a real woman, a flesh and blood woman who existed in a real world; a world filled with happiness and pain, satisfaction and disappointment.

Was she ready to escape the real world for a few moments of fantasy? And in that fantasy world would she discover who she actually was? There was only one way to find the answer to her questions.

Moving off the bed, she raced to the bathroom, reaching for the bathrobe hanging on a hook on the back of the door. Her bare feet were silent as she hurried down the hallway to the staircase. She had made it halfway down when she saw Erick. He stood in the middle of the living room, staring up at her.

He headed toward her, but she held out her hand, stopping his approach. "Okay." The single word was full of promise.

Erick's eyelids fluttered as he registered her acquiescence. "When?"

"I'll come to you." Turning, she retraced her steps up the staircase, not seeing the stunned expression on his face.

SIXTEEN

After Erick's departure, the afternoon passed at a snail's pace, and Morgana savored every minute of it. And for the first time in her life she treasured the solitude.

Settling in the rocker in her bedroom, she opened the journal.

September 10, 1952

My marriage is deteriorating rapidly. Randolph and I sleep together every night—except when I have my menses. And it is not for the first time that I question myself as to why I married him. We barely speak to each other. We cannot continue this way; I will not continue this way.

Katherine opened the door to the library without knocking. Randolph's head jerked up, a frown deepening the lines in his forehead.

"You know better than to come in without knocking."

Closing the door behind her, she folded her arms under her breasts. "I don't need to knock on doors, Randolph. Especially in my own home."

He waved a hand, not wanting to argue with Katherine. Not tonight. "What do you want?"

She walked across the room and sat down on a chair beside his desk. "I need to talk to you."

"About what?"

"Us."

He glared at her. "What about us?" Most people in Salvation retreated whenever Randolph Johnson glared at them, but Katherine wasn't most people.

"Our marriage."

He replaced the cap to his fountain pen, then laced his fingers together. He smiled, but there was no warmth in the expression. "Are you saying you're not happy? Have you come to me because you want a divorce?"

"Don't try to put words in my mouth, Randolph. And don't ever attempt to think for me."

Picking up the pen, he unscrewed the top, his gaze fixed on his manicured fingers. He had successfully curbed the urge to slap her. This was the second time she'd warned him about what he could and could not say to her. Swallowing his rage, he said, "I'm very busy tonight. Whatever it is you want to say to me will have to wait until another time."

Katherine shook her head. "No, Randolph. *I want to talk to you now.*" She had enunciated each word.

He glared at her under lowered lids. "Make it quick."

She tried recalling the words she had rehearsed over and over, but suddenly her mind went blank. A wave of apprehension swept through her, gnawing away at her confidence.

"I feel more like a stranger than your wife."

His eyes narrowed. "Why?"

Taking a deep breath, she pulled back her shoulders. "You claim you love me but I don't believe you."

"Why not?"

"We do nothing together. I shouldn't have to beg you to take me out."

Randolph snorted. "We don't go out because I'm busy. Starting up an insurance business is time consuming."

"If that's the case, then I'm going to go out with my friend."

"Who is this friend?"

"You don't need to know who." She refused to tell him the friend was Caroline.

"I better not catch you with another man."

Katherine almost laughed aloud. "Why, Randolph? Are you afraid I'll meet someone who won't choke me?"

"Dammit, Katherine. I told you I was sorry."

"It never should've happened." She glanced at the pattern on the imported rug. "There's something else I want to tell you."

"What?"

She looked at him. "I'm moving out of the bedroom."

"You've got the gall to come in here and interrupt me with this bullshit?"

"It's not bullshit, Randolph. You jump on me, then get off, not caring whether you hurt me."

His free hand came down hard on the top of the desk, startling her. "That's exactly what it is. I think you're upset because I don't want you." It was his turn to be defensive. "Why would I want to make love to a woman who just lays there with her eyes closed, waiting for me to finish?" Her eyes widened, and he pressed his attack. "I'm willing to bet that if I fucked a cadaver at the funeral home I'd get more of a reaction from it than I get from you." Much to Randolph's surprise, Katherine smiled.

"Do you think you can hurt me with hateful words?"

Scrawling his signature across the bottom of a document, he drawled, "Good night, Katherine."

She went completely still. He had summarily dismissed her. Within seconds something in her died. Any love she'd had for Randolph died with his dismissal.

Pulling back her shoulders, she stared at his bowed head. "Good night, Randolph." Turning on her heels she walked out of the library, closing the door softly behind her.

September 14, 1952

I am now teaching Sunday school. I love working with young children.

Randolph left Salvation Friday morning to spend the week in Atlanta on insurance business so I will share dinner with my parents.

Katherine waited until the dishes were washed and put away before she approached her father. He sat on a worn leather recliner, staring out the set of French doors overlooking the backyard. A glass of scotch sat on a table near his right hand.

"Daddy?"

Shifting on the chair, he stared at his daughter. "Come closer, baby girl."

Closing the distance between them, she sat on the arm of the chair, curving an arm around his neck. "Daddy, I need to talk to you."

He glanced up, seeing the moisture shimmering in her eyes. "What's wrong?"

"I don't know if I'm going to stay with Randolph."

Edward sat up straighter, sobering quickly. What was Katherine saying? She and Randolph hadn't been married three months, and already she was talking about leaving him.

"What's the matter?"

"We're not getting along too well."

"What do you mean not getting along?"

"It's just not working, Daddy. I moved out of our bedroom."

Reaching up, he patted her hair. "Married life isn't easy, especially the first year. I'm certain it's even more difficult for you and Randolph, because you didn't have a normal courtship."

"That's because he didn't want a normal courtship. He claims he didn't want people to talk about us. I think it has something to do with his being fifteen years older than me."

"He did it to protect you."

"That's what he said."

He pulled her closer. "I'll talk to him, baby girl."

"Thank you, Daddy." Sighing, she laid her head on Edward's shoulder, her anxiety easing with his promise to confront Randolph.

Katherine drove home after spending the afternoon with her parents. She went to her bedroom and changed into a sleeveless blouse, slacks, and a pair of sandals.

The house seemed peaceful without Randolph. Whenever he was home he usually spent most of his time in the library, yet she had felt his presence even when she didn't see him.

She picked up John Steinbeck's *East of Eden* from the bedside table and went downstairs to the kitchen to get a glass of lemonade. Minutes later, she sat on the porch glider reading and drinking.

The sound of a car's engine caught Katherine's attention. Looking up, she saw Julian park his car in the driveway. He had taken a temporary position as an admitting doctor at a colored hospital in Savannah and had bought a car for the commute. Although he lived with her and Randolph, she rarely saw him because he spent long hours at the hospital.

He walked up to the porch, his step slow and heavy. Katherine took in everything about him in one glance: a short-sleeved white shirt open at the throat, a pair of pale blue seersucker pants, and white bucks. He had tucked a newspaper under one arm while carrying the black leather doctor's bag with his left hand.

"Hi, Julian." His head came up, and he looked at her as if she were a stranger.

He smiled. "Good afternoon, Katherine."

She placed a marker in her book. "Did you eat?"

"Yes, I did."

Julian stared at Katherine. He'd been living with Randolph and Katherine for two weeks, and when he wasn't working double shifts at the hospital he was sleeping.

He had shared dinner with his brother and sister-in-law twice, finding it odd that the newlyweds did not speak to each other except to ask the other to pass a serving bowl. The dinners were so uncomfortable that he had gone out of his way to avoid eating with them again.

Katherine pointed to the paper under his arm. "Is there anything in there worth reading?"

He shrugged a shoulder. "The only thing that caught my attention was an article about Dwight Eisenhower. He was campaigning in Little Rock, Arkansas, several weeks back. He claims to have warned white southerners they could lose their rights by not protecting the rights of Negroes."

"Ike must be shell-shocked. Does he really think southern whites care about protecting the rights of Negroes?"

Julian smiled. "You're right about that. What concerns me more is the war in Korea."

"Do you think it's the beginning of another world war?"

"I don't know. What worries me are the soldiers who are coming back home addicted to drugs."

"What kind of drugs?"

Julian placed his bag and the newspaper on a small table between the glider and a rocking chair, and sat down. Leaning back, he rocked gently.

"Narcotics."

Katherine listened as Julian told her of the scores of young people he'd treated in New York City who injected an opiate called heroin into their veins. Addicts sold their bodies, robbed, burglarized, and even killed to get money to support their habits.

"Have you ever been to Harlem?"

Julian nodded. "I had an apartment there."

"Please tell me about New York City. Especially Harlem."

Julian's eyes crinkled behind his glasses. Katherine reminded him of a child begging for a sweet treat. He had to remind himself that she was not a child, but a woman. A very beautiful woman.

"New York City is large, noisy, and a very exciting city. It would take several days just to tell you about Harlem."

Katherine wanted to tell Julian that she had hours, days. Randolph wasn't expected to return to Salvation for another six days.

"Randolph has promised to . . ." As soon as she mentioned Randolph's name, the words died on her lips. Randolph had promised to take her to New York next summer but she doubted whether that would become a reality now.

Julian stopped rocking, leaning forward. "He has promised you what?"

She turned her head, and the hair she had secured in a ponytail swept over one shoulder. "We had planned to take a delayed honeymoon to New York next summer."

Julian raised an eyebrow. "Has Randolph changed his mind?"

"No. Would you like a glass of lemonade?" she asked, changing the topic. She did not want to talk about Randolph.

"Yes, I would. Thank you."

Katherine stood, Julian rising with her. He did not sit down again until she returned with a glass and a pitcher of lemonade. He watched her delicate hands as she poured lemonade into a glass for him, then refilled her own.

He took a sip of the cold drink. It was perfect, tart and sweet. Stretching out his legs, he began, "New York City is made up of neighborhoods either by race or nationalities. Sociologists call them ghettos. There are enclaves of Germans, Poles, Negroes, Chinese, Italians, Jews, Russians living in groups in all of the five boroughs that make up New York City."

Katherine listened as Julian spoke of going to Ebbets

Field to cheer on Jackie Robinson and the Brooklyn Dodgers. He became animated when he talked about going to the Apollo Theatre on Amateur Night, dancing at the Savoy, and hearing Paul Robeson speak at a Civil Rights Congress rally at Madison Square Garden where the actor-activist called on President Truman to stop sending troops to Korea.

"Robeson was incensed that Negro soldiers were being sent to fight Koreans. I'll never forget him saying, 'I have said it before and I say it again, that the place for the Negro people to fight for their freedom is here at home.' The crowd gave him a standing ovation."

"What other famous people did you see or meet?"

"I heard Congressman Adam Clayton Powell Jr. preach at the Abyssinian Baptist Church. I had the honor of meeting Dr. Muriel Petioni who had opened a medical practice on One Hundred Thirty-first Street. Dr. Petioni, whose father was also a Harlem physician, is a pioneer in the successful treatment of drug addiction."

Katherine listened to Julian speak of places she wanted to see for herself. Atlanta had tall buildings but not skyscrapers like New York City's Empire State and Chrysler Buildings. She wanted to experience what it felt like to walk over the Brooklyn Bridge, visit Chinatown and eat Chinese food, stroll the narrow winding streets of Greenwich Village, and go to the New York Public Library's 135th Street Branch Library to examine thousands of books, manuscripts, newspapers and assorted items of African and African-American history and culture in the Schomburg Collection of Negro Literature and History.

By the time dusk had settled over the countryside and crickets began their nocturnal chorus Julian's voice had faded.

He sat on the rocker, his chin resting on his chest. He had fallen asleep.

Katherine reached over and shook his arm but he did not stir. Moving off the glider, she leaned down, gently touching the side of his face. His head jerked up at the same time his hand caught her wrist in a firm grip.

"I'm . . . I'm," she began to apologize. "You had fallen asleep."

He released her hand and looked at his watch. "I'm sorry I fell asleep on you. I must be more tired than I realize." He smothered a yawn.

Katherine moved back as Julian stood up. She smiled up at him. "Thank you."

"For what, Katherine?"

She felt his heat and inhaled the cologne on his skin and clothes. The fragrance was clean, masculine. "For your company."

Julian tried making out her features in the waning light but he did not have to see Katherine's expression because the three words spoke volumes. She was lonely.

In that instant he cursed Randolph for his selfishness. He had married Katherine, yet had continued the lifestyle of a bachelor. Whenever Julian had called to speak to Randolph Mrs. Pitt usually answered the phone telling him Mr. Randolph was away on business.

"I thank you for listening."

She smiled. "Good night, Julian."

"Good night, Katherine." He stared at her for a few minutes, then turned and picked up his bag and newspaper. She hadn't moved when he opened the screen door and closed it softly.

The sound of Katherine's voice, her smell and the softness

of her skin when he had touched her lingered with Julian even after he had showered and slipped into bed. It only faded after he had fallen asleep.

September 16, 1952

Julian called me at school today to ask me if I would share dinner with him at a restaurant in Savannah. He had worked the eight-to-three shift and since I got off at three we could eat together. I told him yes.

Katherine felt her pulse quicken as she watched Julian come closer. He wore a dark suit that flattered his tall frame. It was the first time she had seen him wear a hat, and he had pulled down the short brim. The style gave him a rakish look.

She extended her gloved hand but he ignored it, bending over and kissing her cheek. "You look very nice."

Katherine blushed. "Thank you." Today she wore a navy blue suit with a slim skirt and peplum jacket, white silk blouse, navy heels and a single strand of pearls with matching studs in her pierced lobes.

Julian tucked her hand into the bend of his arm. "We'll leave your car here and come back for it later."

"Where are we going?"

He smiled at her. "It's a surprise."

"I don't like surprises, Julian."

He tightened his hold on her hand. "Please, Katherine. Just this once."

She met his amused gaze, then nodded. "Okay."

Julian led Katherine to where he had parked his car, waiting until she was seated before he rounded the five-year-old Dodge. He had decided to buy a used car rather than a new one because he wanted to save money to set up his practice.

He took off his hat and jacket, placing them on the rear seat. Katherine was staring at him when he slipped behind the wheel. "How was your day?"

There was silence before she said, "It was very good." A frown furrowed her forehead. Randolph had never asked about her work. It was always his business they had talked about.

Julian turned the key in the ignition, shifted into gear and pulled away from the curb in front of her school. He switched on the radio, trying for a station that did not have too much static. The voice of Nat King Cole came through the speakers.

He drove south, stopping in Darien where they took a ferry to Sapelo Island. Katherine stared with wide eyes at the unspoiled beauty of the island. She had lived in Georgia all of her life, yet had not bothered to travel beyond the environs of Savannah. Of course, she had gone to Atlanta but only because she had enrolled in Spelman.

Julian led her into a tiny restaurant that wasn't much larger than her living room. Wooden tables and benches made the space appear even smaller. They were the only customers. They sat down near a window that overlooked the water.

An elderly man approached their table to take their order, and Katherine let Julian order for her. She stared out the window sipping sweet tea.

"How did you find this place?"

"I went to grade school with a boy who was born on Sapelo. Joe was a Geechee, and he used to tell me stories that had been passed down through countless generations about the ghosts that followed Africans from West Africa to this country."

Katherine's gray eyes grew wider. "What kind of ghosts?"

"He said there's still talk of people being ridden by witches at night. It's supposed to be an ancient belief of the Vais.

According to the Vais legend, when a witch comes in the door he takes off his skin and lays it aside in the house, rides the victim through the night and returns him to his bed in the morning."

"That's preposterous. It's like people believing in voodoo and roots."

"It isn't when you believe it."

Katherine gave him a long stare. "You're a scientist, Julian, and scientists believe in what can be proven."

"I'm not saying I believe in witches and spells, but I never judge or criticize someone's belief system."

She lifted her eyebrows. "You think I'm judgmental?"

"Maybe a little opinionated."

"You're probably right about that."

Julian told her he had bought a parcel of land half a mile from where Randolph had built his house, and had been meeting with an architect to look at the blueprints for his home/office.

"If all goes according to plan, construction should be completed in early spring. I intend to use a wing for my family practice."

"If you need help picking out furnishings, I'd be more than willing to help you. That is, unless you have someone else in mind."

"And who would that be?"

She shrugged her shoulder. "I don't know. Maybe you have a girlfriend or a fiancée back in New York—"

"I don't have a girlfriend or fiancée, Katherine," he said, interrupting her. "I don't plan to marry until after I'm established."

Katherine wanted to tell Julian that his plans meant nothing to women who were looking for someone as eligible as he.

Coupled with the fact that he was a doctor made him ever more suitable to young Negro women.

The waiter returned, setting a tray filled with platters of fried clams, oysters, catfish fritters and shrimp on the table. Side dishes included buttered corn on the cob, cole slaw, and chow-chow. Tiny bowls held hot pepper and tartar sauces.

Katherine smiled across the table at Julian. "It looks delicious."

He picked up his fork. "It tastes better hot."

She picked up her fork, speared a large shrimp, biting into it and moaning in ecstasy. "This is the best shrimp I've ever tasted." Julian nodded, unable to talk because his own mouth was filled with food.

Katherine could not believe she and Julian had eaten everything, leaving only crumbs on their plates. They decided to walk along the beach before returning to the ferry. She went into the restaurant's minuscule bathroom, took off her stockings and put them in her purse. She walked barefoot along the narrow strip of the beach, experiencing a freedom she had not felt since she was a child.

She did not want her outing with Julian to end but it did end when he drove her back to her car in the school's parking lot. They returned to Salvation, Julian following her in his own car.

They were silent as they climbed the porch steps. Key in hand, Katherine made no attempt to unlock the door. "Thank you, Julian, for dinner." She bit down on her lower lip. "I seem to be thanking you a lot lately."

He stared at the back of her head. Her hair was styled in a neat twist. "There's never a need to thank me, Katherine."

"Why?" The word was a whisper.

"Because there isn't anything I wouldn't do for you. All you have to do is ask."

She stood motionless, replaying his statement. She replayed it over and over in her mind that night and every night until Randolph returned from Atlanta.

The instant she saw Randolph walk into the house she was reminded that she was a married woman.

SEVENTEEN

November 2, 1952

I am at my wit's end because I do not know what I am going to do about the wives, sisters and female cousins of Randolph's business associates. They come by with the pretense of visiting me, but in reality it is Julian they wish to see. The fact that he is only 28, unmarried and a doctor make him a "good catch."

The first few times I invited the women in, but after a while I had Mrs. Pitt inform them that I was feeling poorly, and therefore was not accepting visitors. When I mentioned this to Julian, he seemed unfazed by their attention. Nothing in his expression revealed if he was flattered or amused.

The construction company laid the foundation for his house two weeks ago, and days later the frame went up. He visits the site twice a week to monitor the progress.

We are spending more time together, but only because we both work in Savannah. Whenever he is scheduled to work a morning shift we will drive in and return home together.

My situation with Randolph has improved slightly. I am not certain whether Daddy spoke to him; however, he is now speaking to me, and I find myself relating to him with polite kindness. We are still sleeping apart. Mrs. Pitt and Julian are aware of our sleeping arrangements, but I am past caring or pretending all is well between Randolph and me.

Caroline, who enrolled in a graduate program at Georgia State, called to tell me she is engaged. Her fiancé is the son of one of her father's colleagues. He, like his father, is also a doctor. I am certain the Gaskins can now breathe a sigh of relief now that she is going to become a doctor's wife.

November 25, 1952

Thanksgiving was held at our house this year. My sisters-in-law and Mrs. Pitt did most of the cooking. Delano and Charles's wives volunteered only because they are housewives. With 7 children between them they are always busy doctoring colds and other childhood illnesses, washing, ironing, cooking and cleaning.

Miss Mattie embarrassed me when she asked when was I going to make my mother and father grandparents. Everyone at the table stared at me before they turned their attention to Randolph. I ended the tense moment, saying we are still on our honeymoon. I knew he was angry with

Miss Mattie, but he held his tongue. Mother blushed while Daddy stared down at his plate. He had barely touched his food, preferring instead to drink glass after glass of Concord grape wine.

As I stared at my father I realized he is not aging well. He is 47, yet he looks older than Randolph Sr., who turned 65 in August. On occasion I have noticed his hands trembling. I wonder when was the last time he went to a doctor for a checkup.

Katherine sat on the porch, staring up at the millions of stars dotting the nighttime sky. Everyone had left, all of the food had been put away, the kitchen had been cleaned, and now she wanted to be alone.

She hadn't realized how much she disliked entertaining until today. All of the time and effort that went into cleaning, cooking and preparing for an event ended within hours. She was tired of being gracious to guests who blurted out whatever they wanted.

The screen door opened and closed with a soft clicking sound. Randolph stood in the shadows staring at Katherine. "Are you coming in?"

She shook her head. "No. I just want to stay here and unwind."

He moved closer. "I'm sorry about my mother."

"There's no need for you to apologize for your mother, Randolph. She is who she is."

"Just like I am who I am."

Resting the back of her head on the cushion, Katherine closed her eyes. "If you came out here to fight with me, then I'm going to disappoint you. I want you to go away and leave me in peace."

Taking two long strides, he stood over her. "Is that what you really want, Katherine? Do you want me to leave you alone?"

"Yes." She hadn't bothered to open her eyes to look at him.

Turning on his heel, he left the porch, walking in the direction of the garage. Minutes later, the sound of a car's engine disturbed the tranquillity of the night.

Randolph pounded on the door, cursing and mumbling under his breath. "The bitch is crazy. First she fights with me to spend more time with her, and now she wants me to leave her alone."

Lenora opened the door, her eyes widening in shock. She hadn't seen Randolph since the day after she had moved into her new home. He'd come to give her the money she needed to buy furniture for the additional bedroom. Her slanted eyes narrowed in a knowing smile.

She had shared Thanksgiving dinner with a few nurses at the hospital after their shift had ended, but never in her wildest dreams did she think she would have anything to be thankful for this year. The exception was her new house.

"Hello, Daddy."

He returned her smile. "Hi, Lenny. Aren't you going to invite me in?"

"Why should I?"

His smiled faded. "Because you want me as much as I want you."

"Are you still with your wife?"

"Yes. But, what does that have to do with us?"

"You told me you wouldn't come to me after you married."

Bracing a hand on the door, he forcibly pushed it open,

causing Lenora to stumble backward. Reaching out, he caught her wrist to steady her.

"So, I lied," he crooned. He kissed her hard, stopping her protest. Picking her up with one arm, he kicked the door closed, and headed for her bedroom.

Lenora undressed Randolph slowly, knowing he would be hot and ready for her once she opened her legs to him. She had given up hope that he would come back to her, but the old woman had reassured her he would.

She lay on the bed, her gaze caressing the hard thick length of his erection throbbing between his thighs. Slowly, deliberately, she spread her legs and opened her arms. She was not disappointed when he moved between her legs and pushed into her body. They sighed in unison.

Randolph tempered his passion, wanting it to last all night. His hips rocked back and forth before moving in an up and down motion. He had come home. There was no woman like his Lenny. Waves of ecstasy throbbed through him as he rode her long and hard. He held back as long as he could. A jolt of electricity streaked through his groin, and he exploded, groaning. His breath came in surrendering moans as he collapsed on Lenora's bucking frame.

They lay motionless, listening to the runaway beating of each other's hearts. Once he recovered his strength, Randolph reversed their positions, their bodies still joined.

They fell asleep, and when he awoke hours later he found Lenora sitting astride his hips, riding his rigid flesh like a woman possessed.

Morgana closed the first volume, her mind reeling. She didn't know how, but she felt Katherine's frustration. Her mother had asked Randolph what every woman wanted from a husband: love and consideration. Why, she thought, had it been so difficult for him to give her that? She couldn't read any more. She had to take time to digest what she had uncovered so far.

Glancing at her watch, she noted the time. It was after seven. She reached for the telephone and dialed Bernice's number.

The phone rang several times before the answering machine picked up. "Hi, Bernice. This is Morgana. Call me . . ."

"Hello, Morgana. Hold on a moment. I just walked in."

It was another two minutes before Bernice picked up the receiver. "I'm sorry to keep you waiting. I forgot to throw out last night's Chinese takeout, and the smell was something awful. How's it going?"

"Good. How are you doing?"

"Wonderful, especially since Mrs. Butterfield is putting in the extra hours."

"How's business?"

"We're doing quite well."

"We should do even better with some new merchandise." She told Bernice about Erick's photographs, unaware of the change in her voice as she told of the special process for making new photos look dated.

"You sound very excited about this."

"I am. The photographer said the prints should be ready in about a week. After they are matted and framed, I'll ship them to you."

"It's funny you called, because I was going to call you."

"For what?"

"I saw Franklin today."

A cold knot formed in her stomach. "Had he come into the shop?"

"No. He was with Sandra. Morgana, I don't know how to say this."

The knot tightened. "Say it, Bernice."

"If it hadn't been for Sandra, I wouldn't have recognized him. He's lost a lot of weight and is now wearing a beard."

What did her partner expect her to say? That she would come running back to Maryland to take care of her suffering husband?

"He'll be all right. Sandra called the other day to tell me he was staying with her."

"I'm sorry for interfering."

"You have nothing to apologize for."

"How are things going there?"

Morgana was relieved that Bernice had changed the topic. She didn't want to discuss Franklin.

"The realtor has set up two appointments to show the house this week. I'm hoping someone will like it enough to make an offer. Right now I'm willing to accept any reasonable offer."

"From the photographs I've seen of the house, you should have no problem unloading it."

Even if a potential buyer went to contract within two weeks, Morgana knew the earliest they could close was within another four to six weeks. That would be more than enough time for her to catalogue, pack and ship everything to Baltimore.

"I'll call you again in a few days."

"And I'll call you once I get the photographs. After I see them I'll have to find a place to display them."

"How about the café?" She and Bernice had added a small

area in the back of the shop where they offered lattes and French pastries to those who came in to buy or browse.

"Excellent choice. I keep telling you that you're the artistic partner, while I'm the hustler."

Morgana laughed, because Bernice never permitted a customer to walk out empty-handed. Even if they bought a pack of blank note cards, she felt satisfied knowing she had made a sale.

Rolling over on her side, Morgana stared at the clock on the bedside table. It was only 9:35. The last time she had looked it had been 8:55. She knew this was one night she wasn't going to get much sleep. Her mind was too active.

She reached down to pull the sheet up over her legs, and the scent of coconut wafted in her nostrils, reminding her of Erick.

He used a coconut-scented hair dressing to keep his twists from unlocking. Rolling over on her belly, she buried her face in a pillow, moaning softly as she recalled the feel of his mouth and tongue when they'd shared a kiss.

She tossed and turned restlessly until she finally swept back the sheet and headed to the bathroom. After showering she selected underwear, T-shirts, shorts and a pair of jeans. A quarter of an hour later, she slipped behind the wheel of her car, and drove into Savannah.

Erick sat up, listening intently. He heard it again. Someone was knocking. Swinging his legs over the side of the bed, he reached for a pair of shorts on a bench at the foot of the bed. He walked on bare feet to the door and opened it. He stared at his night visitor, speechless.

"I said I'd come."

Moving closer, he cradled Morgana to his chest as if she were a fragile piece of porcelain. He lowered his head, breathing a kiss under her ear.

"Thank you," he whispered, closing the door and sweeping her into his arms.

She forgot everything and everyone, even her own name as she opened herself to Erick, welcoming him into her body.

His lovemaking was slow as he sculpted every dip and curve of her body. He kissed her taut nipples, combed his fingers through her short hair, rocking his hips against hers until she cried out for release.

Sensations she had forgotten existed settled at the base of her spine as the walls of her vagina convulsed. "Erick, Erick." She crooned his name over and over until an orgasm curled her toes.

Erick quickened his movements. It had become flesh to flesh, man to woman, lover to lover. Morgana's breasts pressed against his chest, her legs wrapped around his waist, and her soft moans as she writhed beneath him aroused him to a passion that was pure and explosive. Lowering his head, he buried his face against her neck, groaning out his own awesome climax.

Morgana couldn't get up because of the weight bearing down on her legs. She opened her eyes, peering over a shoulder. Erick lay on his side, his leg resting over hers.

He pressed a kiss on the nape of her neck. "You have the sexiest neck of any woman I've ever seen."

"How many necks have you seen?"

"More than I've ever wanted to see." Removing his leg, he wrapped an arm around her waist and flipped her onto her back.

Reaching up, she held his hair off his face. "Last night was incredible."

"That's because you are incredible." His lips descended slowly to meet hers. "And I want more, Morgana. I'll take as much as you are willing to give me before . . ." He didn't complete his statement.

She closed her eyes against his intense stare, nodding. "Before it ends. And it is going to end, Erick."

Rubbing the pad of his thumb over her mouth, he coaxed her lips apart. "It's not going to end, sweetheart. At least not this morning."

"Don't you teach today?"

"Not until the afternoon."

Curving her arms around his neck, she pulled his head down to her naked breasts. He teased her nipples with his teeth and she moaned.

Taking her hand, Erick guided it to his arousal, establishing a rhythm that left them both gasping. He paused to slip on a condom before easing his hardness into her moist heat. Together they found a tempo that bound them together.

Breathing heavily, Morgana lay in the drowsy warmth of Erick's embrace, amazed at the sense of fulfillment he had given her. She wondered if she should feel some guilt for the pleasure she found in his arms. She hungered, and Erick fed the hunger; she was hurt, and he had soothed the pain; she felt alone, and he had offered companionship.

"I have to get up, Erick."

Lifting her left arm, he glanced at the hands on her watch. It was almost ten o'clock. It had been years since he'd lain in bed beyond sunrise.

Straddling Morgana's body, he smiled down at her. "Will you stay long enough for me to feed you breakfast?"

She traced the outline of his eyebrows with a forefinger

before moving down the bridge of his nose. "Yes. But first I need you to do a favor for me."

His expression stilled, becoming serious. Sleeping with Morgana had ruined him for every other woman he would ever meet. There was no shy reticence as she whispered what she wanted him to do to bring her ultimate pleasure. And he had complied willingly, dismissing male pride because she had taken the lead. Their coming together had been strong and uncomplicated, and when he lay gasping from the ecstasy she extracted from his soul, he had to acknowledge that she was not his fantasy, but a very real flesh and blood woman.

"What?"

"I need you to get an overnight bag I left in my car."

He smiled, admiring graying reddish curls falling over her forehead. A shaft of sunlight fell across the bed, the golden rays illuminating her face like a spotlight. He was momentarily stunned by the brilliance of her gray-green eyes.

"Your parents should've named you Catherine, because your eyes remind me of a cat's."

Morgana gasped. "How did you know?"

His brow furrowed. "Know what?"

"My middle name is Katherine. It was my mother's name. It's spelled with a K."

"Morgana Katherine Johnson. It flows nicely."

She wanted to tell him she wasn't Morgana Johnson, but Wells. She had already told him more about herself than he needed to know. Everything she had and would share with Erick would come to an end in less than seven weeks.

Moving off the bed, she picked up her handbag, feeling the heat of Erick's gaze on her naked body. She retrieved her keys, turned and handed them to him. He grasped her hand.

"You're perfect, Morgana. Everything about you is perfect."

"No," she protested softly. "I'm not perfect. I have flaws, but I hide them well."

Gathering her to his chest, he buried his face in her wayward curls. A flash of anguish tore at his heart as he anticipated leaving Morgana. If only he had met her a year ago, before he committed to returning to California. He released her, slipped into his shorts, and went to retrieve her overnight bag.

EIGHTEEN

Morgana held a journal in one hand while she balanced a cup of coffee in the other. She walked into the sunporch, sat down and began reading.

December 26, 1952

Yesterday was my first Christmas as Katherine Johnson, and I am very proud of myself. I did not cry. I refused to cry. If it were not for Julian I believe I would have lost my mind.

He takes me out when Randolph goes away. We have shared dinners and sometimes an occasional movie. What I enjoy most is going on long drives with him. Most times we do not talk. When we do talk it is always about his experiences when he lived in New York.

The exterior of his house is completed, and all that

remains is installing the plumbing. School is in recess this week and I told Julian I now have time to go over catalogues with him to select furnishings for his beautiful home.

Julian's home is in the low-country plantation style, and surrounded by at least two acres of land. There is the main house and two smaller wings connected by a wide veranda. One wing will serve as his office, and the other as an intimate guest house.

We celebrated Christmas dinner at Miss Mattie's. Though Randolph and his brothers paid to enlarge and modernize the house I still find it small and cramped.

Randolph left before dinner ended, saying he had to check on a local family who had lost their son two days ago in a traffic accident. I wanted to tell him it was the pastor's responsibility, not his, to console a grieving family, but I held my tongue.

Mrs. Pitt is away on vacation. She travels to Philadelphia every year to celebrate Christmas and New Year's with her sister's family. She is not expected back until January 5th. Randolph left this morning for Atlanta. He said he has meetings with the executives of his insurance company's home office.

Katherine closed her journal, slipping it into a half-filled box of sanitary napkins in the back of her closet. Writing had saved her, kept her sane.

She hadn't bothered to put on her slippers as she made her way down the carpeted staircase to the first floor. The house was empty and quiet, the way she preferred it. Julian was scheduled to work the three-to-eleven shift, and with Randolph and Mrs. Pitt away she was alone.

She walked into Randolph's library. She referred to it as his sanctuary; it was a place where he hid himself behind the door, shutting her and the world out whenever he tried to come up with an idea for a new business venture. It was where on Friday nights eight of the prominent businessmen in Salvation met for a weekly poker game, and it was where her father came to play cards and sometimes drink too much. Lately, more often than not, she woke up on Saturday mornings to find her father sleeping in one of the guest rooms.

Standing in the middle of the room, she shook her head, wondering what the pull was that kept Randolph within its walls for hours, and sometimes days.

She walked over to the towering armoire, opening the decoratively carved doors. Shelves were crowded with wines and liquors, some of them bearing labels with foreign names. Massive decanters with silver tags were labeled with their contents. Exquisite crystal glassware, suspended from built-in hooks, caught the light from a table lamp. Reaching for a glass and a decanter of whiskey, Katherine placed them on a side table. She wasn't much of a drinker, but she had come to enjoy a small amount of mash whiskey. It never failed to relax her.

She sat down on a leather love seat, pulled her bare feet under her body, and began sipping the golden liquid. She drank the first ounce; she felt free, freer than she had ever felt in her life. It was after the third ounce that she could not remember where she was or who she was.

~

Julian walked into the house, bone-tired. His three-to-eleven shift had stretched into a three-to-three. There was a constant flow of patients coming into the emergency room. He'd treated knife and gunshot wounds, delivered two babies, and performed an emergency D&C after a woman inserted a coat hanger into her vagina in an attempt to abort an unwanted pregnancy.

He headed for the staircase, but stopped when he saw light coming from the library. He squinted. Had Randolph come back from Atlanta?

His footfalls were silent as he walked into the library. The lines of fatigue ringing his mouth vanished as he smiled at Katherine sprawled on the love seat, the fabric of her nightgown twisted around her legs.

As he neared her he saw the glass and decanter. It was apparent she had been drinking. It was also obvious she wasn't much of a drinker, because she hadn't been able to make it back to her bedroom. Gathering her off the love seat, he cradled her in his arms, amazed at her fragility. She stirred, but did not wake up.

Julian stood motionless, staring down at the cloud of red hair flowing over the sleeve of his jacket. He forced himself not to stare at the swell of creamy breasts above the lacy décolletage.

She's your brother's wife.

Moisture dotted his brow as he reminded himself that he was lusting after his sister-in-law. He had seen hundreds of naked women since embarking on a career in medicine, but he could not understand his reaction to seeing Katherine's partially-clothed body. He left the library, taking the stairs two at a time. He had to get away from her before his body betrayed him again.

Living with Randolph and Katherine made him aware of things he did not want to know or see. And it was for that reason he could not wait to move into his own home. Whenever the three of them shared dinner the silence was deafening. There was only the polite command to pass a dish.

He was also aware that Randolph no longer slept in the same bedroom with his wife. They had celebrated their six-month anniversary, and already their marriage was in trouble. Julian loved his older brother, had become quite fond of Katherine, but would never question Randolph about his relationship with his wife.

Walking into the bedroom, he placed Katherine's body on the bed. As he covered her with the sheet, her eyes opened.

Katherine blinked, trying to focus on the face inches from her own. A lopsided smile parted her lips. "Hi." The greeting was low, seductive.

Julian returned her smile, his eyes crinkling behind the lenses of his glasses. "Hi. How do you feel?"

Her lids lowered, lashes brushing the tops of her high cheekbones. "I'm a little drunk."

He lifted an eyebrow. "Only a little."

"Okay," she crooned, staring directly at him. "Slightly drunk."

"Do you want me to bring you a cup of hot coffee?"

Shaking her head and patting the side of the mattress, she said, "I want you to stay with me." Unbidden tears filled her eyes. "I thought I wanted to be alone, but I don't."

Julian placed a hand alongside her face. "I can't, Katherine."

Tears shimmered in her eyes. "Please, Julian. Just tonight."

Her tears unnerved him, and he knew at that moment that he could not deny Katherine anything.

In the last four months he had watched her wilt before his eyes. He silently cursed Randolph for marrying Katherine. She was young, full of life, and she deserved better than a man fixated with making money. He'd wondered if his brother had ever taken her out dancing, or away on an overnight trip.

Randolph told him that he had promised Katherine he was going to take her on a delayed honeymoon for Christmas, but even that had been canceled.

Rising to his feet, he removed his glasses, jacket, shoes, and socks then lay down beside her. Katherine turned toward him, her arm going around his neck. Julian felt the whisper of her breath on his throat, inhaled the perfume on her body mingling with the liquor, and gritted his teeth when her full breasts brushed his chest.

He listened for the change in her breathing. She had fallen asleep. A rush of fatigue swept over him and he joined her in sleep.

Katherine woke two hours later, her stomach churning and head spinning. Moaning, she sat up, scrambling over the body sprawled on the bed next to her, and raced to the bathroom. Bending over the commode, she vomited. The sour odor of undigested food caused another bout of retching. It continued until she slumped to the cool tiles, her face streaked with tears.

"Feeling better?"

She opened her eyes. Julian towered over her, frowning. He looked different without his glasses. Weakly, she shook her head.

"No-ooo."

He bent down, cradling her head in his hands. "I hope you'll remember this day when you think about drinking again."

"Please, don't yell at me, Julian."

"I'm not yelling, Katherine."

"Your voice sounds loud to me."

"That's because you have a hangover." He lifted her off the

floor. "You need to eat. You're practically skin and bones." He sat her on a wicker stool, one arm supporting her sagging body. "Try to sit up, Katherine. I'm going to give you a shower, then get you to eat something."

Turning on the faucets in the tub, he adjusted the water temperature. He removed Katherine's nightgown and carried her to the bathtub. She sagged against the wall as he pulled the curtain around the tub.

"It's too cold." Her voice was muffled behind the plastic curtain.

"It should be cool." The curtain snapped open and Katherine glared at him. Her hair hung around her face in limp strands. "Where the hell do you think you're going?" he roared as she attempted to step out of the tub.

"I'm going to catch my death in here."

Moving quickly, Julian picked her up and stepped into the tub. His shirt and slacks were pasted to his body as he held her head under the water. He forced her to fill her mouth with water. She coughed and spewed mucus.

Katherine flailed and fought him like a cat, but he held her firmly. Vanquished, she fell against his chest, sobbing. He stroked her wet hair. "Cry, darling. Let it all out."

She did cry. She cried for the sadness she had carried for the past six months. She cried for the loss of her innocence to a man so undeserving of the precious gift. And she cried for the dreams that would never come true.

She held on to Julian as if he had become her lifeline. Julian, her quiet, gentle brother-in-law. Lifting her chin, she stared at him staring down at her. Her lower lip trembled as much from the cool water beating over her body as from uncertainty.

How had she missed it? How hadn't she acknowledged

what had been apparent the moment Julian stepped out onto the porch to introduce himself. It was the first time that she had questioned whether she had married the wrong man.

Reaching up, she cradled Julian's face between her palms. Tears and water spiked her lashes. "Thank you for helping me to see what I have to do." Rising on tiptoe, she brushed her mouth over his.

The innocent gesture of gratitude sparked an inferno that roared through Julian like hot lava. Tightening his grip on her waist, he deepened the kiss.

Reaching around her, he turned off the water and hoisted her out of the tub. His heat spread to her as she climbed up his body like a cat in heat. He set her aside, stripping off his wet clothes; naked, he carried her back into the bedroom.

They fell on the bed, limbs entwined. Cradling her face, Julian pressed a kiss on her eyelids, tip of her nose and then her mouth. He charted a path down her body, and in his quest to stake his brand and possession he tasted every inch of her flesh.

Katherine gasped, moaning in delight. Julian's hands and mouth were magical. He kissed her behind her knees, under her armpits and along her spine. She writhed and groaned, unable to believe the sensations threatening to take her over the edge.

Everything she had ever experienced before paled in comparison as Julian eased his hardness into her throbbing flesh. He filled every inch of her. She gloried in the powerful thrusting of his hips and arched to meet every thrust, their bodies slamming into each other until it came to an end, her legs around his waist, fingernails biting into his firm buttocks and a piercing scream that faded in a lingering sigh of ultimate satisfaction.

Threading his fingers through Katherine's hair, Julian lowered his head and growled deep in his throat, spilling his love inside her.

In the aftermath of their passion he realized he'd repressed his desire for his brother's wife since coming under their roof.

Then the truth came upon him like a silent fog.

He was in love with Katherine.

NINETEEN

The days, hours, minutes, seconds sped by quickly, too quickly for Morgana. She showed the house to two couples. The elderly couple rejected it, declaring it was too large to maintain. A younger couple, both dentists in their mid-thirties, proclaimed it perfect. With one preschool-age child and another expected by the end of the year, they wanted to close and move in before the start of the new school year. A bank had preapproved them, which meant an early closing was imminent.

Most of her daylight hours were spent cataloguing and filling cartons with china, silver and beddings. Most nights she slept with Erick, making love or talking about every topic imaginable. What they refused to talk about was the future. It was as if that topic had become taboo.

She sat on the floor next to Erick in his studio, studying the prints he had taken of her. She was drawn to the poses of her in bed. They screamed sensuality.

Erick pointed to one. "I like this one." It was the one he had taken after he'd ravished her mouth. Her lips were swollen and pouty, her eyes half-closed in what could be interpreted as an expression of blatant seduction.

"I look like I'm modeling for those 1-900-SEX-ME-UP ads."

Rubbing her back, he kissed her ear. "What you look is wholly female. See the curve of your shoulder, the swell of breasts under the silk cover-up."

"I look wanton."

"That's because you are wanton. You try to downplay it with tailored clothes, but it's still there, Morgana. I prefer seeing you in a pair of jeans and a tank top. That way you leave nothing to the imagination about your femininity."

"Do you know you're good for a woman's ego?"

Erick eased her down to the floor. "No." Leaning closer, he brushed his mouth over hers. "I'm going to have to begin work on your painting if I want to finish before I leave."

She nodded. It was nearing the end of June. "How long do you think it's going to take you?"

"Probably three weeks. That means I have to work on it anytime I get a spare moment."

"I'll stay home nights so you can finish it."

"If you won't come here, then I'll come to you," he countered. "That's if you don't mind my coming to your place."

She smiled up at him. "I don't mind."

"If I'm really into it, then it may be late when I come by."

Curving her arms around his neck, she pulled his head to her chest. "Don't worry about the hour. Just come."

Erick swept her up off the floor and carried her to his bedroom. They had so few moments together—time was precious and fleeting.

Morgana spent the next afternoon on the glider reading.

March 4, 1953

Julian moved into his house yesterday. I am relieved, and I know he is, too. It has not been easy to see him every day and remain unaffected. We have not made love again since that night. It should never have happened.

Randolph and I have called a truce. He said now that Julian is no longer living with us we should try to get along with each other. He promises to spend more time at home. I did not say anything. He will have to prove it to me that he can change.

Daddy has not been feeling well lately. He complains of stomach discomfort, but refuses to see a doctor. I spoke to Mother about him, and she appeared totally disinterested. She said he has always complained about his stomach. I was somewhat put off by her apathy. I am noticing things about Mother that I had ignored in the past. She is more concerned about staying thin than with my father's health.

When Daddy comes for his Friday night poker game I am going to talk to him about his drinking and smoking.

Morgana gasped, rereading what Katherine had written: *We have not made love again since that night.*

Her mother had slept with her uncle!

Flipping pages, she scanned the dates and entries, coming to one that pulled her in.

April 29, 1953

Randolph and I have grown a little closer. He has kept his promise to spend more time at home. We still sleep in separate bedrooms.

This is of no import to me because I have been reading books on human sexuality and have learned to take care of my own physical needs. At first I felt uncomfortable stimulating myself, but that all changed the first time I brought myself to an orgasm. That one encounter with Julian taught me a lot about my own body. I have come to realize that foreplay is as gratifying as penetration.

I am going to surprise Randolph today. I prepared his favorite meal: pot roast with potatoes and carrots, brown gravy with mushrooms and cornbread.

He called from the funeral home to tell me he would be working late, so I decided to deliver it personally.

Katherine placed the picnic hamper on the passenger-side seat. She backed slowly out of the driveway, heading for downtown Salvation. The distance from her house and the funeral home took less than five minutes.

As she parked her car, she noticed there was one other car in the lot beside Randolph's. Picking up the hamper, she walked around to the side of the building to Randolph's private office. She inserted a key into the lock; the door opened easily. She was practically tiptoeing when she approached his office. The door was slightly ajar. Moving closer, she listened for a sign of movement.

"Do it to Daddy, Lenny."

Katherine froze, her eyes widening. The voice she heard coming from behind the door was Randolph's. He'd called someone Lenny. Realization dawned. He'd mumbled that name on their wedding night.

Shifting quietly, she peered through the slight opening. Standing with his hips braced against his desk, pants down around his ankles, was her husband. The woman kneeling in front of him had his penis in her mouth.

The sound of her licking and sucking him, and the look of unbridled pleasure on Randolph's face wouldn't permit Katherine to move. She stood, frozen in place as she watched the woman stand, raise her skirt and straddle Randolph's thighs. She bounced up and down on him, while he moaned deep in his throat, urging her to go faster.

She had seen enough!

Katherine didn't remember picking up the picnic hamper, closing the outer door, or returning to her car. She did not know how she drove with tears streaming down her face and obscuring her vision.

All she knew was that she couldn't go home. She did not want to see anything that reminded her of the man she'd married. She drove to Julian's house, but stayed in her car, staring through the windshield. She couldn't get out of the car and ring the doorbell. Yet she couldn't drive away.

Julian turned onto the road leading to his house and recognized Katherine's Thunderbird in the sweep of his car's headlights as he parked in the driveway. He got out of his car and peered through the window of Katherine's car. She was asleep, her head resting at an odd angle.

He tried her door, sighing in relief when it opened. He shook her gently. "Katherine."

She came awake, her eyes blinking rapidly. "Julian." His name came out in a sob.

"Shh-hh, darling. Come."

Katherine stepped out, collapsing against his body. She had come to him because he was all she had. He was the only one she could trust.

Julian carried her into his house and up the staircase to his bedroom. Combing his fingers through her hair, he stared at her red, swollen eyes. "What's the matter, Kat?"

She told him everything she had heard and seen. "I'm leaving him, Julian. I can't continue to live this way. Not with the lies and false promises."

Julian felt fingers of fear squeeze his heart. Didn't she know he was in love with her? That he would always love her, even from afar. "Where will you go?"

"I don't know. All I know is that it has to be away from Salvation."

"Let me talk to him."

"No, Julian. I don't want you to get involved."

"But I am involved, Katherine."

"What are you talking about?"

"I love you. If I hadn't been, I never would've slept with you."

Her eyes welled with moisture. "Why didn't you tell me before?"

"Because you're my brother's wife. I've broken two of the Lord's commandments by coveting my brother's wife and committing adultery." He stroked her cheek. "Let me talk to Randolph. I'll try to convince him to give you a divorce."

"And if he doesn't?"

"Then wherever you go I'll follow you."

She shook her head. "You can't, Julian. You just built a house, and you're in the process up setting up your practice. I can't let you sacrifice that for me."

"It's not for you, Katherine. It's for us."

Katherine tried weighing the events turning her life and world upside down. "Randolph won't give me a divorce. He considers me one of his prized possessions."

"He will after I talk to him."

There was something in Julian's gaze that frightened her. He radiated a danger that reminded her of Randolph. She touched his lean jaw. "No, Julian. I won't let you fight my battles. I'll confront him myself."

"When?"

"Soon."

"I want you to stay with me tonight."

"I can't stay here with you."

"Yes, you can." Reaching across her body, he picked up the telephone receiver on a table, and dialed the number to the funeral home.

"Katherine came to me because she's not feeling well. I don't believe it's anything to worry about. I'm suggesting she stay here tonight so I can monitor her. No, Randolph. There's no need for you to come by. I'm going to give her something to help her sleep. Sure. Good night."

He hung up, meeting Katherine's startled gaze. "You did it."

"I just told him the truth."

Rising to her knees, she hugged him. "I don't want anything to make me sleep."

Julian breathed a kiss under her ear. "What do you want?"

"You."

"Wait," he moaned as her hand swept up his inner thigh.

"I can't," she panted, unbuttoning his shirt.

Julian wanted to protect Katherine, but she would not be denied. Their coupling was filled with a furious passion. He entered her and she moaned his name. They both climaxed, he chanting her name as he left his seed in her body.

May 2, 1953

I refuse to speak to Randolph. He had the nerve to come home and greet me as if all was right in our world. He asked how I felt and I told him wonderful.

He presides over our table like a pompous ass, the image of respectability. He did not look so respectable with that woman on her knees with his DICK in her mouth! His precious Lenny can have him. I don't care if she sucks him dry. If he attempts to touch me ever again I'll cut him. The only place I have to decide is where.

May 30, 1953

Julian and I had our first big fight. I had promised him that I would talk to Randolph about granting me a divorce. However, the time is never right. Julian warned me, saying if I do not tell Randolph that we are in love with each other, then he will.

What frightens me more than confronting Randolph is that I suspect I am carrying Julian's baby. My menses is almost 2 weeks late. My breasts are fuller, the nipples so sensitive that I cannot bear to touch them. And if I am pregnant, then Randolph will definitely have to grant me a divorce.

Katherine sat in the waiting room with three other patients. The door opened, and a nurse said, "Mrs. Johnson."

She rose, following her into Julian's office. He stood up, seemingly shocked to see her. "Good afternoon, Katherine."

She offered him a small, shy smile. "Good afternoon, Julian."

He gestured to a chair in front of a large desk. "Please sit down. " His dark eyes followed her every gesture. "How can I help you?"

"My menses is late."

Julian recoiled as if he'd been struck across the face. "How late?"

Her gaze never wavered. "Two weeks."

He felt as if someone was sitting on his chest; if Katherine was pregnant, it had to be his child she was carrying. "I'm going to need a urine sample."

Opening a burlap bag, she set a small jar filled with yellow liquid on the desk. "I collected it this morning as soon as I got up."

Julian stared at the jar. "I'll send it over to the hospital for them to test it. I'll call you when I get the results."

"When will that be?"

"In a couple of days."

Morgana sat on the glider, eyes closed, her head resting on the cushioned back.

"My father is not my father. My uncle is my father."

Katherine had lied to her. Randolph had lied to her. Julian had lied to her. And how many more lies would she uncover before the final truth was told?

She did not want to blame Katherine for sleeping with Julian because Randolph was a son of a bitch. Not only had he hit Katherine, but he had also cheated on her, driving her into the arms of another man who happened to be his brother.

She opened her eyes, staring at the ivy climbing around the porch columns. The ancient trees shading the property were witness to a drama played out more than half a century before.

Katherine did not leave Salvation or divorce Randolph.

Julian also stayed in Salvation, unable to claim the fruit of his illicit affair with his brother's wife as his own.

"They were all losers," she whispered, although there was no one around to overhear her.

TWENTY

Julian maneuvered into the driveway as Morgana retrieved a stack of mail order catalogues from the mailbox on a post near the road. Tapping lightly on the horn, he waved to her.

She waited for him to alight from the sedan, her gaze sweeping over him. He knew she was his daughter, yet had relinquished his right as her father to another man. Angling his head, he smiled at her—a tender fatherly smile.

Closing the distance between them, Morgana hugged and kissed him. "How was your reunion?"

"Tiring. But I had a good time."

Curving her arm through his, she led him into the house. "Will you stay for dinner?"

"Of course." He stared at the many cartons crowding the living room. "You've been busy."

"I'm almost finished."

"Do you have a buyer?"

"Yes, a young black couple with one child, and another on the way. They're both dentists."

He nodded his approval. "We could use a few more dentists around here. Do you have a closing date?"

"They've set a tentative date for mid-August." She saw Julian staring at her with a strange expression on his face. "What's the matter?"

"You look wonderful." And she did. Her body was tanned, radiating an air of good health. Her hair had grown out, thick curls falling over her forehead and along the nape of her neck.

"I'm feeling much better, Uncle Julian. Inside and out."

Morgana knew exactly who she was, where she was going, and what she wanted to do with her life. Reading Katherine's journals and her relationship with Erick had helped in her journey of rediscovery.

"Why don't you wash up before my guest arrives."

Julian went completely still. "Look, Morgan, I don't have to stay."

"But I want you to stay. You know I always cook more than enough."

"It's not the food. I don't want to intrude."

Taking his hand, Morgana pulled him toward the small half-bath. "You would never be an intruder, Uncle Julian. Remember what you told me about blood being thicker than water. You're blood and my guest is water."

Julian washed his hands, staring at his reflection in the mirror over the sink. He hadn't enjoyed his stay on Hilton Head because he knew Katherine wouldn't be waiting for him upon his return. When he wasn't grieving the loss of his best friend he'd agonized over her daughter, praying Morgana would find the elusive peace within her grasp.

He heard a strange male voice and hesitated before returning to the kitchen. He'd hoped the guest was Franklin. Pulling back his shoulders, he entered the kitchen. He studied the tall slender man, dressed entirely in black, talking quietly with Morgana.

She glanced up. "Here's my uncle." Reaching for Erick's hand, she led him to Julian. "Erick, Julian Johnson. Julian, Erick Wilson." The two men shook hands, while exchanging polite greetings.

"Morgana told me you are a doctor."

Julian gave Erick a direct stare. "I'm a retired doctor. And what do you do, young man?"

"I teach art."

"Where?"

"At SCAD. I'm a visiting instructor."

"When are you leaving?"

"Uncle Julian!" Morgana had registered the censure in his voice.

Erick held up a hand, stopping her protest. "It's okay, Morgana. My last day is August eighth. I'm driving back to California the next day."

"So, you're from the West Coast?" Julian's voice had taken on a softer quality.

"Yes, sir."

Morgana tapped Julian's arm. "Why don't you fix Erick a drink? We should be ready to sit down to eat in twenty minutes."

"Can I get something for you, Morgan?"

"No, thank you. I'll wait."

Morgana breathed a sigh of relief after Julian led Erick away. Without warning, Julian's paternal instincts had surfaced. She would be fifty years old in February and the man whom she had always regarded as a surrogate father had felt the need to protect her from a strange man. If the secret behind her paternity hadn't been so shocking, she would have laughed hysterically.

Dinner had become a friendly, relaxed affair. Morgana had prepared orange-ginger Cornish hens stuffed with wild rice, julienne string beans with slivers of toasted almonds and a salad of field greens tossed with a garlic-vinaigrette.

Erick did most of the talking. "I'm working on a painting with Morgana as the subject."

Julian raised his snow-white eyebrows. "I'd like to see it."

"You will once I complete it."

"Do you plan to show it?"

"No. I'm giving it to your niece as a gift."

"Bernice and I plan to display some of Erick's photographs at The Registry," Morgan added, deftly changing the subject. She wasn't anxious to have Julian view a painting of her scantily clad body.

Angling his head, Julian smiled at Erick. "You must be very talented."

"That's not for me to say, sir."

"Don't be so modest," Morgana chided softly. "He happens to be incredibly talented."

Julian stared at the food on his plate, wondering which talents Morgana was extolling. It was obvious the young artist had put the fire back in her eyes and glow in her cheeks. He was grateful that Erick had come along when he did, but despite Franklin's philandering Julian wanted Morgana to reconcile with her husband. They shared children and a legacy—a legacy that would continue long after he ceased to exist.

Touching a napkin to his mouth, he pushed back his chair. "I'm going to pass on dessert tonight. I'm still a little fatigued from my drive back." Reaching across the table, he offered Erick his hand. "It's been a pleasure."

Erick leaned over and shook his hand. "I'm honored to have met you."

Morgana stood up. "I'll walk you to the door."

Julian affected a frown. "I'm not so old that I can't find my way to the door unaided." Leaning over, he kissed her cheek. "Thank you for dinner. It was delicious, as usual."

"I'll give you a few days to settle back in your routine before I come visiting."

Erick stared at Morgana as she watched Julian's retreating figure. "Your uncle is an elegant man," he intoned reverently.

"He has always been that way. Quiet, gentle, and very humble."

"Do you think he knows?"

She looked at Erick. "Knows what?"

"That I've been sleeping with his niece."

"I'm not sure."

Erick wanted to tell Morgana that Julian saw him as an interloper, a temporary obstacle to her reconciling with her husband. A small part of him wanted her to go back to her husband. There were too many innocent victims of divorce. He was also selfish enough to want her for himself, hoping and praying she would consider relocating to California.

He cleared his throat. "I've decided not to stay over. I'll probably stay up late painting."

Morgana was not surprised. She was mature and realistic enough to know what she and Erick shared was nearing its conclusion; she could not see herself waiting for August to experience sexual and or emotional withdrawal.

"I don't think we should see each other so often anymore."

"Why, Morgana?"

"It's not going to get easier the closer we get to the day of reckoning—at least not for me."

"For you?"

"Okay. Us."

Erick flashed a sad smile. "I'll go along with whatever you want."

She bit down on her lower lip to still its trembling. "Thank you."

Morgana lay in bed reading later that night.

June 5, 1953

I am pregnant. My lover, the father of my unborn child, confirmed the results of my urine test three days ago. I did not know whether to laugh or cry. Laugh because I have always wanted a baby. Cry because I live with a man whom I have come to detest.

I am waiting for Randolph to come home to tell him. It is certain to change all our lives.

Katherine sat on the edge of the sofa in the living room, waiting for Randolph. From her vantage point, she would see him the moment he walked through the door.

She heard the key in the lock, the fall of the tumblers. Sitting up straighter, she watched the door open slowly.

He stepped into the entryway, weaving unsteadily.

Rising off the cushion, she took one step, then another.

Randolph's gait was off, as if one leg were shorter than the other.

He saw her, a lopsided grin twisting his mouth. "What do we have here? Up waiting for me, baby?"

Katherine's impassive expression did not change. "Yes, Randolph, I've been waiting for you."

He leered at her. "If I want you to move back into the bedroom, then the answer is yes."

"You're drunk and delusional. I don't want you, Randolph. What I want is a divorce."

He took a step, arms flailing before he regained his balance. "Divorce?" Saliva sprayed from his mouth. "Did I hear you say d–divorce?"

Her fingers curled into tight fists. "Yes, Randolph. I said divorce."

Randolph made it over to an armchair, falling and nearly upending it before he sat. Slouching, his legs sprawled in front of him, he shook his head from side to side. "No, Katherine. That cannot happen. I bought you, and I don't give refunds."

She went completely still, not even to blink. "What are you talking about?" Randolph sat motionless, his chin resting on his chest. "Answer me!" she shouted.

His head came up slowly, dark deep-set eyes glittering dangerously. "Who the hell do you think you're talking to?"

Katherine folded her hands on her hips. "I don't see anyone else, so I must be talking to you."

Bracing his hands on the arms of the chair, Randolph pushed to his feet. Glaring, he showed his teeth. "I'm going to give you two minutes to get out of my sight. If not, then I'm going to beat—"

"No, you are *not,*" she said quietly, interrupting him. "You will not touch me, and you *are* going to give me a divorce."

A flash of humor suddenly softened the harsh lines in his face. "You must be sick, Katherine. You're talking out of your head."

She knew it was time she brought the verbal sparring to an end. "I'm pregnant, Randolph."

Rocking back and forth, he closed his eyes, grinning. "You're pregnant? Pregnant," he whispered as if measuring the word. He opened his eyes. "You're having a baby?"

Pulling back her shoulders, Katherine nodded slowly. "Yes, Randolph. I am having a baby."

She never saw him move. His hands snaked around her throat, cutting off precious air to her lungs. "No!" he bellowed like a wounded animal. "Whore! Bitch!"

Katherine clawed at his hands, drawing blood. She had to free herself or he would choke her to death. His face swam before her eyes. "Don't!" She could not hear her own voice because of the roaring sound in her ears.

Randolph shook Katherine as if she were a rag doll, his eyes bulging. The color in her face had changed from red to blue, and without warning he released her throat.

"I will not give another man's bastard my name."

Gasping and holding her bruised throat, Katherine backpedaled, stopping when the back of her knees hit the sofa. She knew she had to get away from him before he hurt her.

"I want a divorce." Her voice came out in a croaking sound. "And you don't have to concern yourself with the baby's name, because it will be a Johnson."

Something she said sobered Randolph as if he'd been doused with icy-cold water. His gaze narrowed. "What?"

Katherine's bravado returned. "The baby I carry is a Johnson."

Randolph stared at the woman he had coveted from the moment his gaze caressed her face. She had been a beautiful girl and had bloomed into a beautiful woman. Katherine was his. He'd bought her. Didn't she know he owned her, and that he would never let her go?

"What are you talking about?"

Raising her chin, she fought the urge to touch her bruised neck. "I'm in love with Julian. It's his child I'm carrying."

Randolph repeated her words to himself. A red haze shimmered before his shocked gaze as he turned and stumbled to the door. Standing on the porch, he stared at the night sky and bellowed, "No! I'm going to kill him!" The threat echoed in Randolph's head as he made his way to his car. He was going to kill Julian for taking what belonged to him.

He continued to shout as he fell into his car, turned the key, and backed out of the driveway. He drove, accelerating until the speedometer inched close to ninety miles per hour. When he glanced into the rearview mirror, he thought he saw someone in the backseat laughing at him.

He shook his head. There couldn't be anyone in the car with him. It was just his imagination. It was the liquor. He had drunk too much at the party and he was hallucinating. But whenever he looked into the mirror he could see the gaping mouth and hear the maniacal laughing. They were chasing him. The faster he went the closer they came.

"No! Get away!" It was as if all the demons in hell were following him. They were out to get him. They wanted to kill him.

Randolph laughed and jerked the wheel to the right. He would outsmart them. He would take another route. One they did not know. He left the paved road for a narrow rutted path. It was the longer route to Julian's but that no longer mattered. He had outrun the demons.

He reversed direction and did not see the dark object blocking the road. The front end of the Jaguar slammed into a fallen tree trunk, before flipping over and coming to rest in a swamp.

Randolph held his chest, believing his heart was pumping outside his body. He had crashed his precious car, but he was still alive. The car had landed on its right side. If only he could open his door, he would be able to get out.

It took two attempts before he was able to open the door. A warm sticky substance trickled down his cheek into his mouth. He tasted it. It was blood. Reaching up, he touched his head. It was wet, wet with his blood. He wasn't sure where he was, but knew he had to get back to the road where he could flag down someone to take him to the hospital.

Randolph fell out of the car, breathing heavily. He lay on the damp ground, gathering strength. Pushing off his elbows, he attempted to stand, but his legs wouldn't support his weight. He tried it again, falling back to the ground. His legs refused to work. He did not understand why he couldn't stand up. There was no pain in his legs.

He crawled on his elbows for more than an hour, pulling the rest of his body along through the odorous earth littered with rotting leaves and wildlife waste before his world went completely dark.

TWENTY-ONE

July 10, 1953

Randolph is coming home today after spending more than a month in the hospital. He has been examined and evaluated by every prominent neurologist in the state, and their finding is the same: he will never walk again. Once I heard the news I cursed God for not making me a widow.

It has taken time, but I have asked for forgiveness because I have sinned. I lay down with another man, my husband's brother, and now I am carrying a child from that sinful union. I have not spoken the word divorce since that eventful night. No matter how great the love I feel for Julian, I know I cannot leave Randolph.

Katherine stood in the entryway, watching two men carry wheelchair-bound Randolph up the porch steps. He sat in the chair, head bowed, arms hanging limply over the armrests.

"Where do you want him, ma'am?"

"Please follow me."

She had rearranged the furniture in Randolph's library to accommodate his physical limitations. A hospital bed replaced his desk, a table and several chairs. A closet was converted to a bath with a commode and shower stall.

Mrs. Pitt stood next to the bed, hands folded to her chest in a prayerful gesture. She blinked back tears. "Welcome home, Mr. Randolph."

Randolph's head came up slowly. He smiled at her. "Thank you, Mrs. Pitt. I must admit it's good to be back home."

The housekeeper gave Katherine a hopeful look. "I'll take care of him now, Mrs. Johnson. Why don't you go sit down and put your feet up? You look tired."

"I am." She offered the older woman a warm smile. "Thank you, Mrs. Pitt."

Katherine walked up the staircase, hoping she would make it to her bedroom before her legs gave out. Being pregnant had drained every ounce of energy she could muster, and sitting in the hospital for hours had taken its toll on her legs and ankles. They were frightfully swollen.

She would accept Mrs. Pitt's advice and assistance, knowing she had to take care of herself. Come February not only would she have to care for an invalid husband, but also a new baby.

Julian walked into the living room, and Katherine felt a shiver of excitement ripple through her body. Just seeing him still made her ache. She loved and missed him so much.

They hadn't been alone since the night before Randolph's accident. During the past month he had come to the hospital to see Randolph and confer with the specialists. But at no time had she sought him out—until now.

Julian's gaze was fixed on Katherine as she sat several feet from his brother. A smile touched his mouth. Impending motherhood agreed with her, he thought. She glowed.

Katherine returned his smile. "Please sit down, Julian." She waited for him to take a chair facing her and Randolph. "I wanted us to meet because I feel we must clear up a few things." The two men looked at each other.

"I'm pregnant," she continued, "and unless I miscarry I look forward to delivering a child early February. The child I carry is a Johnson; nothing can change that. However, I'm faced with a dilemma because while I'm in love with one man and carry his child I'm still legally married to another."

She turned to stare at Randolph. "I came to you, asking for a divorce, and you refused. Perhaps if you had consented you would not be confined to that chair. I don't love you. In fact, I despise you. But you are still my husband. I'm saying all of this because I've had to search my conscience and pray for guidance to come to this decision."

Randolph's expression did not change. He had had more than a month to come to grips with the fact that he would never walk again. He had thought Katherine hypocritical when she came to see him every day, sitting by his bedside like a loyal, grieving wife. He'd called her a whore because that's what she was. She had whored with his brother right under his nose. She despised him and he despised her.

Katherine's gaze shifted to Julian. "I will not leave Randolph. Not as long as he is alive or confined to a wheelchair. I will have your baby, but you will have no claim to it."

Randolph's smile was triumphant. "You lost all around, Julian."

Julian felt as if he had been conspired against. His hands tightened into fists. He had lost everything: the woman he loved and his child. He glared at Randolph. "You son of a bitch!" He shot up, reaching for Randolph, but Katherine moved quickly, holding on to his arm.

"No, Julian! Please."

He stared at her. Tears filled her eyes. "How can you do this, Katherine?"

"What else is there for me to do? Do I divorce Randolph and marry you? Or do I stay with Randolph and tell everyone that the child I carry is yours? We are living in Salvation, Georgia. Everyone knows everyone's business. How long would you have a practice if the word got out that you slept with your brother's wife?" Tears were running down her cheeks.

She turned to Randolph. "You're wrong about Julian being a loser. You're the loser, Randolph. You've lost me, and any love I've ever had for you. I'm not ashamed to admit that I love Julian. I will love him with my dying breath. And the child I carry will be a Johnson, but it will never be yours."

She released Julian's arm and walked out of the room.

Julian stared at the floor. Katherine's statement had cut deep. She was still alive, yet he had lost her. Lost her to a man so undeserving of her loyalty.

His head came up slowly. "Katherine had her say, and you yours. Now it's my turn. I'm not leaving Salvation, Randolph. I'm going to stay here and watch my son or daughter grow to maturity. I'm going to practice medicine until I get tired, then I'm going to take down my shingle.

"I love Katherine and I know I will love her forever. And if you should leave this earth before I do, then I'm going to spend whatever time I have left giving her the happiness she so rightfully deserves."

Bitterness distorted Randolph's features. "Even though I'm sitting in this wheelchair, I'm still the better man, little brother, because I have what you want. And I'm not going to make it easy for you by dying. If that were going to happen I never would've crawled out of that car.

"I'm going to live a long, long time. And every time you hear your son or daughter call me Papa you will be reminded that not only do I claim your woman but also your child."

Bending over, Julian thrust his face close to Randolph's. "You were never a man, *brother.* If you were it would be your seed in Katherine's body, not mine. And every time she stays out late or fails to come home you'll wonder whether she's with me." He felt perverted pleasure in seeing shock in Randolph's eyes. "I'm not going to lie and say if she does come to me that I will send her away. I will accept her anywhere, anytime or anyplace. What I will do is make certain she will not get pregnant again. I won't permit her to become the brunt of gossip when folks whisper about how can she get pregnant from a man who is dead below the waist."

Straightening, Julian turned, walked out of the house, closing the door on his past.

Closing the book, Morgana could not stop her hands from trembling. Randolph had used and abused Katherine, yet she had stayed with him.

Had she stayed out of guilt, a commitment to her wedding vows, or because of small-town gossip?

She raced out of the house to her car. Reading the entries had evoked too many memories. Events she had forgotten came rushing back: the prolonged periods of silence between Katherine and Randolph, her mother's disappearing acts, and the tension between Randolph and Katherine whenever Julian was present.

Morgana arrived at the lake, maneuvering her car into the last available space. Walking along the path she found a bench, and sat down. The area was teeming with life: children chasing one another, couples boating, barking dogs chasing ducks and geese, and lovers exchanging kisses in secluded spaces behind shrubs and trees.

It wasn't what she saw that shocked her as much as what she felt. She had slept with a man other than her husband for the first time in thirty years, and in doing so had rediscovered passion.

And in reading her mother's journals, she had discovered her biological father.

Franklin was an adulterer.

Katherine was an adulteress.

Julian had coveted his brother's wife.

Randolph was an adulterer.

I'm not perfect, she mused. She was not the perfect daughter, wife or mother. She'd become judgmental and unforgiving. How could she expect forgiveness if she did not forgive?

Could she forgive Franklin? Go back to Chevy Chase to pick up the pieces of her life as if there had been no pause? Only time would tell because she had less than three weeks to make a decision.

She returned to her car, driving without purpose or direction. Three quarters of an hour later she found herself standing over her mother's grave. The words on the gravestone were branded into her brain: *Katherine Faith Graham Johnson: Wife, Patient and Loving Mother.*

Katherine had selected her own inscription. When Morgana had insisted it read *Wife of Randolph,* Katherine had snapped at her. She had left explicit written instructions that she not be buried in the same plot as Randolph. His remains lay in a plot next to his parents.

Now, Morgana thought, *where do I bury Julian?*

She searched the cemetery for the graves of her grand- and great-grandparents. There had been a time when there were so many family members, and now there was one: Julian.

"Daddy," she whispered, testing the word. She'd called Randolph Papa, but she knew instinctively Julian would have been Daddy.

Erick opened the door to her knock. He seemed shocked to see her. "May I come in?"

"Of course. I . . . I didn't expect to see you again."

Morgana stepped into the minuscule entryway, smiling. "I know we agreed not to meet." She blew out her breath.

Erick ran his fingers along her cheek. "What's the matter?"

"I need someone to talk to."

Grasping her hand, he led her into his bedroom. They lay across the bed, Morgana curved along the length of his body. An oscillating fan in a corner did little to dispel the sultry Savannah humidity.

Dropping a kiss on the top of her head, Erick held her until she felt comfortable enough to tell him everything she had read in her mother's journals.

"The man who I thought was my uncle is my father."

"I suspected that," Erick stated smugly.

Pulling away from him, Morgana sat up. "How?"

His eyes sparkled with amusement. "You have to be a guy to recognize when you're being interrogated by a girl's father. And it doesn't matter how old she is. Daddy just wants to protect his baby girl."

Morgana laughed softly. "What else did you pick up?"

"He wants you to go back to your husband."

She sobered. "Did he tell you that?"

"He didn't have to, Morgana. You're all he has left and he wants to make certain you're protected."

"Protected?"

He nodded. "Even the most liberated woman needs a man's protection. Whether you want to acknowledge it or not, your husband has protected you physically, financially and emotionally."

She pondered Erick's statement. Winding her arms around his waist, she kissed his mouth. "I'm going to miss you."

He closed his eyes and nodded. He did not have to ask the question. She had given him his answer. "I should be finished with the painting sometime next week. You still don't want to see it?"

"No." Her voice was muffled against his chest. "I want to be surprised."

"I'm certain you will be surprised."

"Bernice called to tell me your prints are selling faster than any new item in the shop. You should leave me a forwarding address for the reorders."

"There are not going to be any reorders."

Morgana sat up again, lines appearing between her eyes. "Why not?"

"I gave you those as a gift, and you chose to sell them."

"I didn't sell all of them. I still have my copies."

He ran a finger down the length of her nose then leaned forward and kissed her. "Then you'd better hold on to them. They may be worth more than a few pennies one day."

"What aren't you telling me?"

"A publisher is interested in buying them for a large coffee table book."

"Oh, Erick!" She straddled him, kissing his face. "That's wonderful. We should go out and celebrate."

He held her arms, shaking his head. "No, Morgana. No more celebrating. You're the one who said we have to pull back. I agreed to it because I know in the end it's for the best. I love you. Not the all-consuming passion that makes people crazy, but a gentle, healing love has allowed me to offer a prayer of thanks because I'm alive. A love that taught me that I can love again, and maybe I'll find that special woman who will want to share my life and a future with me."

Her gaze moved slowly over his face, committing to memory his neatly twisted hair, flat cheekbones, long narrow nose, and the stubborn set of his strong chin. "I will never forget you, Erick. You've taught me a lot about myself." She pressed her open lips to his. "I've heard that a woman can't love two men. Whoever said that is wrong. I love you." She kissed him again.

He didn't try to stop her as she slid off the bed. He was still sitting in the same position long after she drove away. Folding his arms behind his head, he lay down and stared up at the cracks in the ceiling.

A wide smile curved his mouth. Morgana Johnson had streaked into his life like a falling star. She was there and then she was gone. He hoped her husband would appreciate his second chance at happiness.

"Don't blow it again, fool," he said softly.

He knew she was going back to her husband. She needed

him and he needed her. They had shared too much not to give their marriage a second chance.

His chest rose and fell heavily as he expelled a lungful of air. "Good-bye, Morgana, and good luck."

TWENTY-TWO

Morgana's eyes were burning but she couldn't stop reading.

November 4, 1976

I have been a widow for three months. More than enough time to mourn a man I did not love. It took more than a month for me to believe that I was free. Free to live and to love without guilt.

All of the Johnsons have left Salvation—everyone but Julian. Miss Mattie called her sons' wives "ungrateful heifers" who would have never had anything if it weren't for Randolph. Three months after Miss Mattie cursed her daughters-in-law she died of a massive heart attack. Randolph Sr. followed four months later. People were saying that someone put a curse on the Johnsons.

Julian is coming for dinner. It has been a long time.

Katherine opened the door, smiling up at Julian. "Please, come in."

Julian noticed the bouquet of flowers on the table in the entryway. The vase was filled with yellow roses. He handed her a bouquet.

"I keep forgetting you grow your own."

She took the flowers. "I can never get enough yellow roses."

He stared at the hair brushing her shoulders. She had cut her waist-length hair. He sniffed the air. "I smell lamb."

Katherine smiled at him over her shoulder. "I remembered it was your favorite."

Reaching out, he caught her arm and turned her to face him. "I've missed you, Katherine."

She moved into his embrace, her arms curving around his neck. "Not as much as I've missed you." She kissed him tentatively, as if she feared he would disappear. "Come," she urged, leading him to the staircase.

Julian followed her to the second floor and into the bedroom where he had made love to her the first time. They took their time undressing each other, loving each other with all of their senses.

When Katherine finally felt him moving in her, she sighed. It felt so good. She had waited so long for this moment.

Their passions peaked at the same time and afterward they lay motionless, listening to the other's heart.

Cradling her face between his palms, Julian brushed a kiss over her mouth. "I love you."

She smiled, nodding. "And I'll love you to my dying breath."

Morgana packed the journals in a box, each volume telling a story of its own. She had opened the door to the past, devouring the secrets and yearnings like a voyeur.

The third volume began with Katherine giving birth to a daughter. She and Julian, not Randolph, had named her. Morgan was Julian's middle name, so she had become Morgana Katherine Johnson.

It had taken Morgana a week to read all of the journals. She existed on four hours of sleep because she wanted to finish them all before she returned to Maryland.

She had thought about burning them, then changed her mind. She would pack them away for the next generation to read.

The doorbell chimed, startling her. She closed the box and raced down the stairs. The bell chimed again. "I'm coming." Opening the door, she stood there, shocked.

"Hello, Mo. I hope I haven't caught you at a bad time."

She blinked. "No, Franklin. In fact, it's a good time. Please, come in."

Morgana took her time closing the door in an attempt to slow down her runaway heart. He was in the living room, standing amid dozens of labeled boxes when she strolled in. Nothing in her expression mirrored her shock of seeing him. Bernice was right. He had lost weight, a lot of weight. However, it did not detract from his overall attractiveness. A short, neatly barbered salt-and-pepper beard added fullness to his lean face.

"We'll sit in the kitchen."

Franklin breathed a sigh of relief. He had expected Morgana to send him packing again. His gaze caressed the curves in her body as he followed her into the kitchen. She looked different. Hell, she looked damn good.

"You look good, Mo." He spoke his thoughts aloud.

"Thank you. I feel good." She opened the refrigerator door. "Can I offer you something to drink?"

Franklin wanted to tell Morgana that he wasn't a stranger whom she had to impress. He was her husband. "What do you have?"

"Water, iced tea, and wine."

"Wine."

Morgana placed a bottle of Chardonnay on the countertop along with two glasses. The gesture was so automatic that she hadn't realized it until she'd filled the first glass. It had been a ritual with them that they would never drink alone. Sitting on a stool opposite Franklin, she lifted her glass and took a sip. The chilled liquid slid down the back of her throat, settling in her chest. Within the span of one magical minute she felt relaxed enough to challenge Franklin.

Waiting until he had taken a sip, she peered closely at him. "Why are you here, Franklin?"

"I came because I want you to forgive me."

Morgana wanted to tell him that she had already forgiven him. "Forgive you for what?"

"For my deceit, and for being a fool." He put the wineglass to his mouth, draining it in one swallow. "I'm sorry, Mo. I don't know how else to say it."

She refilled his glass before topping off her own. "You said it."

His jaw dropped. "What?"

Turning her head, she hid a smile. "I said you said it. I accept your apology."

His hands were shaking as he gulped down his second glass of wine. "Give me another one."

Morgana shook her head. "No, Franklin. I don't want you getting drunk on me. Have you eaten?"

"Yes . . . I mean, no."

She gave him a tender smile. "Neither have I. Give me a few minutes to change."

Franklin reached for Morgana's glass, then changed his mind. She was right. He didn't want to get drunk. Burying his face in his hands, he tried holding back the hot tears welling up behind his eyelids. He hadn't believed it was going to be that easy.

When he felt her warmth beside him, he dropped his hands and turned on the stool. Morgana stared at him, her gaze filled with concern.

"Are you all right, Franklin?" He shook his head, his face collapsing. Pride, ego and cockiness fled as he laid his head on her shoulder and cried.

Morgana wrapped her arms around his neck, pulling his face to her breasts. "It's okay, darling. Whatever happened is in the past. It's behind us. Now it's time to go forward."

Franklin cried until spent. Morgana handed him a towel. He blotted the moisture from his face, experiencing relief rather than shame. Cradling his face between her soft, cool palms, she brushed a light kiss over his mouth.

"Would it bother you if we didn't go out to eat? The truth is I'm exhausted. My flight was canceled and I had to wait four hours before I could get on another one."

"No, Franklin, I don't mind. Why don't you go up and bed down for the night."

Moving closer, he kissed her. "Thank you. I love you," he crooned.

"I know."

Morgana dropped her hands. She picked up her glass of wine and sipped it. She sat on the stool long after she'd emptied the glass. Finally, when the clock over the sink chimed midnight, she climbed the staircase to the second level.

The lamp on the table in her bedroom illuminated the

space. She stared at the bed where she'd slept as a child, where she'd slept with Franklin as her husband, and where she sometimes lay when reading her mother's secret desires.

The bed was empty.

Walking down the hall, she peered into another bedroom. The glow from a near-full moon illuminated her husband, who lay on his back, naked. She smiled. Franklin had always slept in the buff.

She turned, retreating to her bedroom. It would take a long time for them to rebuild the trust, but not as long for them to fall in love all over again.

After sharing dinner with Morgana and Franklin at a new soul food restaurant in Savannah, Julian drove them back to Katherine's house. "Morgan, are you expecting a delivery?" Julian asked, when he spotted a package on the porch.

"No." She waited for Franklin to open the door for her. A large package wrapped in brown paper lay against a post on the porch. "I wonder who could've sent it."

"I'll get it," Franklin volunteered, picking up the box. "It's addressed to you, Mo."

Her name was written in a familiar calligraphy. It was from Erick. "It's a painting."

Franklin looked at her. "You ordered a painting?"

"No. Someone did a painting of me. Open it up, Franklin."

Julian and Franklin sat on the porch, staring at the oil Erick had done of her. Julian shook his head while Franklin stared, slack-jawed.

Morgana was equally shocked. Erick hadn't missed a detail. He'd painted every eyelash, freckle, curve and muscle in her body. The sensual drape of the blood-red shawl, the mysterious green centers in her gray eyes, and the vibrant color of her just-kissed lips screamed wantonness.

Franklin's stunned gaze shifted from the painting to his wife and back again. She looked like a woman who had just been made love to.

Julian broke the silence, saying, "I'm not a gambling man, but I'm willing to bet that boy's work is going to hang in a museum before long."

"I believe you're right, Uncle Julian." She stood up. "Franklin, please put it in the living room when you come in. I'll pack it up later."

Julian pushed to his feet. "I'd better be getting back home. The Braves are playing the Mets tonight."

Franklin nodded. "Good night, Julian."

Julian waved at him. "Good night, son."

Morgana stood under the spray of the shower, luxuriating in the pulsing waters beating down on her shoulders. A sly smile softened her mouth as she thought about the painting she planned to hang in her sitting room in Maryland.

Her smile vanished when the curtains around the tub opened. Franklin stood motionless, naked, staring at her. "Do you mind if I join you?"

Morgana nodded. He stepped in, pulling the curtains around them. He covered her breasts with his hands, cradling and measuring their weight.

"You are magnificent, Mo." His lids and voice lowered. "In and out of bed."

Moving closer, her legs sandwiched between his, Morgana kissed Franklin, her tongue slipping into his mouth and simulating his hardness sliding in and out of her body.

Groaning deep in his throat, Franklin lifted her and pushed into her heat. They moaned in unison. Time stood still as they reconciled with each other in the most intimate way possible.

Franklin couldn't believe what he had missed. This woman above all women never failed to take him to heaven and back. He loved her hard and long, and when their passions soared, they screamed out their release, swallowing the other's breath.

He slid down to the bottom of the tub, taking Morgana with him. Staring up at her he recognized the same expression she'd had in the painting.

The water pouring down on them had cooled, but neither seemed to notice. Morgana laid her head on his shoulder. "I love you."

"I know," he whispered.

Her head came up and she gave him a dazzling smile. His gaze softened as a knowing expression flittered over his face. "Do you want to know something?"

"What, darling?"

His dark burning eyes would not permit her to move, breathe. "Now, we are even."

EPILOGUE

Morgana opened the door, dropping her handbag on a chair. "I'm back." Her voice carried easily in the expansive kitchen.

Franklin met her, helping her out of her jacket. He kissed her. "Your mouth is cold."

She snuggled against his warmth. "That's not all that's cold. Don't, Franklin," she gasped as his hand searched under her skirt. "You keep forgetting we don't live alone."

Morgana had convinced her uncle to leave Salvation and live with her and Franklin. He'd balked for several months after she had closed on Katherine's house, then without warning he changed his mind, asking if her invitation was still open. He admitted he liked Maryland, except for the cold weather.

Franklin hung her jacket in a closet off the kitchen. "Sandra called from the car. She and Kenneth picked up my mother and are on their way over."

"Where's Justin?"

"He's still asleep."

A frown marred her forehead. "There can't be that much jet lag in the world. He's been asleep for at least twelve hours."

"His circadian rhythms are all screwed up. Remember he was in the Philippines before he flew back to the States yesterday."

"I just don't want him to miss dinner. It's been a long time since we've had our families together at one time." It was Christmas Eve, and she and Franklin had opened their home for a festive gathering.

Curving an arm around her waist, Franklin pulled Morgana to his chest. He couldn't believe how much his life had changed in six months. He'd cut back on his hours at the firm, hadn't slept over at the hotel since the night of Katherine's passing, and had moved his elderly mother into a nearby housing complex for assisted living. She, like Julian, complained of the cold weather. However, she hadn't complained so much that she wanted to move back to Birmingham. Even his relationship with his sisters had improved. They called weekly to check on their mother.

The doorbell rang and Morgana glanced at her watch. "That must be the caterers."

"Relax, Mo. You go upstairs and change. I'll take care of everything."

"Are you sure?"

He kissed her again. "Of course I'm sure."

"If you guys are going to stand there and suck face, then I'll get the door." Franklin and Morgana sprang apart, smiling at their son. Justin winked at them. "A word of caution. Not too much screaming tonight. Especially with everyone sleeping over."

Morgana buried her face against Franklin's chest to hide the blush in her cheeks. He patted her back in a comforting gesture. "It's all right, baby. He's just jealous."

She peered up at him. "No, he's not!"

"Your son's idea of action is taking off and landing on a carrier."

"Why is he *my son?"*

"Because Sandra has always been *my daughter."*

Morgana nodded in agreement. "I'll see you later."

Morgana sat at the table in an enclosed patio, clasping hands with Justin on her right and Sandra on her left. Her voice, though soft, carried easily in the large room. Blinking multicolored lights from a towering Christmas tree outside the glass walls added to the festive atmosphere.

"And finally, watch over everyone gathered at this table. The mothers." She smiled at her mother-in-law. "Fathers." Her gaze settled on Franklin before it shifted to Julian, who had bowed his head. "Uncle. Sisters, brothers, sons and daughters. Amen."

Julian raised his head and his gaze met Morgana's. He gloried in the shared moment.

It had taken fifty years for him to claim his daughter. She didn't know he was her father, and those who did were gone.

It had been their secret, but now it was his and his alone. A secret he would carry to his grave. A secret never told.

Secrets Never Told

Rochelle Alers

A Reading Group Guide

ABOUT THIS GUIDE

The suggested questions are intended to help your reading group find new and interesting angles and topics for discussion for Rochelle Alers's *Secrets Never Told*. We hope that these ideas will enrich your conversation and increase your enjoyment of the book.

Reading Group Guide for *Secrets Never Told*

1. Who is the book's narrator? Why does the author set the story in a town called Salvation? Who finds salvation there? Pick a passage and share how the author uses description and setting to tell the story.

2. What are the secrets never told? Why does Edward make the deal with Randolph?

3. Describe Franklin, Morgana, Randolph, and Katherine as if you are describing them to a friend. Share what they look like, their habits, where they come from, and what kind of people they are.

4. What are the parallels between the marriages of Franklin and Morgana and Katherine and Randolph? How do the couples' sexual relations relate to the functioning of their marriages?

5. To what is Morgana referring when she says of Katherine, "even in death she affected a mysterious

smile"? When did you realize that Morgana Johnson-Wells is Julian's daughter? Share whether or not you are surprised to be more involved, early on, in Katherine's story rather than Morgana's. Why does Rochelle Alers construct the book this way?

6. How could Morgana have missed the signs that Franklin was fooling around? Discuss why his cheating may not have had anything to do with his wife. Why would he cheat if he believes his marriage to be "something sacred, something so vital"?

7. Look at the paragraph in Chapter 3 that describes Katherine's hair. Discuss what information is imparted and what puzzle pieces of the story are put in place.

8. How does Morgana treat Franklin after she learns of his philandering? Share whether or not you believe she still loves him, and why. What does it mean that Morgana celebrates her 28th wedding anniversary with another man? Discuss Franklin's unraveling after he visits Morgana on their anniversary.

9. Why does the author utilize diaries in *Secrets Never Told?* What does Morgana learn from the diaries? How do they affect her life? Discuss whether or not you keep a diary and how you would feel if someone looked at it now as well as after your passing. What would you do if you found the diaries of one of your parents?

10. Why is Katherine so repulsed by Randolph? Even though Randolph didn't tell Katherine about "winning" her, does Katherine know about it? Looking at Katherine's journal entry in Chapter 12, what does she say about her life with Randolph? About her feelings about gambling?

11. Share your reaction to Katherine being Randolph's prize. Is Randolph's attraction based on Katherine's hair and skin color? Consider how and why men confer different status to women in *Secrets Never Told.* Does Randolph really love Katherine, or is something else involved?

12. Think about "black magic" and working "roots." Discuss why people believe in them. Why

would Lenny want to harm Randolph even though she is told that he would come back to her? What is going on when Randolph has his accident? Does black magic have anything to do with it?

13. What is the "miracle Jesus wrought in Cana"? When and why does this reference appear in the book? Why is it significant for *Secrets Never Told?*

14. Discuss Uncle Julian. When did you figure out he was more than Morgana's "Uncle"? Trace his life and his accomplishments as an African American in the twentieth century.

15. How does Morgana justify sleeping with Erick? How does having a time-frame for her affair with Erick affect Morgana?

16. In Chapter 19, Morgana says that Randolph, Julian, and Katherine "were all losers." Why does she feel this way?

17. Share whether or not you are satisfied with the book's outcome, and why.

A Conversation with Rochelle Alers

1. What inspired you to write *Secrets Never Told?*

As a child I overheard my parents and relatives from the South talk about people with whom they'd grown up or known. Whenever I asked a question, their retort was to "stay out of grown folks business." Therefore, I learned at an early age to listen surreptitiously without interrupting. Using this practice I heard tales about cheating husbands, wives, women "dressing" their unfaithful husbands, secret children, and black women being kept by white men.

2. The name Salvation is loaded with meaning. Why did you choose it?

I chose to name the town Salvation because it was founded and settled by emancipated slaves and free people of color. For them it represented deliverance from the power and effects of sin: slavery. As an historically all-black town, the inhabitants were then responsible for their own successes and/or failures.

3. Writers often write about events close to them. Is this the case with *Secrets Never Told?*

I am familiar with some of the events in *Secrets Never Told*, but not all of them. Although a native New Yorker, I do have Southern roots: Florida and Georgia. I have some relatives whose marriages were based on the hue of one's complexion or social standing. I know relatives who lived double lives all of their lives, and those who, if subjected to DNA testing, would be surprised to find out that Daddy is *not* really Daddy.

4. You've written many other books, and *Secrets Never Told* is your most expansive. Your characters here defy stereotypes. What was the most challenging aspect of weaving together so many three-dimensional characters throughout such a long time frame?

What I found challenging once I began writing *Secrets Never Told* was keeping the characters true to their respective time period. The social mores and manners of 1950s Salvation are quite different from what would become today's Salvation, Georgia. A woman's position in society and the way she related to men or her husband was more subordinate than this century's more liberated woman. I had to keep in mind that even the manner of dress spanning the half century has changed. During the 1950s men wore hats year-round, and women were expected to wear hats, gloves, and hose whenever they ventured out of the house. As a writer who has lived through several of the time periods depicted in *Secrets Never Told* and as a history enthusiast, I was able to put myself in the period, making certain the historical facts are accurate, and to see what the characters were seeing and feeling during that time.

As to personality types, a detailed character dossier on each of the six major characters permitted me to "know" who they are and who they will become. There are similarities between Julian and Erick, Franklin and Randolph, and Morgana and Katherine. Yet, despite the similarities there are distinct differences that make them unique unto themselves: profession, place of birth, and social and economic class.

5. The struggles and happiness of the women in *Secrets Never Told* are at the center of the story. Both Morgana and Katherine are emotionally strong and independent. What do you most want readers to know about them?

Women have and will always be faced with the issue of infidelity. Their first question will always be "why?" Both Morgana and Katherine had husbands who were adulterers, yet each handled their situations differently despite their strength and independence.

I want readers, especially women, to understand that one can only become a victim if one gives someone else the authority to victimize them. Everyone has the power to choose to confront, leave, stay, or reconcile. Morgana chose to confront, leave, and then reconcile, while Katherine did not confront Randolph once she discovered his infidelity, but then opted to stay without reconciling.

6. Which character in the book do you like the most, and which the least? Why?

I like Dr. Julian Johnson because of his gentleness, however, I am partial to Erick Wilson. The least—Randolph Johnson became a man I truly wanted to hate.

Sensitive and romantic Erick Wilson unknowingly becomes Morgana's conscience and her voice of reason. He selflessly opens up to her, and in doing so he is able to exorcise his personal demons. Readers will probably complain because they believe Erick should have ended up with Morgana, but he was mature and realistic enough to know that what he had shared with Morgana was incomparable to the thirty years she had with Franklin.

All of Randolph Johnson's positive qualities are overshadowed by his lust for success and control. And despite his generosity, he is unable to give of himself. For him everything and everyone has a price tag. He is a manipulative man blinded by power, and in the end he loses everything, including the two women who love him unconditionally.

7. How did you decide to use diaries as a storytelling device?

Using diary entries as a storytelling device is one I had used quite successfully in another novel. To me diary entries are as intimate as opening one's bedroom door. The reader becomes a voyeur to one's longings, joy, and pain. I am considering writing a novel using only diary entries and letters between several characters.

8. Morgana could have given up on Franklin, but she doesn't. What makes her go back to him?

Morgana goes back to Franklin because she loves him. There was never a time when she had stopped loving him. What she needed was time away from him to come to the realization that what she had thought of as "perfect" was indeed not so perfect—including herself as a wife. Sleeping with Erick helped her to see how easy it was to succumb to the temptations which had plagued Franklin and his father.

9. Will readers be seeing more of Morgana, Franklin, and Erick?

Morgana and Franklin's story has been told. I have been asked if I would write Erick's story, and only time will tell if that will become a reality. I have learned to say, "Never say never."